THE NEW JEDI ORDER

TRAITOR

Other titles by Matthew Stover:

IRON DAWN
JERICHO MOON
HEROES DIE
BLADE OF TYSHALLE

Books published by The Ballantine Publishing Group
are available at quantity discounts on bulk purchases
for premium, educational, fund-raising, and special
sales use. For details, please call 1-800-733-3000.

STAR WARS

THE NEW JEDI ORDER

TRAITOR

MATTHEW STOVER

BALLANTINE BOOKS • NEW YORK

A Del Rey® Book
Published by The Ballantine Publishing Group

www.starwars.com
www.starwarskids.com
www.delreydigital.com

ISBN 0-345-42865-X

Manufactured in the United States of America

First Edition: August 2002

OPM 10 9 8 7 6 5 4 3 2 1

for the teachers

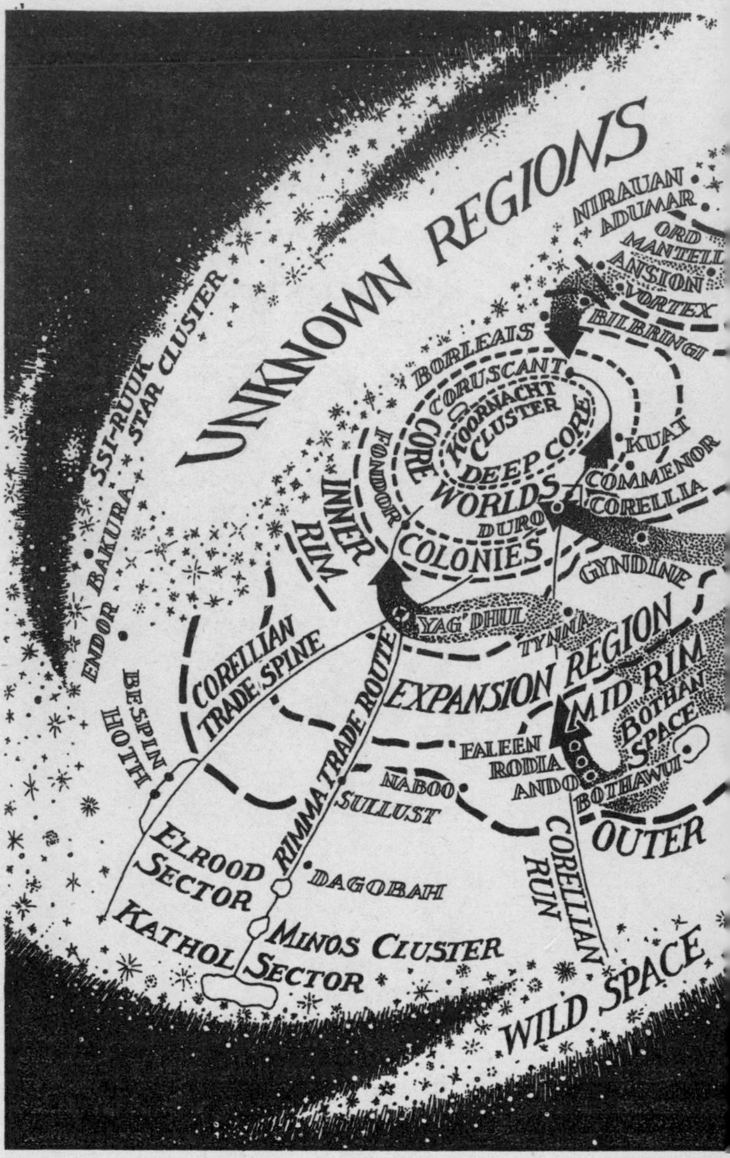
UNKNOWN REGIONS
NIRAUAN
ADUMAR
ORD
MANTELL
ANSION
VORTEX
BILBRINGI
BORLEAIS
CORUSCANT
KOORNACHT CLUSTER
DEEP CORE
CORE WORLDS
KUAT
COMMENOR
CORELLIA
FONDOR
INNER RIM
COLONIES
DURO
GYNDINE
YAG'DHUL
TYNNA
EXPANSION REGION
MID RIM
BOTHAN SPACE
BOTHAWUI
FALEEN
RODIA
ANDO
NABOO
SULLUST
OUTER
CORELLIAN RUN
SSI-RUUK STAR CLUSTER
BAKURA
ENDOR
BESPIN
HOTH
CORELLIAN TRADE SPINE
RIMMA TRADE ROUTE
ELROOD SECTOR
DAGOBAH
MINOS CLUSTER
KATHOL SECTOR
WILD SPACE

THE STAR WARS NOVELS TIMELINE

 44 YEARS BEFORE STAR WARS: A New Hope

Jedi Apprentice series

33 YEARS BEFORE STAR WARS: A New Hope

Darth Maul: Saboteur
Cloak of Deception

32.5 YEARS BEFORE STAR WARS: A New Hope

Darth Maul: Shadow Hunter

32 YEARS BEFORE STAR WARS: A New Hope

*STAR WARS: EPISODE I
THE PHANTOM MENACE*

29 YEARS BEFORE STAR WARS: A New Hope

Rogue Planet

22.5 YEARS BEFORE STAR WARS: A New Hope

The Approaching Storm

22 YEARS BEFORE STAR WARS: A New Hope

*STAR WARS: EPISODE II
ATTACK OF THE CLONES*

20 YEARS BEFORE STAR WARS: A New Hope

STAR WARS: EPISODE III

10-0 YEARS BEFORE STAR WARS: A New Hope

The Han Solo Trilogy:

The Paradise Snare
The Hutt Gambit
Rebel Dawn

5-2 YEARS BEFORE STAR WARS: A New Hope

The Adventures of Lando Calrissian:

Lando Calrissian and the
Mindharp of Sharu
Lando Calrissian and the
Flamewind of Oseon
Lando Calrissian and the
Starcave of ThonBoka

The Han Solo Adventures:

Han Solo at Stars' End
Han Solo's Revenge
Han Solo and the Lost Legacy

 **STAR WARS: A New Hope
YEAR 0**

*STAR WARS: EPISODE IV
A NEW HOPE*

0-3 YEARS AFTER STAR WARS: A New Hope

Tales from the Mos Eisley
Cantina
Splinter of the Mind's Eye

3 YEARS AFTER STAR WARS: A New Hope

*STAR WARS: EPISODE V
THE EMPIRE STRIKES BACK*

Tales of the Bounty Hunters

3.5 YEARS AFTER STAR WARS: A New Hope

Shadows of the Empire

4 YEARS AFTER STAR WARS: A New Hope

*STAR WARS: EPISODE VI
RETURN OF THE JEDI*

Tales from Jabba's Palace

The Bounty Hunter Wars:

The Mandalorian Armor
Slave Ship
Hard Merchandise

The Truce at Bakura

DRAMATIS PERSONAE

Ch' Gang Hool; master shaper (male Yuuzhan Vong)
Ganner Rhysode; Jedi Knight (male human)
Jacen Solo; Jedi Knight (male human)
Nom Anor; executor (male Yuuzhan Vong)
Tsavong Lah; warmaster (male Yuuzhan Vong)
Vergere (female Fosh)

TRAITOR

PROLOGUE

THE EMBRACE OF PAIN

Outside the universe, there is nothing.

This nothing is called hyperspace.

A tiny bubble of existence hangs in the nothing. This bubble is called a ship.

The bubble has neither motion nor stillness, nor even orientation, since the nothing has no distance or direction. It hangs there forever, or for less than an instant, because in the nothing there is also no time. Time, distance, and direction have meaning only inside the bubble, and the bubble maintains the existence of these things only by an absolute separation of what is within from what is without.

The bubble is its own universe.

Outside the universe, there is nothing.

Jacen Solo hangs in the white, exploring the spectrum of pain.

In the far infrared, he finds cinders of thirst that bake his throat. Higher, up in the visible wavelengths, gleam the crimson wire-stretched ligaments that sizzle within his shoulders; grinding glass-shard screams howl from his hip joints like the death shrieks of golden Ithorian starflowers. There is green here, too—bubbling tongues of acid hungrily lick his nerves—as well as lightning-blue shocks that spasm his overloaded body into convulsion.

And higher still, now far beyond the ultraviolet betrayal that brought him here—the betrayal that delivered him into the hands of the Yuuzhan Vong, the betrayal that gathered him into the Embrace of Pain, the betrayal by Vergere, whom he had trusted—he finds silent shattering gamma-ray bursts sleeting into his brain.

Those gamma-ray bursts are the color of his brother's death.

Anakin, he moans, somewhere deep within himself. *Anakin, how can you be dead?*

He has faced deaths in his family before; more than once, he thought Jaina lost, or his father, or mother or Uncle Luke. He has grieved, mourned them—but it was always a *mistake,* it was a *misunderstanding,* sometimes even a deliberate *trick* . . . In the end, they always came back to him.

Until Chewbacca.

When the moon crashed on Sernpidal, it shattered not only Chewbacca's life but also the magic charm that had always seemed to guard them all. Something in the universe has tilted to one side and opened a gap in reality; through that gap, death has slipped into his family.

Anakin . . .

Jacen saw him die. *Felt* him die, through the Force. Saw his lifeless body in the hands of the Yuuzhan Vong.

Anakin didn't even fade.

He only died.

In one impossible instant, Anakin ceased to be the brother Jacen played with, teased, looked after, played tricks on, fought with, cared for, trained with, loved— and became . . . what? An object. Remains. Not a person, not anymore. Now, the only *person* who is Anakin is the image Jacen carries in his heart.

An image that Jacen cannot even let himself see.

Each flash of Anakin—his reckless grin so like their father's, his eyes smoldering with fierce will mirroring their mother's, his effortlessly athletic warrior's grace, so much like Uncle Luke's—these are the gamma bursts that burn the marrow of his bones, that cook his brain until its boil threatens to burst his skull.

But when he looks away from Anakin, there is nothing to see but pain.

He cannot remember if he is on a ship, or still planet-bound. He finds a vague memory of capture aboard a Yuuzhan Vong worldship, but he's not sure if that happened to him, or to someone else. He cannot remember if such distinctions mean anything. All he knows is the white.

He remembers that he's been captured before. He remembers Belkadan, remembers his vain dream of freeing slaves, remembers the blank terror of discovering that his Force powers meant nothing against the Yuuzhan Vong; he remembers the Embrace of Pain, remembers his rescue by Uncle Luke—

Master Luke. Master Skywalker.

He remembers Vergere. Remembering Vergere brings him to the voxyn queen, and the voxyn queen sends him slithering back down a despair-greased slope to Anakin's corpse. Anakin's corpse floats on a burning lake of torment far deeper than anything that can happen to Jacen's body.

Jacen knows—intellectually, distantly, abstractly—that once he lived outside the white. He knows that he once felt happiness, pleasure, regret, anger, even love. But these are only ghosts, shadows murmuring beneath the roar of pain that fills everything he is, everything he will ever be; the simple fact that the white had a beginning does not imply that it will have an end. Jacen exists beyond time.

Where Jacen is, there is only the white, and the Force.

The Force is the air that he breathes—a cool whisk of sanity, a gentle breeze from a healthier world—though he can no more grasp its power than he might hold on to the wind. It surrounds him, fills him, accepts his suffering, and sustains his sanity. It whispers a reminder that despair is of the dark side, and that ceaseless murmur gives him the strength to go on living.

Distantly on that cool breeze he feels a knot of anger, of black rage and hurt and despair clenching ever harder, compressing itself to diamond and beyond, crushing itself back into carbon powder—he feels, through the bond they have shared from birth, his twin sister falling into the dark.

Jaina, he begs in a quiet corner of his heart. *Don't do it. Jaina, hold on—*

But he cannot let himself touch her through the Force; he cannot ask her to share his torment—she is in so much pain already that to suffer his would only drive her darker yet. And so even his twin bond has become a source of anguish.

Jacen has become a prism, reintegrating the glittering spectrum of pain into pure blazing agony.

Agony is white.

Snow-blind in an eternal Hoth ice-noon of suffering, Jacen Solo hangs in the Embrace of Pain.

The touch of a hand along his jaw leaked time into the white. This was not a human hand, not Wookiee, not family or close friend—four fingers, mutually opposable, hard-fleshed as a raptor's talons—but the touch was warm, and moist, and somehow not unfriendly. Pain retreated toward the back of his mind until he could think again, though he felt it lurking there, waiting. He knew that it would overtake him again, would break in waves across him, but for now—

The tides of agony rolled slowly out, and Jacen could open his eyes.

The hand that had brought him out of the white belonged to Vergere. She stood below him, looking up with wide alien eyes, her fingers light upon his cheek.

Jacen hung horizontally, suspended facedown two meters above a floor of wet, slick-looking greens and browns—its surface corded, viny, as though with muscle and vein. The walls oozed oily dampness that smelled darkly organic: bantha sweat and hawk-bat droppings. From the darkness above swung tentacles like prehensile eyestalks, ends socketed with glowing orbs that stared at him as the tentacles wove and danced and twisted about each other.

He understood: the enemy was watching.

Something that felt like claws, sharp and unyielding, gripped his skull from behind; he could not turn his head to see what held him. His arms were drawn wide, pulled to full extension and twisted so that his shoulders howled in their sockets. A single strong grip crushed his ankles together, grinding bone on bone—

Yet the greatest pain he now suffered was to look on Vergere and remember that he had trusted her.

She withdrew her hand, clenching and opening it while she stared at it with what, on a human, might have been a smile—as though her hand were an unfamiliar tool that might turn out to be a toy, instead.

"Among our masters," she said casually, as though continuing a friendly conversation, "it is not considered shameful for a warrior in your position to pray for death. This is occasionally granted, to honor great courage. There are some on this very ship who whisper that your action against the voxyn queen has earned this honor for you. On the other hand, our warmaster claims you for his own, to be a sacrifice to the True Gods. This, too, is a very great honor. Do you understand this?"

Jacen understood nothing except how much he hurt, and how terribly he had been betrayed. "I—" Speaking tore his throat as though he coughed splinters of trans-paristeel. He winced, squeezing shut his eyes until galaxies flared within them, then gritted his teeth and spoke anyway. "I *trusted* you."

"Yes, you did." She opened her hand, turning her quadrifid palm upward as if to catch a falling tear, and smiled up at him. "Why?"

Jacen could not find his breath to give answer; and then he found he had no answer to give.

She was so *alien*—

Raised on Coruscant, the nexus of the galaxy, he had no memory of a time when there had not been dozens—hundreds, even thousands—of wildly differing species in sight whenever he so much as peeked out the holographic false window of his bedroom. All space lanes led to Coruscant. Every sentient species of the New Republic had had representatives there. Bigotry was utterly beyond him; Jacen could no more dislike or distrust someone simply because she belonged to an unfamiliar species than he could breathe methane.

But Vergere—

Body compact and lithe, arms long and oddly mobile as though possessed of extra joints, hands from which fingers opened like the gripping spines of Andoan rock polyps, back-bent knees above splay-toed feet—he was acutely, overpoweringly aware that he had never seen any of Vergere's kind before. Long bright eyes the shape of teardrops, a spray of whiskers curving around a wide, expressive mouth . . . but expressive of what? How could he know what the arc of her lips truly signified?

It resembled a human smile, but she was nothing resembling human.

Perhaps her species used the crest of iridescent feathers along her cranial ridge for nonverbal signals: right now, as he stared, feathers near the rounded rear of her oblate skull lifted and turned so that their color shifted from starlight silver to red as a blaster bolt. Was that what corresponded to a smile? Or a human's deadpan shrug? Or a predator's threat display?

How could he possibly know?

How could he have ever trusted her?

"But you—" he rasped. "You saved Mara—"

"Did I?" she chirped sunnily. "And if I did, what significance do you attach to this?"

"I thought you were on our side—"

One whiskered eyebrow arched. "There is no 'our side,' Jacen Solo."

"You helped me kill the voxyn queen—"

"Helped you? Perhaps. Perhaps I *used* you; perhaps I had my own reasons to desire the death of the voxyn queen, and you were a convenient weapon. Or perhaps *you* are my true interest: perhaps I gave of my tears to Mara—perhaps I helped you survive the encounter with the voxyn queen—perhaps everything I have done was intended to bring you here, and hang you in the Embrace of Pain."

"Which—" Jacen made himself say "—which was it?"

"Which do you think it was?"

"I—I don't know . . . How *can* I know?"

"Why ask me? Should I presume to instruct a Jedi in the mysteries of epistemology?"

Jacen stiffened in the grip of the Embrace of Pain; he was not so broken that he did not know he was being mocked. "What do you want from me? Why have you done this? Why are you here?"

"Deep questions, little Solo." Her ridge feathers rippled through a shimmering rainbow like a diamond-edged sabacc deck riffled by an expert dealer. "It is near enough to the truth to say that I am a messenger of melancholy—a herald of tragedy, bearing gifts to ease the grieved. A mourner, with grave goods to decorate the tomb. A hierophant, to perform the sacred offices for the dead—"

Jacen's head swam. "What are you talking about? I don't—I can't—" His voice failed, and he sagged exhaustedly.

"Of course you can't. It's enough that the dead suffer their demise; would it be fair to ask them to understand it as well?"

"You're saying . . ." Jacen licked his lips, his tongue so dry it scraped them raw. *I can face this,* he told himself. *I may not be much of a warrior, but I can die like one.* "You're saying you're going to kill me."

"Oh no, not at all." From Vergere's mouth came a musical chiming like a spray of Endorian wind-crystals; he guessed this must serve her for laughter. "I'm saying you're already dead."

Jacen stared.

"You are forever lost to the worlds you knew," she went on with a liquidly alien gesture that might have been a shrug. "Your friends mourn, your father rages, your mother weeps. Your life has been *terminated*: a line of division has been drawn between you and everything you have ever known. You have seen the terminator that sweeps across the face of a planet, the twilit division between day and night? You have crossed that line, Jacen Solo. The bright fields of day are forever past."

But not everything he knew was gone, not while he lived. He was a Jedi. He reached out with his feelings—

"Oh, the Force," Vergere chirped dismissively. "The Force is *life*; what has life to do with you?"

Suffering and exhaustion had bled away Jacen's capacity for astonishment; he did not care how Vergere knew what he was doing. He opened himself to the Force, let its clean cascade wash through him, dissolving his pain and confusion—and found at his side a connection to the Force as profound as his own.

Vergere crackled with power.

Jacen murmured, "You're a Jedi . . ."

Vergere laughed. "There are no Jedi here," she said, and made a gesture, eyeflick-swift.

Inside Jacen's head, a swirl of interstellar gases fell in upon itself, kindling a protostar behind his eyes. The protostar swelled, gathering power, ramping up intensity until the light inside his skull washed away the woody glow of the chamber in which he hung. In the whited-out blaze, he heard Vergere's voice, cold and precise as the light of a distant quasar.

"I am your guide through the lands of the dead."

Beyond that, he heard and saw no more.

A silent supernova erupted within Jacen's brain, and blasted away the universe.

Seconds or centuries passed in oblivion.

Consciousness swam back into him, and he opened his eyes to find himself still hanging in the Embrace of Pain, Vergere still standing below him, on her face the same alien facsimile of cheerful mockery.

Nothing had changed.

Everything had changed.

The universe was *empty*, now.

"What? . . ." Jacen croaked, his throat raw as though he'd spent days screaming in his sleep. "*What have you done to me? . . .*"

"You have no business with the Force, nor it with you. Let *you* have the Force? The idea! It must be some kind of human thing—you mammals are so impulsive, so reckless: infants teething on a blaster. No, no, no, little Solo. The Force is much too dangerous for children. A great deal more dangerous than those ridiculous lightsabers you all seem to like to wave about. So I took it away from you."

The emptiness of the universe howled inside his head.

There was *nothing out there.*

Only vast interstellar vacuum.

All his training, all his talent, his gift, meant nothing to the limitlessly indifferent cosmos; the Force was only the ghost of a dream from which he had now awakened.

Jaina— He thrust desperately into the bond that had always been there, seeking his sister, his twin; he poured his terror and loss into the void that yawned where that bond had always been.

Only silence. Only emptiness. Only *lack.*

Oh, Jaina—Jaina, I'm sorry . . .

With the Force-bond between them shattered, even Jaina would think he was dead.

Would *know* he was dead.

"You—there's no way—you can't *possibly*—" He barely recognized this tiny, lost-in-the-dark whisper as his own voice.

"But I have. Really, this Force business, you're better off without it. If you're a good boy, I'll give it back when you grow up."

"But . . ." How could his universe be so fragile? How could everything he was be so easily broken? "But I'm a Jedi . . ."

"You *were* a Jedi," she corrected him. "Haven't you been paying attention? What part about being dead do you not understand?"

"I don't . . ." Jacen's eyes drifted closed.

Tears gathered in his eyelashes, and when he opened his eyes the tears dripped straight from his eyeballs to splash on the floor beside Vergere's feet. One of the room's prehensile eyestalks twisted itself lower to examine them. "I don't understand *anything* . . . Nothing makes *sense* to me anymore . . ."

Vergere straightened her back-bent legs and rose onto her toes, bringing her wide whiskered mouth within a decimeter of Jacen's ear.

"Jacen Solo. Listen well." Her voice was warm and kind, and her breath smelled of spices grown in alien soil. "Everything I tell you is a lie. Every question I ask is a trick. You will find no truth in me." She came close enough that her whiskers tickled his ear, and whispered, "Though you believe nothing else, you may rest your faith on this."

Jacen stared into eyes as blackly encompassing as interstellar space. He whispered, "What *are* you?"

"I am Vergere," she said simply. "What are you?"

She waited, motionlessly patient, as though to confirm that he had no answer, then she turned away. A hatch sphincter dilated in the wall—a wet sound like lips opening for a kiss—and Vergere left without a backward glance.

The walls and ceiling creaked like an old man's joints as the grip of the Embrace of Pain tightened again. Jacen Solo was once more swallowed by agony.

Now there is no more Force for Jacen—no more cool breath of life and sanity, no more Jaina, no more life.

Where Jacen is, there is only the white.

PART ONE

DESCENT

ONE

COCOON

In the dust-swept reaches of interstellar space, where the density of matter is measured in atoms per cubic meter, a small vessel of yorik coral blinked into existence, slewed through a radical curve that altered both its vector and its velocity, then streaked away, trailing a laser-straight line of ionizing radiation, to vanish again in the gamma burst of hyperjump.

Some unknown time later, an unguessable distance away, in a region indistinguishable from the first save by the altered parallax of certain stellar groups, the same vessel performed a similar manuver.

On its long journey, the vessel might fall into the galaxy any number of times, and each time be swallowed once more by the nothing beyond.

Jacen Solo hangs in the white, thinking.

He has begun to riddle out the lesson of pain.

The white drops him once in a while, as though the Embrace of Pain understands him somehow: as though it can read the limit of his strength. When another minute in the white might kill him, the Embrace of Pain eases enough to slide him back into the reality of the room, of the ship; when the pain has crackled so hot for so long that his overloaded nerves and brain have been scorched too numb to feel it, the Embrace of Pain lowers him entirely to the floor, where he can even sleep for a time, while other devices—or creatures, since he cannot tell the difference anymore, since he is no longer sure that there *is* any difference—bathe him and tend wounds scraped or torn or slashed into his flesh by the Embrace's grip, and still more creature-devices crawl over him like spider-roaches, injecting him with nutrients and enough water to maintain his life.

Even without the Force, his Jedi training gives him ways to survive the pain; he can drive his mind through a meditative cycle that builds a wall of discipline between his consciousness and the white. Though his body still suffers, he can hold his mind outside the pain. But this wall of discipline doesn't last forever, and the Embrace of Pain is patient.

It erodes his mental walls with the inanimate persistence of waves against a cliff; the Embrace's arcane perception somehow lets it know that he has defended himself, and its efforts slowly gather like a storm spinning up into a hurricane until it batters down his walls and slashes once more into everything Jacen is. Only then, only after it has pushed him to the uttermost limit of his tolerance then blasted him beyond that limit into whole new galaxies of pain, will the Embrace slowly relent.

He feels as if the white is *eating* him—as if the Embrace eats his pain, but never so much that he can't recover to feed it again. He is being managed, tended like wander-kelp on a Chadian deepwater ranch. His existence has become a tidal rhythm of agony that sweeps in, reaches an infinite crest, then rolls out again just far enough that he might catch his breath; the Embrace is careful not to let him drown.

Sometimes, when he slips down from the white, Vergere

is there. Sometimes she crouches at his side with the un-blinking predatory patience of a hawk-bat; sometimes she stalks around the chamber on her back-bent legs like a dactyl stork wading through a swamp. Often, she is incongruously kind to him, tending his raw flesh herself with oddly comforting efficiency; he sometimes wonders if she would do more, would say more, if not for the constant monitoring stares of the eyestalks that dangle from the ceiling.

But mostly he sits, or lies, waiting. Naked, blood seeping from his wrists and ankles. More than naked: utterly hairless. The living machines that tend to his body also pluck out his hairs. All of them: head, arms, legs, pubis, armpits. Eyebrows. Eyelashes.

Once he asked, in his thin, weakly croaking voice, "How long?"

Her response was a blank stare. He tried again. "How long . . . have I been here?"

She made the liquid ripple of her flexible arms that he usually took for a shrug. "How long you have been here is as irrelevant as where you are. *Time* and *place* belong to the living, little Solo. They have nothing to do with you, nor you with them."

His questions always meet with answers like this one; eventually he stops asking. Questions require strength, and he has none to spare.

"Our masters serve stern gods," she said, the second or fifth or tenth time he awoke to find her at his side. "The True Gods decree that life is suffering, and give us pain to demonstrate their truth. Some among our masters seek favor with the True Gods by seeking pain; Domain Shai was legendary for this. They used the Embrace of Pain the way you or I might take a bath. Perhaps they hoped that by punishing themselves, they might avert the punishments of the True Gods. In this, one must suppose they were . . . ah, *disappointed*. Or perhaps—as Domain Shai's detractors like to whisper—they grew to *enjoy* the pain. Pain can be a drug, Jacen Solo. Do you understand this yet?"

Vergere seemed never to care if he didn't answer; she seemed perfectly content to prattle away endlessly on any random subject, as though interested in nothing beyond the sound of her own voice—but if he so much as lifted his head, as soon as he croaked an answer or murmured a question, the subject somehow turned to pain.

They had plenty to talk about; Jacen had learned a great deal about pain.

His first actual clue to the lesson of pain came once when he lay upon the corded floor, trembling with exhaustion. The branchlike grips of the Embrace of Pain still held him, but loosely, maintaining contact, no more. They hung in slack spirals overhead, dangling from bunched, knotted bundles of vegetative muscle that shifted and squirmed above the leather-barked ceiling of the chamber.

These periods of rest hurt Jacen almost as much as the Embrace's torment: his body slowly but inexorably dragged itself back into shape, resocketing his joints and achingly releasing the overstretched tension of his muscles. And without the constant agony of the Embrace of Pain, he could think of nothing but Anakin, of the gaping wound that Anakin's death had opened in his life—and of what Anakin's death had begun to do to Jaina, driving her toward the dark—and of how his parents must be suffering, having lost both their sons—

More to distract himself than out of any desire for conversation, he had rolled over to face Vergere and asked, "Why are you doing this to me?"

"This?" Vergere gazed at him steadily. "What am I doing?"

"No—" He closed his eyes, organizing pain-scattered thoughts, then opened them again. "No, I mean the Yuuzhan Vong. The Embrace of Pain. I've been through a breaking," he said. "The breaking makes a kind of sense, I guess. But this . . ."

His voice broke despairingly, but he caught himself, and held his tongue until he could control it. *Despair is of the dark side.* "Why are they torturing me?" he asked, clearly and simply. "No one even *asks* me anything . . ."

"*Why* is a question that is always deeper than its answer," Vergere said. "Perhaps you should ask instead: *what?* You say *torture*, you say *breaking*. To you, yes. To our masters?" She canted her head, and her crest splayed orange. "Who knows?"

"This isn't torture? You should try it from my side," Jacen said with a feeble smile. "In fact, I really wish you would."

Her chuckle chimed like a handful of glass bells. "Do you think I haven't?"

Jacen stared, uncomprehending.

"Perhaps you are not being tortured," she said cheerily. "Perhaps you are being *taught*."

Jacen made a rusty hacking sound, halfway between a cough and a bitter laugh. "In the New Republic," he said, "education doesn't hurt this much."

"No?" She canted her head to the opposite angle, and her crest shimmered to green. "That may be why your people are losing this war. The Yuuzhan Vong understand that no lesson is truly learned until it has been purchased with pain."

"Oh, sure. What's this supposed to *teach* me?"

"Is it what the teacher teaches?" Vergere countered. "Or what the student learns?"

"What's the difference?"

The arc of her lips and the angle of her head might have added up to a smile. "That is, itself, a question worth considering, yes?"

There was another time—before, after, he could never be sure. He had found himself huddled against the leathery curve of the chamber's wall, the Embrace's grips trailing upward like slack feeder vines. Vergere crouched at his side, and as consciousness trickled through him he seemed to recall that she had been coaxing him to take a sip from the stem of an elongated, gourdlike drink bulb. Too exhausted for disobedience, he tried; but the liquid within— only water, cool and pure—savaged his parched throat until he gagged and had to spit it out again. Patiently, Vergere had used the bulb to moisten a scrap of rag, then gave it to him to suck on until his throat loosened up enough that he could swallow.

The vast desert inside his mouth absorbed the moisture instantly, and Vergere dampened the rag again. This went on for some considerable while.

"What is pain *for*?" she murmured after a time. "Do you ever think about that, Jacen Solo? What is its function? Many of our more devout masters believe that pain is the lash of the True Gods: that suffering is how the True Gods teach us to disdain comfort, our bodies, even life itself. For myself, I say that pain is itself a god: the taskmaster of life. Pain cracks the whip, and all that lives will move. The most basic instinct of life is to retreat from pain. To hide from it. If going *here* hurts, even a granite slug will go *over there*; to live is to be a slave to pain. To be 'beyond pain' is to be dead, yes?"

"Not for me," Jacen answered dully, once his throat opened enough that he could speak. "No matter how dead you say I am, it still hurts."

"Oh, well, yes. That the dead are beyond pain is only an article of faith, isn't it? We should say, we *hope* that the dead are beyond pain—but there's only one way to find out for sure." She winked at him, smiling. "Do you think that pain might be the ruling principle of death, as well?"

"I don't think anything. I just want it to stop."

She turned away, making an odd snuffling sound; for half a moment Jacen wondered if his suffering might have finally touched her somehow—wondered if she might take pity on him . . .

But when she turned back, her eyes were alight with mockery, not compassion. "I am such a fool," she chimed. "All this time, I had thought I was speaking to an *adult*. Ah, self-deception is the cruelest trick of all, isn't it? I let myself believe that you had once been a true Jedi, when in truth you are only a hatchling, shivering in the nest, squalling because your mother hasn't fluttered up to *feed* you."

"You—you—" Jacen stammered. "How can you— after what you've done—"

"What I have done? Oh, no no no, little Solo child. This is about what *you* have done."

"I haven't done *anything*!"

Vergere settled back against the chamber's wall a meter away. Slowly, she folded her back-bent knees beneath her, then laced her fingers together in front of her delicately whiskered mouth and stared at him over her knuckles.

After a long, long silence, during which *I haven't done anything!* echoed in his mind until Jacen's face burned, Vergere said, "Exactly."

She leaned close, as though to share an embarrassing secret. "Is that not the infant's tactic? To wail, and wail, and wail, to wriggle its fingers and kick its heels . . . hoping an adult will notice, and care for it?"

Jacen lowered his head, struggling against sudden hot tears. "What *can* I do?"

She sat back again and made more of that snuffling noise. "Certainly, among your options is continuing to hang in this room and suffer. And so long as you do that, do you know what will happen?"

Jacen gave her a bruised look. "What?"

"Nothing," she said cheerfully. She spread her hands. "Oh, eventually, you'll go mad, I suppose. If you're lucky. Someday you may even die." Her crest flattened back and became blasterbore gray. "Of *old age*."

Jacen stared, openmouthed. He couldn't face another *hour* in the Embrace of Pain—she was talking about *years*. About *decades*.

About *the rest of his life*.

He hugged his knees and buried his face against them, grinding his eye sockets against his kneecaps as though he could squeeze the horror out of his head. He remembered Uncle Luke in the doorway of the shed on Belkadan, remembered the sadness on his face as he cut through the Yuuzhan Vong warriors who had captured Jacen, remembered the swift sure pressure as Luke gouged the slave seed out of Jacen's face with his cybernetic thumb.

He remembered that Uncle Luke wouldn't be coming for him this time. Nobody would.

Because Jacen was dead.

"Is that why you keep coming here?" he muttered into his folded arms. "To gloat? To humiliate a defeated enemy?"

"Am I gloating? Are we enemies?" Vergere asked, sounding honestly puzzled. "Are you defeated?"

Her suddenly sincere tone caught him; he raised his

head, and could find no mockery now in her eyes. "I don't understand."

"That, at least, is very clear," she sighed. "I give you a *gift*, Jacen Solo. I free you from hope of rescue. Can you not see how I am trying to help you?"

"Help?" Jacen coughed a bitter chuckle. "You need to brush up on your Basic, Vergere. In Basic, when we talk about the kind of things you've done to me, *help* isn't the word we use."

"No? Then perhaps you are correct: our difficulties may be linguistic." Vergere sighed again, and settled even lower, folding her arms on the floor in front of her and arranging herself on top of them in a way more feline than avian. Secondary inner lids shrouded her eyes.

"When I was very young—younger than you, little Solo—I came upon a ringed moon shadowmoth at the end of its metamorphosis, still within its cocoon," she said distantly, a little sadly. "I had already some touch with the Force; I could feel the shadowmoth's pain, its panic, its claustrophobia, its hopelessly desperate struggle to free itself. It was as though this particular shadowmoth knew I was beside it, and screamed out to me for help. How could I refuse? Shadowmoth cocoons are polychained silicates—very, very tough—and shadowmoths are so delicate, so beautiful: gentle creatures whose only purpose is to sing to the night sky. So I gave it what I think *you* mean by *help*: I used a small utility cutter to slice the cocoon, to *help* the shadowmoth get out."

"Oh, you didn't, did you? Please say you didn't." Jacen let his eyes drift closed, sorry already, for how he knew this story would end.

He'd had a shadowmoth in his collection for a short time; he remembered watching the larva grow, feeling its happy satisfaction through his empathic talent as it fed on stripped insulation and crumbled duracrete; he remembered the young shadowmoth that had emerged, spreading its dusky, beautifully striated wings against the crystalline polymer of its viewcage; he remembered the shadowmoth's thrilling whistle of moonsong, when he had released it from its viewcage and it had soared away under the mingled glows of Coruscant's four moons.

He remembered the desperate panic that had beat in waves against him through the Force, the night the shadowmoth had fought free of its cocoon. He remembered his ache to help the helpless creature—and he remembered why he hadn't.

"You can't help a shadowmoth by cutting its cocoon," he said. "It needs the effort; the struggle to break the cocoon forces ichor into its wing veins. If you cut the cocoon—"

"The shadowmoth will be crippled," Vergere finished for him solemnly. "Yes. It was a tragic creature—never to fly, never to join its fellows in their nightdance under the moons. Even its wingflutes were stunted, and so it was as mute as it was planetbound. During that long summer, we sometimes heard moonsong through the window of my bedchamber, and from my shadowmoth I would feel always only sadness and bitter envy, that it could never soar beneath the stars, that its voice could never rise in song. I cared for it as best I could—but the life of a shadowmoth is short, you know; they spend years and years as larvae, storing strength for one single summer of dance and song. I *robbed* that shadowmoth; I stole its destiny—because I *helped* it."

"That wasn't helping," Jacen said. "That's not what *help* means, either."

"No? I saw a creature in agony, crying out its terror, and I undertook to ease its pain, and assuage its fear. If that is not what you mean by *help*, then my command of Basic is worse than I believed."

"You didn't understand what was happening."

Vergere shrugged. "Neither did the shadowmoth. But tell me this, Jacen Solo: if I *had* understood what was happening—if I had known what the larva was, and what it must do, and what it must *suffer*, to become the glorious creature that it could become—what should I have done that you would call, in your Basic, help?"

Jacen thought for some time before answering. His Force empathy had enabled him to understand the exotic creatures in his collection with extraordinary depth and clarity; that understanding had left him with a profound respect for the intrinsic processes of nature. "I suppose," he said slowly, "the best help you could offer would be to keep the cocoon safe. Hawk-bats hunt shadowmoth larvae, and they especially like newly cocooned pupae: that's the stage where they have the most stored fat. So I guess the best help you could offer would be to keep watch over the larva, to protect it from predators—and leave it alone to fight its own battle."

"And, perhaps," Vergere offered gently, "also to protect it from other well-intentioned folk—who might wish, in their ignorance, to 'help' it with their own utility cutters."

"Yes . . ." Jacen said, then he caught his breath, staring at Vergere as though she had suddenly grown an extra head. "Hey . . ." Comprehension began to dawn. "Hey—"

"And also, perhaps," Vergere went on, "you might stop by from time to time, to let the struggling, desperate, suffering creature know that it is not alone. That someone cares. That its pain is in the service of its destiny."

Jacen could barely breathe, but somehow he forced out a whisper. "Yes . . ."

Vergere said gravely, "Then, Jacen Solo, our definitions of *help* are identical."

Jacen shifted forward, coming up onto his knees. "We're not really talking about shadowmoth larvae, are we?" he said, his heart suddenly pounding. "You're talking about *me*."

She rose, legs unfolding like gantry cranes beneath her. "About you?"

"About *us*." His throat clenched with impossible hope. "You and me."

"I must go, now; the Embrace has become impatient for your return."

"Vergere, wait—!" he said, struggling to his feet, the Embrace's branch-grips dangling from his wrists. "Wait, Vergere, come on, talk to me—and, and, and shadowmoths—" he stammered. "Shadowmoths are indigenous! They're not a transported species—they're native to *Coruscant*! How could you have found a shadowmoth larva? Unless, unless you—I mean, did you—*are* you—"

She put her hand between the lips of the mouthlike sensor receptacle beside the hatch sphincter, and the warted pucker of the hatch gaped wide.

"Everything I tell you is a lie," she said, and stepped through.

The Embrace of Pain gathered him once more into the white.

Jacen Solo hangs in the white, thinking.

For an infinite instant, he is merely amazed that he *can* think; the white has scoured his consciousness for days, or weeks, or centuries, and he is astonished now to discover that he can not only think, but think *clearly*.

He spends a white eon marveling.

Then he goes to work on the lesson of pain.

This is it, he thinks. *This is what Vergere was talking about. This is the help she gave me, that I didn't know how to accept.*

She has freed him from his own trap: the trap of childhood. The trap of waiting for someone *else.* Waiting for Dad, or Mother, Uncle Luke, Jaina, Zekk or Lowie or Tenel Ka or any of the others whom he could always count on to fly to his rescue.

He is not helpless. He is only alone.

It's not the same thing.

He doesn't have to simply hang here and suffer. He can *do something.*

Her shadowmoth tale may have been a lie, but within the lie was a truth he could not have comprehended without it. Was that what she had meant when she said, *Everything I tell you is a lie?*

Did it matter?

Pain is itself a god: the taskmaster of life. Pain cracks the whip, and all that lives will move. To live is to be a slave to pain.

He knows the truth of this, not only from his own life but from watching Dad and Anakin, after Chewie's death. He watched pain crack its whip over his father, and watched Han run from that pain halfway across the galaxy. He watched Anakin turn hard, watched him drive himself like a loadlifter, always pushing himself to be stronger, faster, more effective, to *do more*—this was the only answer he had to the pain of having survived to watch his rescuer die.

Jacen always thought of Anakin as being a lot like Uncle Luke: his mechanical aptitude, his piloting and fighting skills, his stark warrior's courage. He can see now that in one important way, Anakin was more like his father. His only answer to pain was to keep too busy to notice it.

Running from the taskmaster.

To live is to be a slave to pain.

But that is only half true; pain can also be a teacher. Jacen can remember hour after hour of dragging his aching muscles through one more repetition of his light-saber training routines. He remembers practicing the more advanced stances, how much it hurt to work his body in ways he'd never worked it before, to lower his center of gravity, loosen his hips, train his legs to coil and spring like a sand panther's. He remembers Uncle Luke saying, *If it doesn't hurt, you're not doing it right.* Even the stinger bolts of a practice remote—sure, his goal had been always to intercept or dodge the stingers, but the easiest way to avoid that pain would have been to quit training.

Sometimes pain is the only bridge to where you want to go.

And the worst pains are the ones you can't run away from, anyway. He knows his mother's tale so well that he has seen it in his dreams: standing on the bridge of the Death Star, forced to watch while the battle station's main weapon destroyed her entire planet. He has felt her all-devouring horror, denial, and blistering helpless rage, and he has some clue how much of her relentless dedication to the peace of the galaxy is driven by the memory of those billions of lives wiped from existence before her eyes.

And Uncle Luke: if he hadn't faced the pain of finding his foster parents brutally murdered by Imperial storm-troopers, he might have spent his whole life as an unhappy moisture farmer, deep in the Tatooine sand-wastes, dreaming of adventures he would never have—and the galaxy might groan under Imperial rule to this very day.

Pain can be power, too, Jacen realizes. Power to change things for the better. That's how change happens: someone hurts, and sooner or later decides to *do something about it.*

Suffering is the fuel in the engine of civilization.

Now he begins to understand: because pain *is* a god—he has been in the grip of this cruel god ever since Anakin's death. But it is also a teacher, and a bridge. It can be a slave master, and break you—and it can be the power that makes you unbreakable. It is all these things, and more.

At the same time.

What it is depends on who you are.

But who am I? he wonders. *I've been running like Dad—like Anakin. I think they stopped, though; I think Dad was strong enough to turn back and face it, to use the pain to make himself stronger, like Mom and Uncle Luke. Anakin did, too, at the end. Am I that strong?*

There's only one way to find out.

For indefinite days, weeks, centuries, the white has been eating him.

Now, he begins to eat the white.

Executor Nom Anor toyed idly with a sacworm of dragweed broth while he waited for the shaper drone to finish its report. He sat human-style on a fleshy hump to one side of the unusually large villip to which the drone addressed its monotonous, singsong analysis of the Embrace chamber's readings on the young Jedi, Jacen Solo.

Nom Anor had no need to pay attention. He knew already what the drone would say; he had composed the report himself. This particular Embrace chamber was equipped with an exceptionally sophisticated nerve-web of sensors, which could read the electrochemical output of Jacen Solo's nerves down to each individual impulse and compare the pain they registered with its effect on his brain chemistry. The shaper drone mumbled on and on in its description of minute details of its data collection, and its deadly dull murmur was excruciating—

Perhaps that's why we call them drones, Nom Anor thought with a humorless interior smile. He did not share this observation with the third occupant of the small, moist chamber. It wasn't even a joke in any language but Basic, and it wasn't that funny, anyway.

Instead he simply sat, sipping broth occasionally from the sacworm, watching the villip, waiting for Warmaster Tsavong Lah to lose his patience.

With vegetative accuracy, the villip conveyed the physical features of the warmaster: his tall narrow skull, bulging braincase, dangerously sharp teeth bristling within his lipless gash of a mouth, as well as the proud array of scars that defined his devotion to the True Way. Nom Anor reflected idly how well some of those intricately scarified designs would look on his own face. Not that he had any real interest in the True Way beyond its use as a political tool; from long experience, he knew that the appearance of piety was vastly more useful than its reality could ever be.

The villip also captured perfectly the frightening intensity of Tsavong Lah's fanatic glare.

That gleam of faith's power in his eye was the reflection of an inner conviction the like of which Nom Anor could only imagine: to *know*, beyond the possibility of doubt, that the True Gods stood at his shoulder, guiding his hand in Their service. To *know* that all truth, all justice, all *right*, shone from the True Gods like stellar wind, illuminating the universe.

The warmaster was a true believer.

To Nom Anor, faith was an extravagance. He knew too well how easily such true believers could be manipulated by those who believe in nothing but themselves.

This was, in fact, his specialty.

The moment he'd been waiting for came during the drone's exhaustive point-by-point cross-species interpolation between Jacen Solo's readings and those of three different control subjects, all Yuuzhan Vong: one warrior caste, one priest caste, and one shaper caste, each of whom had earlier undergone excruciation by the very same Embrace of Pain in which the young Jedi now hung. Anger gathered upon Tsavong Lah's villip image like the ion peak that precedes a solar flare.

Finally, his patience broke. "Why is my time wasted with this babble?"

The shaper drone stiffened, glancing nervously at Nom Anor. "This data is extremely significant—"

"Not to me. Am I a shaper? I have no interest in raw data—tell me what it *means!*"

Nom Anor sat forward. "With the warmaster's permission, I may perhaps be of some service here."

The villip twisted fractionally to fix Nom Anor with the warmaster's glare. "You had better," he said. "My patience is limited—and you personally, *Executor,* have required too much of it already in recent days. You swing from a thin vine, Nom Anor, and it continues to fray."

"All apologies to the warmaster," Nom Anor said smoothly. He gestured dismissal to the drone, which made a hasty obeisance toward the villip, triggered the room's hatch sphincter, and scuttled away. "I mean only to offer analysis; interpretation is my specialty."

"Your specialty is propaganda and lies," Tsavong Lah rasped.

As if there were a difference. Nom Anor shrugged and smiled amiably: gestures he had learned from his impersonations of the human species. He exchanged one quick glance with the other occupant of the chamber—his partner in the Solo Project—then directed his gaze back to the villip. "The import of the Embrace chamber's data is exactly this: Jacen Solo has become capable of not only accepting torment, but thriving on it. As the warmaster will recall, I predicted such a result. He has discovered resources within himself of the sort that we find only in our greatest warriors."

"And?" The warmaster glared. "Make your point."

"It will work," Nom Anor said simply. "That is the point. The only point. Based on our current figures, Jacen Solo will inevitably—provided he lives—turn to the True Way with his whole heart."

"This has been attempted before," Tsavong Lah growled. "The *Jeedai* Wurth Skidder, and the *Jeedai* Tahiri on Yavin Four. The results were less than satisfactory."

"Shapers," Nom Anor snorted derisively.

"Mind your tongue, if you would keep it in your mouth. The shaper caste is holy unto Yun-Yuuzhan."

"Of course, of course. No disrespect intended, naturally. I only mean to point out, with the warmaster's permission, that the methods used in the Tahiri disaster were crude physical alterations—possibly *heretical*." Nom Anor leaned on the word.

Tsavong Lah's face darkened.

"They were performing sacrilegious *research*," Nom Anor went on. "They tried to make her into a Yuuzhan Vong—as though a slave can be altered into one of the Chosen Race. Is this not blasphemy? The ensuing slaughter was far kinder than they deserved, as the warmaster will no doubt agree."

"Not at all," Tsavong Lah countered. "It was *precisely* what they deserved. Whatever the Gods decree is the *definition* of justice."

"As you say," Nom Anor conceded easily. "No such heresy will take place in the Solo Project. The process with Jacen Solo is precisely the opposite: he will remain fully human, yet acknowledge and proclaim the Truth.

We will not have to alter or destroy him in any way. We merely demonstrate; he will do the rest himself."

The warmaster's image chilled over with calculation. "You still have not made clear why I should desire this. Everything you have told me implies that he would make an even greater sacrifice than I had dreamed. Explain why I should await this promised conversion. Should he die in the process, I will have broken an oath to the True Gods: cheated them of their due sacrifice. The True Gods are unforgiving to oathbreakers, Nom Anor."

You couldn't prove it by me, Nom Anor thought smugly, but he spoke with utmost respect. "The symbolic importance of Jacen Solo cannot be overestimated, Warmaster. First, he is Jedi—and the Jedi stand in place of gods in the New Republic. They are looked to as surrogate parents, gifted with vast abilities that legend further magnifies beyond all reason; their purpose is to fight and die for the New Republic's debased, infidel perversions of truth and justice. Jacen Solo is already a legendary hero. His exploits, even as a child and a youth, are known throughout the galaxy; together with those of his sister—his *twin* sister—they rival even those of Yun-Harla and Yun-Yammka—"

"You utter such blasphemies too easily," Tsavong Lah grated.

"Do I?" Nom Anor smiled. "And yet the True Gods do not see fit to strike me down; perhaps what I say is not blasphemy at all—as you shall see."

The warmaster only glared at him stonily.

"Jacen Solo is also the eldest son of the galaxy's leading clan. His mother was, for a time, the New Republic's Supreme Overlord—"

"For a time? How is this possible? Why would her successor let her live?"

"Does the warmaster truly wish a disquisition upon

the New Republic's perverse system of government? It has to do with a bizarre concept called *democracy*, in which ruling power is given to whoever is most skillful at directing the herd instincts of the largest masses of their most ignorant citizens—"

"Their politics are your concern," Tsavong Lah growled. "Their fighting strength is mine."

"The two are, in this case, more closely related than the warmaster might suspect. For a quarter of a standard century, the Solo family has dominated galactic affairs of all kinds. Even the warmaster of the Jedi is none other than Jacen Solo's uncle. This uncle, Luke Skywalker, is popularly considered to have singlehandedly created the New Republic by defeating an older, much more rational government called the Empire. And, I might add, it is fortunate for us that he did; the Empire was vastly more organized, powerful, and potently militaristic. Lacking the internal divisions we have exploited so successfully in the New Republic, the Empire could have crushed our people utterly in their first encounter."

Tsavong Lah bristled. "The True Gods would never have allowed such a defeat!"

"Precisely my point," Nom Anor countered. "They *didn't*. Instead, Luke Skywalker, the Solos, and the Rebel Alliance destroyed the Empire, leaving the galaxy in a state of disarray, a power vacuum that we could exploit— for even then, the Solo clan served the True Gods *without ever knowing it*!"

For the first time, Tsavong Lah began to look interested.

"Now, imagine," Nom Anor said, scenting blood, "the effect on the morale of the remaining New Republic forces when this Jedi, this hero, this scion of the greatest clan of their *entire civilization*, announces to all his people that they have been deceived by their leaders: that the True Gods are the only gods—that the True Way is the *only* way!"

The villip conveyed perfectly a spark kindling in the warmaster's eyes. "We hurt them when we took their capital, but we did not kill their spirit," he murmured. "This would be gangrene in the wound of Coruscant."

"Yes."

"The New Republic could sicken, and finally die."

"Yes."

"You are certain that you can make Jacen Solo submit to the Truth?"

"Warmaster," Nom Anor said intensely, "it is *already happening*. Jacen and Jaina Solo are *twins*, yet male and female, complementary *opposites*. Don't you see it? Yun-Yammka and Yun-Harla. Warrior and Trickster. Jacen Solo will *become* one half of the Twin Gods—to fight in service of the God he *is*! He will be proof no creature of the New Republic could ever refute."

"This may have value," Tsavong Lah admitted.

"May?" Nom Anor said. "*May?* Warmaster, you have personally performed every sacrifice the True Gods demand for victory—every sacrifice save *one*—"

The spark in the warmaster's eyes suddenly blazed into a fusion furnace. "The Great Sacrifice—you speak of the Sacrifice of the Twins!"

"*Yes.* You yourself, Warmaster, must have wondered in your heart of hearts, must have doubted the True Gods' promise of victory, when the final sacrifice could not be performed."

"The True Gods do not mock, and They do not promise in vain," the warmaster intoned piously.

"But Their gifts are not *given*," Nom Anor said. "You know this. They require that we *earn* them: that *we* bring Their prophecies to pass."

"Yes."

"And so on that great day, Jacen Solo will himself capture his sister, his twin—he will drag her to the altar, and he will himself take her life in the Great Twin Sacrifice, and the will of the True Gods shall finally be brought to pass."

"The True Gods' will be done!" Tsavong Lah thundered.

"The True Gods' will be done," Nom Anor agreed.

"You will do this."

"Yes, Warmaster."

"You will not fail."

"If it be within my power, Warmaster—"

"No," Tsavong Lah said. "You do not understand. I tell you, Nom Anor, *you will not fail*. The True Gods are not mocked. Should Jacen Solo *not* turn to the True Path, no breath of this can be whispered; no hint of this can be *thought*. For Nom Anor, there is only victory; lacking victory, the creature that is currently called by the name Nom Anor shall be sacrificed to the True Gods as a nameless thing."

Nom Anor swallowed. "Ah, Warmaster—?"

Tsavong Lah went on inexorably. "All who have breathed the air of this plan shall die, screaming and without names, and their bones shall be scattered to drift between the stars. In every Name of all True Gods, this is my word."

Abruptly, the villip inverted to its quiescent state, folding in upon itself with wet slaps like raw meat smacking bone.

Nom Anor sat back, and discovered that he was trembling. This was not quite how he had expected matters to go. *There's the trouble with fanatics,* he thought. *They're easy to manipulate, but somehow they take everything five steps too far.*

He took a long sip of the dragweed broth in the sacworm that he had held, forgotten, throughout the interview. He turned to the other occupant of the small chamber. "Well, now we are partners in truth: together, we face either total victory or utter destruction," he said heavily. "We are, as the Corellians say, off to a flying start."

Across the quiescent villip, his partner met his gaze with unblinking avian calm.

"Well begun," Vergere said neutrally, "is half done."

TWO

THE NURSERY

Deep in the infinite space above the plane of the galactic ecliptic—in the spark-scattered velvet so far from any stellar system that the place was not, strictly speaking, even a place at all, only a statistical array of vectors and velocities—a small vessel of yorik coral dropped from hyperspace. It was so far from any observable point of fixed reference that its motion was arbitrary: on an Obroa-skai referent, the vessel streaked away at a respectable fraction of lightspeed; referent to Tatooine it swung in a long, lazy arc; referent to Coruscant it infell, gathering velocity.

Its twin dovin basals pulsed, emitting expanding ripples of gravity waves; some considerable time thereafter, those same dovin basals registered other space-time ripples in reply.

The vessel was not alone.

These answering ripples had a direction; the dovin basals of the small vessel were sensitive enough to register the femtosecond-scale difference between the instant one dovin basal detected a wave of space-time and the instant that wave reached its twin.

The small vessel of yorik coral altered course.

The object toward which it curved was a sphere of extravagant construction, hundreds of thousands of times the volume of the small vessel, featureless save for an array of black fins that girdled the globe and intersected at random, like mountain ranges on an airless moon. These fins glowed in the deep infrared, radiating waste heat into the void.

The vessel of yorik coral slowed to intercept the sphere, angling toward one of the smooth fleshy expanses between the radiating fins. As it closed the final few meters, a docking claw like the chelicerae of a spider-roach extended from its nose and gripped the semi-elastic surface. A few moments passed while dovin basals shimmered space-time at each other, and the signals thus exchanged were interpreted by specially bred cousins of villips, which passed on the information to the creatures who served as the guiding wills of the two living structures: shapers of the Yuuzhan Vong.

The smooth plain to which the vessel had attached itself bunched into sudden landscape, gathering into a spasmic impact crater whose rim reached out and out and out. A hundred meters beyond the nether tip of the coral vessel, the rim became lips, the crater a mouth that closed around the vessel, slowly contracting to vacuum-fit itself to the vessel's every angle and curve.

The sphere swallowed.

Within seconds, the place where the vessel had rested was once again a broad, smooth plain of semi-elastic flesh, featureless and warm.

Jacen opened his eyes as the hatch sphincter dilated. Vergere stood outside. She did not seem inclined to enter. "You're looking well."

He shrugged and sat up. He chafed the new scars around his wrists, where the Embrace of Pain had rasped away his skin. The last of his scabs had peeled off two sleeps ago. "I haven't seen you for a while," he said.

"Yes." Vergere's crest fanned an inquiring green. "How have you been enjoying your vacation from the Embrace? I see your wrists have healed. How do your shoulders feel? Your hips and ankles? Can you walk?"

Jacen shrugged again, looking down. He had lost track of how many times he had slept and awakened again since the Embrace of Pain had finally released him. While his body had knit, he had never been able to make himself do more than glance at the branches and tentacles and sensory orbs of the Embrace of Pain. They were still up there, coiled around each other in eel-basket knots, pulsing faintly. Waiting. He didn't know why they had released him.

He was afraid that if he stared at them too long, they would remember he was here.

Vergere extended a hand. "Arise, Jacen Solo. Arise and walk."

He met her gaze, blinking astonishment. "For real?" he asked. "You're taking me out of here? For real?"

A liquid shrug rippled along her too-flexible arm. "That depends," she said sunnily, "on what you mean by *here*. And what you mean by *real*. But to stay where you are, while this chamber is—I believe the Basic word is—*digested*, yes? This you would not enjoy."

"Enjoy . . . Oh, right. I forgot," he muttered. "I'm supposed to be having *fun*."

"You mean you're not?" She tossed him a crude robe that seemed to be woven of coarse, unbleached fiber. "Let's see if we can find you a residence more entertaining, hmm?"

He forced himself to his feet and slipped the robe over his head. The robe was warm to the touch; it writhed gently as he struggled into it, fibers bunching and unbunching like sleepy worms. Putting it on hurt. Slower to heal than his skin, his shoulders and hip joints grated as though packed with chunks of duracrete, but he didn't so much as grimace.

This was merely pain; he barely noticed.

She held something in her other hand: a baling hook of sun-yellowed bone, long and curved and sharp.

He stopped. "What's that?"

"What's what?"

"In your hand. Is that some kind of weapon?"

Her crest flattened and spread again, its green now shimmering with yellow highlights. "Why would I carry a weapon? Am I in danger?"

"I—" Jacen rubbed his eyes. Now only a blur hung from her fist; had he seen what he thought he saw?

"Probably just a trick of the light," Vergere said. "Forget about it. Come with me."

He stepped through the hatch sphincter. The corridor had somehow changed; instead of the resin-smoothed yorik coral passageway he had glimpsed when Vergere would come or go, he now stood inside one end of a tunnel or a tube. The floor was warm and soft, fleshy, and it pulsed faintly beneath his bare feet.

A pair of tall, impassive Yuuzhan Vong warriors stood outside in full vonduun crab armor, right arms thick with the coils of their amphistaffs. "Pay no attention to them," Vergere said lightly. "They speak no Basic, nor have they tizowyrms to translate—and they have no idea who you are. They are here only to ensure that you cause no mischief. Don't make them hurt you."

Jacen only shrugged. He looked back through the closing sphincter. He was leaving a lot of pain in that room.

He was bringing a lot of pain with him.

Anakin . . . Every time he blinked, he could see his

brother's corpse on the inside of his eyelids. It still hurt. He guessed it always would.

But pain didn't mean so much to him anymore.

He fell in at Vergere's side as she stalked away along the slick warm tunnel; it was valved like the inside of a vein. The warriors followed.

Jacen forgot about the hook of bone.

It had probably been just a trick of the light.

Jacen couldn't find a direction or a pattern in the route they walked, through endless tangles of fleshy tubes that seemed to branch and coil and knot themselves at random. Light filtered through the walls from outside, vividly illuminating striated arterial clusters in the tubes' translucent skin. Valves before them opened at Vergere's touch; valves behind closed by themselves. Sometimes the tubes contracted until Jacen had to walk hunched over, and the warriors were forced to bend nearly double. Sometimes they were in large tunnels that flexed and pulsed as though pumping air; a constant breeze huffed at their backs like the breath of a well-fed watchbeast.

The tube-skin vibrated like a huge slack drumhead, making the air hum and rumble, sometimes so low that Jacen could only feel the sound with his hand against the skin wall, sometimes louder, higher, scaling up to a tidal roar of a thousand voices moaning and shouting and screaming in pain.

Often they passed hatch sphincters like the one that had sealed the Embrace of Pain; sometimes these might be open, revealing chambers floored with grassy swamp, woody trunks branching above brownish muck, globular yawns draped with cocoons of alien pupae, or caverns vast and dark where tiny flames of crimson and chartreuse, of vivid yellow or dim, almost invisible violet floated and gleamed and winked like eyes of predators gathered in the night to watch prey huddled around a campfire.

Rarely Jacen caught glimpses of other Yuuzhan Vong: mostly warriors, whose unscarred faces and unmutilated limbs hinted at low status, and once or twice even a few of the shorter, squattier-seeming Yuuzhan Vong, each wearing some kind of living headdress that reminded Jacen of Vergere's feathered crest. These must be shapers; Jacen remembered Anakin's tale of the shaper base on Yavin 4.

"What is this place?" Jacen had been on Yuuzhan Vong ships before, and he'd seen their planetside installations at Belkadan: sure, they had been organic, more grown than built—but they had been *comprehensible.* "Is this a ship? A space station? Some kind of creature?"

"It is all those, and more. The Yuuzhan Vong name for this—ship, station, creature, what you will—translates as 'seedship.' I suppose a biologist might call it an ecospheric blastoderm." She pulled him close and lowered her voice as though sharing a private joke. "This is an egg that will give birth to an entire world."

Jacen made a face like he tasted something foul. "A Yuuzhan Vong world."

"Of course."

"I was on Belkadan. And Duro. There was nothing like this. To do their—what would you call it? Vongforming?—they just sprayed gene-tailored bacteria into the atmosphere—"

"Belkadan and Duro are no more than industrial parks," Vergere said. "They are shipyards producing war matériel. They will be used up, and abandoned. But the world transformed by this seedship—it will be *home.*"

Jacen felt weak. "Home?"

"A planet can be described as a single organism, a living creature with a skeleton of stone and a heart of molten rock. The species that inhabit a planet, plant and animal alike, from microbe to megalossus, are the planet-creature's organs, internal symbionts, and parasites. This seedship itself is composed mostly of incubating stem cells, which will differentiate into living machines—which will in turn construct an entire planet's worth of wild-life with vastly accelerated growth. Animals will mature within a few standard days; whole forests within weeks. Mere months after seeding, the new world will bear a fully functioning, dynamically stable ecosystem: the replica of a planet dead for so many thousand years that it is barely a memory."

"Their homeworld," Jacen muttered. "The Yuuzhan Vong. They're making themselves a new homeworld. That's what this is."

"You might call it that." Vergere stopped and gestured to one of the warriors. She touched a spot on the tube-skin. The warrior stepped forward and twitched his right arm; his amphistaff uncoiled into a blade that ripped a long, ragged slash through the wall. The lips of the slash seeped milky fluid. Vergere pulled one lip aside as though holding open a curtain. She made a slight bow, beckoning Jacen to step through.

"I would call it a work in progress," she said. "Rather like you."

Darkly swamp-smelling fog gusted into the tube, warm and thick and smoke-roiling. Jacen snorted. "Smells like the plumbing broke in your barracks refresher. What's *this* supposed to teach me?"

"There's only one way to find out."

Jacen pushed through the gap, into air smotheringly thick with rot and excrement and hot wet mold. Sweat prickled out over his skin. The milky fluid-blood from the gap trailed pale sticky strings that clung to his hair and his hands. He scrubbed at them with the robe, but the milk liked his skin better than the fiber.

Then he looked up, and forgot about the milk.

This was where the screams had been coming from.

He stood in a world turned inside out.

The tunnel at his back made a knotted hump like a varicose vein across the crest of the hill. From up here, Jacen had a clear vantage over a boil of swamp and jungle all the way to the horizon.

But there was no horizon.

Through storm-swirls of stinking fog, an endless bowl of scum-stained pools and fetid belching quagmires rose higher and higher and higher until he had to squint against the actinic blue-white pinprick that was this place's sun. Then a rift parted the fog above, and he could see beyond the sun: other swamps and jungles and ridges of low hills sealed shut the sky. Blurred in the regathering mist, it seemed that vast creatures roamed those hills in disorganized herds—but then the mist thinned again, and the scene snapped into perspective.

Those creatures weren't huge; they were *human*.

Not just human, but also Mon Calamari, and Bothan and Twi'lek, and dozens of other species of the New Republic.

Those hills overhead were only a klick away, maybe a klick and a half. The "sun" must have been some kind of artificial fusion source, probably not much bigger than Jacen's fist. He nodded to himself; with the fine gravity control wielded by dovin basals, it wouldn't be much of a trick to contain a fusion furnace. Filtering out damaging radiation would be trickier, though. He couldn't guess how they managed it without shield technology; he'd never been technical. His gift had been with animals. For that kind of question, he'd just ask Jaina, or Anakin—

He shook himself, and ground his teeth together until the pain ebbed.

Now he could pick out Yuuzhan Vong among the groups: some warriors—not many—but hundreds and hundreds of what he guessed must be shapers, moving in slow and purposeful paths, taking soil and water samples, collecting leaves and strips of bark, stems, and handfuls of algae, paying no attention at all to what he'd originally taken for herds.

Those herds—

If he'd still had the Force, he would have felt the truth instantly.

Those are slave gangs.

"Magnificent, isn't it?" Vergere said from beside him.

Jacen shook his head. "Madness," he answered. "I mean, *look* at this—"

He swung a hand toward a nearby bog. Along its bank, a crew dug savagely with crude shovels, howling as they threw muck and vegetation and dirt in all directions, trying to excavate what would probably have been some kind of drainage ditch, while another howling gang worked just as savagely to fill the ditch in once more. A little farther away, a knot of shouting, swearing people stuck grain cuttings into the mud, while a handful of others followed behind, moaning through streams of anguished tears while they stamped the cuttings flat. The sphere was filled with similar useless struggle: stone cairns being simultaneously built up and torn down, fields being packed flat with rolled stone while still being plowed, saplings being planted and chopped down, all by half-naked slaves staggering with exhaustion, some cursing, some sobbing, the rest only bellowing and shrieking wordless animal pain.

Even where there was no struggle, the slaves lurched from task to task as though pursued by invisible clouds of stinging insects; a man digging a hole might suddenly spasm as if he'd touched an open power bus, then clamber out to half build a dike, then jerk again and stumble away to uproot marsh grass by the handful and scatter it randomly to the wind.

"This, this *insanity* . . ." Jacen hugged himself, swallowing hard, his breath shallow against a retch that twisted his guts. "How can you call this magnificent?"

"Because I see beyond what it is, to what it shall become." Vergere touched his arm. Her eyes danced. "Follow me."

Coils and knots of veins made footholds up the outer skin of the tunnel. Vergere sprang from one to the next with assured agility, then waited at the crest while Jacen struggled painfully up to join her. The thick reeking air had him gasping, drenched with sweat, half smothered as if he'd been wrapped in a blanket of wet tauntaun hide. The pair of warriors followed, impassive and deliberate.

"But what is *this* place for?" Jacen waved a hand at the pandemonium. "What does this have to do with Vongforming a planet?"

"This?" Vergere's head tilted in a way that Jacen had learned to interpret as a smile. "This is a playground."

"A *playground*?"

"Oh, yes. Is this not what playgrounds are in the New Republic—a place for children to learn the boundaries of behavior? One learns to fight in playground scuffles; one learns politics in playground cliques. It is on the playground that one is initiated into the madness of mobs, the insidious mire of peer pressure, and the final, unthinkable, inarguable *unfairness* of existence—that some are smarter, others stronger or faster, and no force at your command can make you better than your gifts."

Her gesture encompassed the entire sphere. "What you see around you is the work of powerful, undisciplined infants . . . playing with their toys."

"These aren't *toys*," Jacen blurted, appalled. "These are *living beings*—humans, Bothans—"

"I will not argue names with you, Jacen Solo. Call them what you will. Their use remains the same."

"What *use*? What possible value could anybody get out of this—this pointless *suffering*?"

Vergere shook her head pityingly. "Do you think a process so complex as re-creating an entire planetary ecology can be entrusted to chance? Oh, no no no, Jacen Solo. There is *learning* involved. Education. Trial and error—more error than not, of course. And practice. Practice, practice, practice."

She opened a hand like a service droid offering a table in a fancy restaurant, indicating a large pond not far from the base of the hill where they stood. An island bulged from the pond's middle, a huge hulking mound of slick, waxy hexagonal blocks like sealed birth chambers in a hive of Corellian wine-bees—except each of these chambers was large enough to swallow the *Millennium Falcon*.

A ring of Yuuzhan Vong warriors circled the pond, facing outward with weapons at the ready as though to defend it against unexpected attack; another ring of warriors held the shore of the central island itself. Dozens or hundreds of shapers clambered among the blocks, bearing bundles and implements and jiggling sacs of liquid. Occasionally one of the shapers would use an implement to pierce the plug at the end of one of the blocks, passing either a bundle or a liquid-filled sac within before sealing the block again, and Jacen realized that his wine-bee analogy had been unexpectedly apt. Those huge hexagonal blocks must contain some sort of living creatures—something already huge, perhaps the pupal forms of unimaginable giants—

"What are they?" he breathed.

"The real issue is not so much what they are, as what the single one that survives to maturity will become."

Again she smiled, and her crest bloomed vivid orange. "Like all complex creatures," she said, "the Yuuzhan Vong homeworld will require a brain."

The creatures were called dhuryams.

Related to yammosks, dhuryams are fully as specialized as the giant war coordinators, but bred for a different, much more complex type of telepathic coordination. Bigger, stronger, vastly more powerful, dhuryams are capable of mentally melding many, many more disparate elements than the greatest yammosk that ever lived. A dhuryam will be responsible for integrating the activities of the Vongforming organomachines. The dhuryam will be less a servant than a partner: fully intelligent, fully aware, capable of making decisions based on a constant data flow streaming in from the entire planetwide network of telepathically linked creatures, to guide the planet's transformation flawlessly, without any of the chaotic-system fragility that plagues natural ecologies.

When Vergere had finished describing them, Jacen said slowly, "These slave gangs—you're saying they're being mentally controlled?"

Vergere nodded. "You may have noticed the lack of guards, with the exception of the dhuryam hive itself. And those are there only to prevent the dhuryams from using their slaves to murder their siblings."

"Murder—?"

"Oh, yes. Behaviors can be bred, but skills must be learned. Much of what the dhuryams are doing here is learning play—not unlike a pilot training in a flight simulator. Here they hone their skills, of mental mastery and the coordination of many disparate life-forms, that one of them will later use as the World Brain."

"*One* of them . . ." Jacen echoed.

"Only one. The games these children play are more than serious. They are deadly. These infant dhuryams know already the basic truth of existence: win or die."

"It's so—" Jacen's fists clenched helplessly. "—so *horrible.*"

"I would call it *honest.*" She smiled up at him, friendly, cheerful, untouched by the horror around them. "Life is struggle, Jacen Solo. It has always been so: an unending savage battle, red in tooth and claw. This is perhaps the greatest strength of the Yuuzhan Vong; our masters— unlike the Jedi, unlike the New Republic—never delude themselves. They never waste their energy pretending that this is not so."

"You keep saying 'our masters.'" Jacen's knuckles whitened. "You mean *your* masters. This—this *perversion*—this has nothing to do with me."

"You will be astonished, I think, when you discover just how wrong you are."

"No," Jacen said, stronger. "*No.* The only master I've ever had is Master Skywalker. I serve only the Force. The Yuuzhan Vong can kill me, but they can't make me obey."

"Poor little Solo." Her arms rippled in another of her liquid shrugs. "Do you ever get embarrassed at being so thoroughly and consistently mistaken?"

Jacen looked away. "You're wasting your time, Vergere. I have nothing to learn from this place."

"You see? Doubly mistaken: my time is not wasted, nor is this your schoolroom." She lifted her hand—a flickering, blurred gesture—and the two warriors at Jacen's back seized his arms in grips hard as hull metal. Then the blur in her hand resolved into that wicked hook of bone.

The Force, he thought, panic surging into his heart. *She Force-blurred it—she's been carrying it all along!*

"This is your new *home*," she said, and stabbed him in the chest.

THREE

THE GARDEN

Just within the fringe of the galactic event horizon—that battlement of gravity where even infinite hyperspace finds its limit—the seedship fell beyond the reality of the universe for the last time. It became, for the last time, its own universe.

This seed-universe, like the larger one it had left, continued to evolve. Over time that had meaning only within its bubble, the seed-universe differentiated and complexified. The flesh between the radiating fins altered, becoming thicker and harder here, softer and more billowy there, as fetal creature-devices coalesced inside wombs that grew themselves just within its thin skin of reality.

In the directionless nonlocation of hyperspace, this seed-universe began its long, long, slow fall toward the center of the galaxy.

Jacen saw Vergere coming: a small agile silhouette in the misty green gloom that passed for night in the Nursery. She hopped deliberately across the luminescent scum-smeared surface of the vonduun crab bog, her attention on her footing as though she scavenged tide pools.

Jacen's jaw locked.

He looked down again at the wound in the slave's belly: a long curved gash, not too deep. The slave's skin was pink, shading angry red at the lips of the wound; the slave shuddered when Jacen pulled the lips apart. The wound was superficial, only seeping blood—he could see soft tallow within, not hard red muscle or the webbed bulge of gut, and he nodded to himself. "You'll be all right. From now on, stay away from the amphistaff grove."

"How—how can I?" the slave whined. "What choice do I have?"

"There's always a choice," Jacen muttered. He scratched his head: his hair had grown out enough to start to curl. It was caked with greasy dirt, and it itched—though not as much as the thin, patchy teenager's beard that roughened his cheeks and neck. He glanced back up at Vergere.

She was closer now, weaving through the fungal colony mounds of young oogliths. He hadn't seen her since his first day in the Nursery. That had been, by his best estimate, weeks ago.

Possibly months.

He teased open the mouth of a bulging sacworm that lay on the ground beside him, and stuck his hand inside. The clip beetles that filled the sacworm's belly attacked his hand savagely; Jacen waited until twenty or thirty had clamped their mandibles into his skin, then pulled his hand out and let the sacworm's mouth snap closed once more. The clip beetles bristled like a knobbed insectile glove. He used his beetle-gloved hand to pinch the slave's belly wound together. With his free hand he tickled the head joint of a clip beetle until its jaws opened; then he pressed the beetle along the wound until its mandibles engaged once more, clipping the wound together. A quick twist of his fingers snapped off the beetle's body; its head remained in place.

It took twenty-three clip beetles to close the slave's wound. He gently disengaged the living beetles that still clung to his hand and returned them to the sacworm, then tore strips from the lower edge of the slave's robeskin to tie around his middle in a makeshift bandage. The robeskin and the strips alike bled milk from their ripped edges: a sticky resinous blood that glued the strips together and healed them in place.

"Try to keep it dry," Jacen told him quietly. "And don't go anywhere near the amphistaff grove until it heals. I'm pretty sure they can smell wounds. They'll cut you to ribbons."

This amphistaff grove was very different from the one he had found on the worldship at Myrkr; those had been shaped, altered, domesticated. Tamed. The amphistaff grove in the Nursery was the original, the baseline. Nothing about it was tame.

The amphistaff polyps in this grove ranged from one to three meters tall: deep-rooted mounds of leather-fleshed tissue, each with two to five muscular nodules from which sprouted triads of juvenile amphistaffs. Amphistaff polyps are sessile carnivores; the juvenile amphistaffs act as the polyp's arms and weapons, spearing, envenoming, and eventually dissecting a polyp's prey into chunks small enough to be swept into the polyp's fist-sized groundmouth. They will kill and eat any living thing. Only the vonduun crab, the amphistaff polyp's sole natural enemy, can approach them in safety, protected by the shallow curve of their impenetrable topshell.

"But—but if I'm *sent*," the slave moaned. "What then?"

"The slave seed-web is only hooked into your touch-pain nerves. The worst it can do is cause pain," Jacen said. "The amphistaffs will kill you."

"But the pain—the *pain*—"

"I know."

"You *don't* know," the slave said bitterly. "They never make you do anything."

"They don't make *you* do anything either. They can't. All they can do is hurt you. It's not the same thing."

"Easy for you to say! When was the last time they hurt *you*?"

Jacen rose, looking away toward Vergere. "You'd better get some sleep. They'll turn the sun back on soon."

Muttering, the slave dragged himself away, moving toward the rest of the slaves. He didn't say thanks.

They rarely did.

Except when the slaves brought their wounds for him to treat, they barely spoke to him at all. They avoided him. He was too strange, too unlike any of the others, and he wasn't easy to talk to. He walked among them in a permanent bubble of solitude; no one wanted to get too close. They feared him. Sometimes they hated him, too.

Jacen bent down and swept up a handful of the headless beetles. While he watched Vergere approach, he cracked their abdominal shells one by one between his thumb and first knuckle, scooping out the pale purple flesh. Clip beetle flesh was high in protein and fats, and tasted like Mon Cal ice-lobster.

It was the most appetizing thing he ever got to eat.

Vergere picked her way among the sleeping slaves. She looked up and met his eye, smiling, and gave a flickering wave with one hand. Jacen said, "That's close enough."

She stopped. "What, no hug? No kiss for your friend Vergere?"

"What do you want?"

She got that wise smile and opened her mouth as if she was about to give one of her cryptic nonanswers, but instead she shrugged, sighed, and the smile faded. "I am curious," she said plainly. "How is your chest?"

Jacen touched his robeskin over the suppurating hole

below his ribs. His robe had healed weeks ago. Even the bloodstain was gone. He suspected that the robeskins lived on the secretions of the creatures who wore them: sweat, blood, sloughed skin cells, and oils. His was large and healthy, even though he continually ripped strips from it for bandages, both for himself and for the wounded slaves he treated; it always grew back to the original length within a day or two.

His chest, though—

Looking at Vergere, he could feel it happen once more: the bone hook slicing in below his ribs, curving up to puncture his diaphragm. Its point had nicked his lung, then scratched against the inside of his sternum: an icy shuddering nonpain that punched a hole through his strength. He had sagged in the warriors' grips.

Vergere had withdrawn the hook slowly; it skidded through clamped muscle. She examined him at some length, her crest shimmering an iridescent, unreadable rainbow. "Do you feel it yet?"

Jacen had stared down at the sluggish trail of blood that leaked from the hole below his ribs. The hole had been no bigger than the end of his little finger; he'd felt an absurd desire to stick his finger in the hole like the stopper in a bottle of Corellian whiskey.

Only then had Vergere told him what that hook of bone had done: implanted a slave coral seed inside his chest. "Well done," she had said to the weapon cheerfully. "Go; enjoy yourself." The hook had relaxed, coiling around her wrist for a moment like a hug from an affectionate snake, then unwrapped itself and dropped to the ground, slithering away into the underbrush.

"I know you've been implanted before," she had told him. "On Belkadan, yes? That seed, though, grew too slowly and was removed too easily. So I've made your new, improved one less . . . mm, less *accessible.*"

And the agony that had blossomed over his heart—

The slave seed had sprouted in seconds, filaments wriggling like screwworms into his celiac plexus. It said hello by secreting algesic enzymes, triggering a star flare in his chest that slapped him off his feet like a blow from a club. He lay on the knotted hump of vein flesh, curled around his pain.

Vergere and the warriors had left him there. No instructions or orders were necessary; the slave seed—with an efficiency Jacen had come to think of as typically Yuuzhan Vong—had let him know what was required of him, simply and directly.

It had hurt him.

The slave seed was linked telepathically to one of the dhuryams. Whenever Jacen wasn't doing what the dhuryam wanted, the slave seed set his nerves on fire. The only way to escape pain was to discover the dhuryam's desire: he'd try one thing after another until he found an activity that did not hurt.

Often it took a while to figure out. Sometimes a long while.

Here in the Nursery, the sun was extinguished for about a third of each day; instead of moons for light during the artificial night, the Nursery had an abundance of phosphorescent mosses and algae. He could count days now, if he wished, but he didn't bother. He could chart the passage of time by the spread of slave seed filaments webbing his nerves.

He could feel it growing.

As it grew, its control refined; through the increasingly sophisticated slave seed-web, the dhuryam could tell him to go forward by hurting his back. It could tell him to pick something up by hurting his empty hand. At need, it could spike his nerves so sharply that involuntary spasms would jerk an arm or a leg in the appropriate direction.

The injection wound left by Vergere's weapon had gone bad: red and inflamed and crusted with yellow ooze. Jacen pressed his palm against the stiff robeskin-bandage over it. He stared expressionlessly at the alien avianoid creature who had inflicted this on him. "My chest?" he said. "It's all right."

"Let me see."

"Leave me alone."

"Have we not yet discussed, Jacen Solo, the futility of acting like a child?" She hopped nimbly toward him.

"Stay away from me, Vergere. I mean it."

"I believe you," she said. She reached solid ground and stalked up to him. "But what matters your meaning? How will you prevent me? Will you slay?"

Jacen clenched his fists and did not answer.

"Will you maim? Cripple your friend Vergere? No?" She gave him her arm as though inviting him to dance. "Break a bone, then—above the wrist, if you don't mind. It should heal cleanly enough to be a merely temporary inconvenience."

"Vergere—"

"Inflict pain," she offered. "Twist my elbow. Pluck feathers from my crest. Otherwise, sit down and show me your ribs. Orders not backed by force are only suggestions, Jacen Solo."

And her orders are orders, Jacen thought. She could have a squad of warriors here in minutes; she could probably Force-hold him in midair and do whatever she wanted. But still he did not move.

She cocked her head quizzically, smiling sideways up at him. She gathered her four opposable fingers into a point and jabbed firmly, accurately, through the robeskin onto his infected wound.

Pain blazed in his side. Jacen didn't even blink.

"I told you," he said evenly. "It's all right."

She pointed to the ground, to the crushed layers of moss where the slave had lain while Jacen had beetled his wound. "Lie down."

Jacen didn't move.

"Jacen Solo," she said patiently, "you know the Force is with me. Do you think I cannot feel your infection? Am I so blind that I cannot see fever boiling in your eyes? Am I so weak that I cannot knock you down?"

There may come a time, Jacen thought, *when we will answer that last one.* But he sighed and lowered himself to the moss.

Vergere seized his robeskin with both hands, then lowered her face to nip a hole in it with her small sharp dental ridges. She tore the hole wide, then stripped off the bandage beneath. Folding the bandage upon itself, she roughly scrubbed away the infected crust over the wound. Jacen watched her expressionlessly, not reacting to the coarse scrape across his inflamed ribs.

She noted his regard, and winked at him. "Pain means little to you now, yes?"

"Since the Embrace?" Jacen shrugged. "I don't ignore it, if that's what you mean."

"But it does not rule you," she said approvingly. "There are some who say that humans are incapable of overcoming their fear of pain."

"Maybe the people who say that don't know very many humans."

"And maybe they do. Maybe they simply know none like you."

She lowered her head and closed her eyes, cupping the folded bandage in the palm of one hand. Jacen stared, astonished, while she wept.

Liquid gems gathered at the corners of her eyes and

rolled down her muzzle, gleaming in the misty green twilight. *Vergere's tears* . . . He remembered the little vial of tears, and Mara's sudden recovery from the coomb-spore infection that everyone had privately expected would take her life.

Vergere mopped tears from her face with the crusted bandage, then applied that bandage once more to Jacen's wound.

His pain vanished.

"Hold this in place," she said, and when Jacen put his hand on the bandage she began to tear strips from the lower edge of his robeskin.

Jacen couldn't stop himself from lifting the bandage. He had to see.

The inflammation was gone. The skin around his wound was pink and healthy, and the wound itself dripped blood that looked and smelled normal, instead of the thick death-reeking ooze of infection that had leaked from it these many days.

"How—?" he gasped. "How could you *possibly*—"

"Didn't I tell you to keep that in place?" Vergere slapped the bandage flat again, then briskly tied it down with the strips she'd torn from Jacen's robeskin.

"Those tears—what *are* they?" Jacen asked, awed.

"Whatever I choose them to be."

"I don't understand."

"If you still had the Force, it would be obvious. Females of my species have very sophisticated lachrymal glands; even the Force-blind can—could—alter their tears to produce a wide range of pheromonal signals and chemical intoxicants for use on our males. Using the Force, my control is very precise: I can match the molecular structure of my tears to my desire, whether that desire be a systemic cure for coomb-spore infection—or merely a potent topical antibiotic with instant steroidal properties."

"Wow," Jacen breathed. His heart stung with sudden hope. "I mean, *wow*. Vergere, do you think—I mean, would you, uh—could I—?"

She gazed at him steadily. "Ask."

"There are so many—" he began. "There's a slave—a Bothan, Trask—he shattered his ankle. Compound fracture, and it's septic. I'll have to take off his foot. And that'll probably kill him anyway. Pillon Miner, he's human—he was the first one to find out that the amphistaff polyps in that grove over there are mature enough to attack. Peritonitis. He's dying. I have dozens of slaves carrying cuts and slashes, most of them infected—every time a slave goes by there, the amphistaffs attack. We're just lucky their venom glands aren't mature, or none of the slaves would survive at all. The oogliths budding on those hummocks, the ones you came by just now? Two of them got hold of a Twi'lek, across her back, but they're immature, too, and they don't have the antibacterial enzymes of the adults; when their feeder filaments stabbed through her pores, they carried who knows what kind of germs. That's her over there—the one who's moaning. There's nothing I can do for her. I don't think she'll live until morning."

"Nothing you have said is a question, or a request." Vergere blinked once, slowly, then again. "Ask."

Jacen clenched his fists, and opened them again, and placed one against the bandage she had tied around his ribs. "Your tears, Vergere. You could save so many lives."

"Yes, I could."

"Please, Vergere. Will you?"

"No."

"Please—"

"No, Jacen Solo. I will not. Why should I? They are slaves."

"They're *people*—"

She shrugged.

"You helped *me*," Jacen said, desperation and anger starting to gather behind his voice. "Why would you do this for me, and not for any of them?"

"*Why* is a question deeper than its answer." She settled back onto the mossy ground. Her crest lay flat along the curve of her skull. "Tell me this, Jacen Solo: what distinguishes a flower from a weed?"

"Vergere—"

"This is not a riddle. What distinguishes a flower from a weed is only—and exactly—this: the choice of the gardener."

"I'm not a *gardener*," Jacen said, biting down on his temper. He leaned toward her, blood surging into his face. "*And these are not weeds!*"

She shrugged. "Again, our difficulties may be linguistic. To me, a gardener is one who chooses what to cultivate, and what to uproot; who decides which lives must end so that the lives he cherishes may flourish." She lowered her head as though shy, or embarrassed, sighing; she opened her hand toward the headless shells of the clip beetles. "Is that not what you have done?"

He kept his eyes on her, hanging on to his anger. "Those are *bugs*, Vergere."

"So is a shadowmoth."

"I'm talking about *people*—"

"Were the beetles less alive than the slave? Is not a life a life, whatever form it takes?"

Jacen lowered his head. "You can't make me say I was wrong to do it. It wasn't wrong. He's a sentient being. Those were insects."

She gave out a wind-chime spray of laughter. "I did

not say it was *wrong*, Jacen Solo. Am I a moralist? I only point out that you make the gardener's choice."

Jacen had always been stubborn; he was far from ready to give up. "You're the gardener," he muttered sullenly, staring at his hands. "I'm just one of the weeds."

She placed her hand on his arm, her long flexible fingers warm and gentle; her touch was so clearly friendly, even affectionate, that Jacen for one moment felt as though his Force empathy had not deserted him. He *knew*, absolutely and without question, that Vergere meant him no harm. That she cared for him, and regretted his anger, his hostility, and his suffering.

But that doesn't mean she's on my side, he reminded himself.

"How is it," she asked slowly, "that you have come to be the medical droid for your slave gang? Of all the jobs that all the slaves do, how did this one fall to you?"

"There's no one else who can do it."

"No one who can set a bone? No one who can wash clean a cut? No one who can twist the head off a clip beetle?"

Jacen shrugged. "No one who can tell the dhuryam to blow itself out an air lock."

"Ah." That translucent inner lid slid down her eye. "The dhuryam disapproves?"

"Let's say it took some convincing."

"Convincing?"

"Yeah."

She said nothing for a long time. She might have been waiting for him to elaborate; she might have been trying to guess what he had done. She might have been thinking of something else altogether. "And how did you manage to convince it?"

Jacen stared through her, remembering his savage private struggle against the slave seed and the dhuryam that controlled it, day after day of bitter agony. He wondered how much of that story she might know already; he was certain that she had some way of keeping him under observation.

The dhuryam was an intelligent creature; it had not taken long to discover that Jacen could not be moved by pain. But the dhuryam was itself stubborn by nature, and it had been specifically engineered to command. It was not accustomed to disobedience, nor inclined to tolerate it.

After days of straight, simple pain, the dhuryam had taken advantage of the slave seed's growth; it had spent more than a week jerking Jacen's limbs individually by remote control, using the slave seed to give him spasms and cramps that forced him to move, making him twitch and thrash like a holomonster controlled by a half-melted logic board.

The turning point had come when the dhuryam realized that it had been pouring so much energy and attention into its struggle with Jacen that it was neglecting its other slaves. Its domain in the Nursery was falling to ruin, becoming a wasteland among the lush domains of its sibling-rivals. It understood that breaking Jacen was an expensive undertaking: a project whose costs were counted in jobs that did not get done. And it soon began to discover that Jacen could be useful, even unbroken.

Jacen had taken every respite from the pain to minister to his fellow slaves. He didn't have real medical training, but his exotic life-form collection had taught him some basics of exobiology, and in his adventures with the other young Jedi he had garnered a working knowledge of field surgery.

The dhuryam had eventually seemed to understand that healthy slaves can work harder, and soon its domain began to improve again. Jacen had discovered that the dhuryam would let him do pretty much whatever he wanted, so long as it advanced the dhuryam's own interests.

I guess you could say, Jacen thought, *I taught the dhuryam that sometimes partners are more useful than slaves.*

But he said nothing of this.

He owed Vergere no answers.

"I told you before," he muttered solidly. "You can kill me, but you can't make me obey."

Her inner eyelids slid upward again. "And that, Jacen Solo, is why you are a flower among the weeds."

He looked into the bottomless black of her eyes, looked away at the scatter of slaves, resting among the Vong-formed life of the Nursery, then down at his hands, which curled into white-knuckled fists; he relaxed them again, then looked back at her, and finally, after all, he couldn't think of any reason not to just say it.

"You're Sith, aren't you?"

She went very, very still. "Am I?"

"I know a little about the dark side, Vergere. All this garbage about flowers and weeds—I know what you're *really* talking about. You're talking about believing you're *above* people."

"Everything I tell you is a—"

"Save it. You're wasting your time. Jaina and I were kidnapped by the Shadow Academy. They tried to turn us both. It didn't work." He thought briefly of Jaina, of the darkness he'd felt in his last touch through their twin bond. His hands became fists again, and he shook the memory out of his head. He repeated, "It didn't work. It won't work for you, either."

Her first motion: a faint curve at the corners of her lips. "Sith? Jedi?" she said. "Are these the only choices? Dark or light, good or evil? Is there no more to the Force than this? What is the screen on which light and dark cast their shapes and shadows? Where is the ground on which stands good and evil?"

"Save it. I've spent too much time wondering about those questions already. Years. I never got anywhere."

Her eyes lit up merrily. "You got here, yes?" A sweep of her arm took in the Nursery. "Is this not somewhere?"

Jacen shook his head, tired of this. He pushed himself to his feet. "All the answers fall short of the truth."

"Very good!" Vergere clapped her hands and bounced upright like a spring-loaded puppet. "*Very* good, Jacen Solo. Questions are more true than answers: this is the beginning of wisdom."

"*Your* kind of wisdom—"

"Is there any other kind? Does truth come in breeds like nerfs?" She seemed elated; she shivered as though she struggled against an urge to break into dance. "Here's a question of another kind—an easy kind, a friendly inquiry—to which there is an answer not only true, but useful."

Jacen got up. "I don't have time for this. They'll turn on the sun in a few minutes." He started walking toward the resting slaves. There were dressings to be changed before these slaves began their morning work.

Vergere spoke to his departing back. "If the Force is life, how can there be life without the Force?"

"What?" Jacen stopped. He looked over his shoulder. "What?"

"You are born to be a gardener," she said. "Remember this: it is not only your right to choose flowers over weeds, it is your *responsibility*. Which are flowers? Which are weeds? The choice is yours."

"What?"

With a lightning crackle and a wavefront blast of thunder, the Nursery's sun kindled overhead. Jacen flinched, shading his eyes against the sudden flare, and by the time he could see again Vergere was far away, hopping from hummock to hummock across the vonduun crab bog.

He stared after her.

If the Force is life, how can there be life without the Force?

He kept washing and clipping wounds, setting fractures, debriding septic flesh. The sun came on, the sun turned off. Some slaves got better. Some slaves died. Everybody kept working.

The dhuryam's domain flourished. Trees wove into fantastic structures, draped in iridescent epiphytes. Lush grasses on upland hills rippled in the bellows breath pumped through ventilation veins. To Jacen's eye, it seemed that this dhuryam's lands were more sophisticated, more elegant than those of its neighbors; when the mists would part enough that he could see the bowl of lands overhead, he thought that the domain where he lived was, in fact, the most developed in the whole Nursery. He was wryly aware, though, that his opinion might not be entirely objective; maybe he was just rooting for the home team.

If the Force is life, she had said, *how can there be life without the Force?*

He ached for the Force every day—every hour. Every minute. He was constantly, acutely aware of the gaping absence in his life: reminded every time he had to tie a tourniquet, reminded by each groan or squeal of pain that with the Force he could have eased.

Reminded when he had to amputate Trask's foot with an amphistaff he had cautiously, laboriously lured out of the grove by feeding pieces of a dead slave to its polyp until it shed its amphistaffs and they wriggled into the grass in search of new fertile ground to plant themselves—

Reminded when the Bothan died in delirium a few days later.

If the Force is life, how can there be life without the Force?

The question haunted him. It throbbed in the back of his head like an abscessed tooth. Vergere could have been talking about *his* life: how could he live without the Force?

The answer was, of course, that he couldn't. He didn't. The Force was there.

He just couldn't feel it.

Anakin used to say that the Force was a tool, like a hammer. If the Force is a hammer, Jacen decided, then he was a carpenter with his arms cut off. He couldn't even *see* the hammer anymore. He couldn't remember what it looked like.

But—

If I came of a species that had never had arms, I wouldn't recognize a hammer—and I'd have no use for it, even if I somehow guessed what it was. A hammer would have nothing to do with me at all.

Like the Force has nothing to do with the Yuuzhan Vong.

That was half an answer—but the other half kept wriggling, chewing at the inside of his skull.

Because the Force was not just a tool.

If the Yuuzhan Vong existed outside it, the Force must be less than he had been taught it was. Less than he *knew* it was. Because he knew, *bedrock* knew, knew beyond even the possibility of doubt, that the Force was not less than he'd been taught. It was more.

It was *everything*.

If the Force was only about life, how could it be used

TRAITOR 69

to pick up a rock, or a lightsaber, or an X-wing star-fighter? To move something with the Force, you have to *feel* it. A piece of rock has more presence in the Force than a living Yuuzhan Vong.

There was a mystery here, one that nagged at him. Fortunately, he had plenty of time to think about it.

As the days blended one into the next, the dhuryam seemed to gain an understanding of what Jacen did; through the slave seed, the dhuryam had sent occasional small, almost affectionate twinges—more like a pinch from a playmate than the crack of a slave master's whip—and Jacen discovered that if he followed where these twinges directed him, he might find, say, a type of moss with immunostimulant properties, or a secretion of the vonduun crabs that acted as a natural antiseptic.

Almost as though the dhuryam were trying to help . . .

Gradually, through these days, his idea of the dhuryam transformed. He had thought of it, through these bitter weeks, as a hideously alien monster that had reached inside his body with the slave seed, rasping his nerves with its loathsome, inescapable touch; now he discovered that when he thought of the dhuryam in unguarded moments, he felt no horror at all.

I guess you can get used to anything, eventually, he thought.

But it was more than that: he had begun to see the dhuryam as another life-form, an unfamiliar species, dangerous but not necessarily hostile. It had intelligence, will, intention; it was able to see that Jacen was doing more good than harm, and it had apparently consented to a working partnership.

If a species that had always been blind met a species that had always been deaf, how would they communicate? To Jacen, the answer was obvious: they would have to improvise a language *based on a sense that they shared.*

The pain from the slave seed was actually a form of communication, a primitive language that Jacen was slowly coming to comprehend, though he had not yet learned how to reply.

If the Force is life, how can there be life without the Force?

The realization did not come as a blinding revelation, but rather as a slow dawning of awareness, an incremental gathering of comprehension, so that on a steel-colored noon when he looked down from a hillock onto the dhuryam hive-island, he knew, and understood, and was neither suprised nor astonished at his new knowledge and understanding.

This was what he knew and understood: the answer for the Yuuzhan Vong was the same as the answer for himself.

There is no life without the Force.

The human eye does not register electromagnetic energy outside the tiny band of frequencies called visible light—but even though you can't see them, those frequencies exist. The Yuuzhan Vong and their creations must participate in a part of the Force that is beyond the range of Jedi senses.

That's all.

Jacen stood on the hillock, staring down at the dhuryam island with its ring of warrior-guards, and he thought, *The Yuuzhan Vong aren't the only ones who participate in a part of the Force that is outside the range of Jedi senses.*

I do, too.

He had always had a particular gift for making friends with alien species. He used to call it empathy, but it had always been more than shared emotion—

It had been an improvised language that operated through a part of the Force that other Jedi didn't seem able to sense.

That flash of empathy he'd gotten from Vergere—he had thought that was something she had projected, something *she* had done. What if it wasn't? What if his empathy came from part of the Force that he could still touch?

Standing on the hillock under the blue-white fusion-ball noon, Jacen began a cycle of breath that would ease his mind into Jedi focus. He reached down inside himself, feeling for the presence of the slave seed that was the dhuryam's link to him—and his link to the dhuryam.

He felt it, where it coiled along his nerves: an alien animal, sharing his body.

Hey there, little guy, he said inside himself. *Let's be friends.*

The viewspider stood on a spray of nine slim jointed legs that arched high from its central hub before curving down to support its weight on grip-clawed feet. Below its central hub hung a transparent sac large enough to hold a Wookiee, filled to bulging with optical jelly. The central hub also held the viewspider's brain, which integrated telepathic signals channeled from a variety of the slave seeds that drove the creatures in the Nursery. It integrated these signals into a holographic image, created within the jelly medium by the intersection of phased electromagnetic pulses from a cluster of glands where the jelly sac attached to the brain hub.

Nom Anor studied this image with a certain satisfaction, as did Vergere, who crouched on the chamber floor beyond the viewspider. Though he was not inclined to the doctrinaire fanaticism of, say, a Tsavong Lah, the executor had to admit that there were some ways in which

Yuuzhan Vong bioformed creatures truly were far superior to their mechanical counterparts in the New Republic. The viewspider itself, for example. Though not very intelligent, it did at least understand that its task was to maintain a real-time image of the Nursery centered on one specific subject, and to follow that subject wherever he might go. This it did very well.

The subject in question was Jacen Solo.

Nom Anor stretched onto his toes to stroke the viewspider's hub in a specific way, so that Jacen's image shrank, bringing into view more and more of the Nursery around him: the slaves who toiled in the wheel of domains that radiated from the dhuryam hive-island. Jacen seemed to be splinting the wrist of a slave who had taken a hard fall, but to Nom Anor's eye, much of Jacen's attention was clearly directed toward the hive-island in the distance.

"So," he said. "You say the second step is complete? The dhuryam has successfully seduced him?"

"Or he the dhuryam." Vergere leaned to one side to meet his eye through the thicket of viewspider legs. "It is the same. To create the empathic bond, as he has done, requires each of them to downplay their differences, and focus on all they have in common. Yes: the second step is complete."

"So." Nom Anor leaned back, and folded his long, bony fingers across his chest. "Jacen Solo has, for the moment, an alarming degree of freedom."

"Freedom is always alarming," Vergere agreed.

"Though more alarming is that he is now *aware* of it. I wonder if Tsavong Lah may have been overconfident in agreeing to this phase of the plan."

"Don't you mean," Vergere said with a sly half smile, "that you fear *you* were overconfident in proposing it?"

Nom Anor waved this aside. "Giving him room to

act is one thing; giving him that room in this ship is another."

"You believe he could threaten the ship? How?"

"I do not know." Nom Anor shifted his weight forward, resting his chin on his knuckles as he stared into the optical jelly. "But I have not survived this much of the war by underestimating Jedi—particularly the Solo family. I am concerned. Even the slightest threat to this ship is far too great a risk."

He had no need to elaborate; Vergere knew already that the genetic material that had gone into the creation of the seedship was irreplaceable: gene samples preserved through the incalculable millennia of the Yuuzhan Vong's intergalactic voyage aboard the worldships. Samples preserved from a homeworld so long vanished in the dust of history that not even its name survived.

"Ease your mind, Nom Anor. Has not each step gone perfectly so far?"

He scowled. "I distrust such easy victories."

"But easy victories are proof of the True Gods' favor," Vergere said in that irritating chime, a tone that may or may not have been intentionally mocking, Nom Anor had never been able to decide. "To distrust victory smacks of blasphemy—to say nothing of ingratitude . . ."

"Remember to whom you speak." The executor waved a dismissal. "Leave me. Maintain your vigilance. In fact, intensify it. These last few days before seedfall will be especially dangerous. Take no chances."

"As you say, Executor." Vergere favored him with a millimetrically correct bow, then opened the chamber's hatch sphincter and climbed out.

And Nom Anor, in his cautious, methodical way, took his own advice. As soon as Vergere left, Nom Anor sent a message by villip to the commander of a special detachment of warriors; this detachment had been brought aboard and specially trained for just such a moment as this. He issued a short string of orders.

Before the end of the day, warriors in ooglith masquers would begin to infiltrate the other slave gangs in the Nursery. They would stay well away from Jacen Solo, conceal their presence, and wait.

Before seedfall, there would be more than a hundred of them.

And meanwhile, Nom Anor made a mental note to have his coralcraft fed, groomed, and prepped for sudden takeoff.

He would take no chances. He had not survived so much of this war by underestimating Jedi.

When the Devaronian died, Jacen thought, *Okay, maybe I was wrong.*

He knelt on the hive-lake's verge. A mob of injured, wounded, and sick slaves surged and shouted around him, hands and tentacles and talons reaching for him, tugging at his robeskin. His robeskin had soaked up a lot of blood before Jacen had managed to tourniquet the stump of the Devaronian's arm; the Devaronian's silver-based blood was black as tarnish, and smelled of burned sulfur. From his link with the dhuryam through the slave seed in his chest, Jacen could faintly perceive his robeskin's primitive delight at the blood's unusual flavor.

As weeks passed, Jacen and the dhuryam had learned to communicate more precisely, through the medium of the slave seed. Perhaps it was because the dhuryam, like its cousin the yammosk, was innately telepathic to a limited degree even with humans; perhaps it was because Jacen had long, long experience with empathic and telepathic communication. Perhaps it was because the slave seed's web of tendrils had become so intimately entwined with Jacen's nervous system that it was practically a part of his brain. Jacen did not trouble himself with explanations.

Only results counted.

He could now exchange information with the dhuryam, in the form of emotions and images. By using these in combination, they had developed a wide-ranging mutual vocabulary, but their connection had gone beyond this. As his bond with the dhuryam had deepened, Jacen had found he could tap into the dhuryam's own senses: with concentration, he could become as aware of the various life-forms within the Nursery as was the dhuryam itself.

To reach the dying Devaronian, he'd had to fight his way through the mob of shouting, weeping, struggling slaves. Hundreds of them had gathered near the hive-lake, all hoping that Jacen might treat their wounds or illnesses. Many of the slaves had been driven here by other dhuryams, lashed by slave seed-web agony burning their nerves; though the other dhuryams had tried to develop medics of their own, they could neither find nor create other healers of Jacen's skill. His empathic bond with the slave seed let him use the dhuryams' own telepathic connections to feel the extent of wounds and diseases and internal injuries, and to treat them with an efficiency that would have astonished a trained meditech.

At first, his own dhuryam had tried to stop Jacen from treating slaves who belonged to its sibling-rivals; for nearly a day, Jacen and the dhuryam had gone back to their war of unendurable pain against unbreakable will. Through it all, Jacen had kept hearing Vergere's voice echo inside his head.

Which are flowers? Which are weeds? she had said. *The choice is yours.*

He had chosen.

No agony at any dhuryam's command could unmake his choice.

There are no weeds here.

Every slave was a flower. Every life was precious. He would spend the last erg of his strength to save every one of them.

There are no weeds here.

He had built an aid station near the bank of the lake that surrounded the dhuryam hive-island. Since the domains radiated from the lake like sections of longitude, here was the place where slaves from rival domains could reach him while passing through the least amount of enemy territory. His own dhuryam had cooperated to the point of giving Jacen the occasional help of a few members of his slave gang, to gather medicinal mosses and herbs, supplies of clip beetles, and young robeskins that could be used for bandages.

The Devaronian had been one of these temporary assistants. Jacen had sent him upland for a bundle of grain-bearing grasses that grew on a nearby hillock; when ground fine, these grains made an excellent coagulant, and were mildly antibiotic. The Devaronian had given a nod of his vestigial horns, offered a smile full of needle-sharp teeth, and set off willingly, without requiring any spurring from the dhuryam.

Before he could return, the crowd of wounded had grown to a mob. Shoving matches broke out as the competing dhuryams set their injured slaves against those of other sibling-rivals; some of these shoving matches had turned starkly violent before Jacen could intervene. The Devaronian had been caught at the edge of one, and all that his hissing and sharp-toothed threat displays had accomplished was to get himself shoved off around the fringes of the mob. He couldn't fight back without dropping the bundle of grasses Jacen had sent him for, and the two stunted horns that curved from his forehead were far from intimidating. He had tried to skirt the mob by slipping around the hive-pond's shore, since the ring of Yuuzhan Vong warriors around it prevented the mob from extending in that direction.

It was this that had killed him.

Jacen didn't know if the Devaronian had stumbled, or slipped on the scummy reeds that lay flat at the bank of the pond, or if someone in the crowd had knocked into him or even purposefully shoved him. All he knew was that the Devaronian had gotten too close to the ring of warriors.

He'd heard the harsh bark of a warrior's order at the edge of the pond, and he'd looked up in time to see a flicker of amphistaff blade conjure a jet of shimmering black blood. He had pushed and shoved and fought his way through the mob to find the Devaronian lying on his back in a scatter of the grasses he had carried, one hand clutching at the stump of his other arm.

Jacen had done everything he could, which wasn't much. Before he could tie off the stump, the Devaronian was in deep shock; death had followed only a minute or two later.

Jacen had had time to study the Devaronian's face: the bleakly pale hide, the spray of needle teeth behind thick leathern lips, the small forehead horns curving in growth rings that Jacen could count with his fingertips. He'd had time to gaze into the Devaronian's vivid red eyes, to read there a puzzled sadness at the useless, empty, arbitrary death that now swallowed him.

That's when Jacen thought, *Okay, maybe I was wrong.*

There *were* weeds here, after all.

He lifted his head, and met the eyes of a weed.

The warrior who had killed the Devaronian returned

his gaze impassively, black-smeared amphistaff at the ready.

Which are flowers? Which are weeds? It is not only your right to choose flowers over weeds, it is your responsibility.

Vergere's words rang true. But Jacen doubted the truth he'd found in them was the truth she had intended. He discovered that he didn't really care what Vergere had intended. He had chosen.

Expressionlessly, he rose and turned his back on the warrior, and moved away into the mob.

He'd decided who the weeds were.

You want gardening? he thought with icy clarity. *Just wait. I'll show you gardening.*

Just you wait.

FOUR

THE WILL
OF THE GODS

A battered, barren world circled a blue-white spark of fusion fire. This world had seen the rise and fall of nation after nation, from simple provincial states to planetary confederations to interstellar empires and galactic republics. It had been the scene of a million battles, from simple surface skirmishes to the destruction of whole civilizations. It had been ravaged by war and reconstruction until its original environment survived only beneath sterile polar ice caps; it was the most artificial world of a galactic culture devoted to artifice. The whole planet had become a machine.

This was about to change.

Its new masters began by stealing its moons.

Stripped from orbit by dovin basal gravity drives, the three smaller moons were steered well away, while the largest was pulverized by tidal stress created by pulses from other yammosk-linked dovin basals. A refined application of similar techniques organized the resultant mass of dust and gravel and lumps of hardening magma into a thick spreading ring-disk of rubble that rotated around the planet at an angle seventeen degrees from the ecliptic.

This, while dramatic in itself, was only a prologue.

Dovin basals had been grown on the planet's surface.

The effect of gravity can be profitably described topo-graphically, as an altered curvature of space-time. The dovin basals on the planet's surface altered the curve of local space-time in such a way that the direction of the planet's orbit became, roughly speaking, uphill.

The planet slowed. Slowing, it fell inward, toward its sun.

It got warmer.

On its long slow fall toward its sun, the planet suffered a bombardment of small meteors, carefully sized and with their angle of atmospheric entry precisely calculated so that they would reach an average temperature sufficient to vaporize their primary mineral, without cracking it into its constituent molecules of hydrogen and oxygen. The pri-mary mineral of these small meteors was a mineral only in the black chill of interplanetary space; by the time it reached the warming surface, it had lost its crystalline structure, and was simply water.

For the first time in a thousand years, natural rain fell across the face of the planet.

Once the planet had spiraled into its revised orbit, the dovin basals quieted, and space returned to its custom-ary topography. The three remaining moons were moved back into new, more complex orbits, whose tidal effects would eventually braid the striated disk of rubble that ringed the planet into a permanent sky-bridge of rain-bow lace.

By the time the seedship fell back into normal space and moved toward an orbital intercept, the planet duplicated—in its gross elements of orbital length, rota-tion, moons, and rings—the eon-lost homeworld of the Yuuzhan Vong. It remained only to remake the surface, and bring Life to the shattered remnants of what once had been a single planetwide city, so that the planet could grow into the name it would bear: Yuuzhan'tar, the Crèche of God.

Coruscant was ready for seedfall.

In the Nursery, it was the *tizo'pil Yun'tchilat*: the Day of Comprehending the Will of the Gods.

In these last few hours before seedfall, teams of shapers fanned out through the dhuryams' domains, measuring, calculating, indexing, and evaluating. Each shaper team walked in company with a squad of towering, lanky warriors: heavily armored, weapons at the ready, glittering eyes scanning ceaselessly, moving with the ponderously sinister threat of reeks in mating season.

Four squads guarded the shreeyam'tiz: a small, specialized subspecies of yammosk, this speeder-sized creature existed only to emit a powerful interference signal in the telepathic band used by yammosks and dhuryams alike. The squads had carried the barrel-bodied shreeyam'tiz into the Nursery in a huge basin filled with nutrient fluid. This was the first act of the *tizo'pil Yun'tchilat*, because each dhuryam knew that this was the day that would decide life or death. The shreeyam'tiz ensured that none of the dhuryams could use its slaves for any desperate act of sabotage or self-defense.

These slave seeds are designed with a fail-safe: when telepathic contact with a dhuryam is severed, each slave seed automatically immobilizes its slave by driving him mercilessly toward its parent, the coraltree basal from which slave coral was harvested. Shrieking sudden inexplicable agony, the slaves scrambled for each domain's coraltree basal. Only actual physical contact with the coraltree basal could quiet a slave's pain; even the sick and wounded had dragged themselves over rocks and through swamps, howling. This organized the slaves into neat little clusters, keeping them safely out of the way until they could be most conveniently disposed of.

To the slaves, it didn't matter which dhuryam won.

None of them were supposed to live long enough to find out.

Nom Anor glared at the image in the viewspider's sac of optical jelly. "Why doesn't he *do* something?"

Vergere shrugged liquidly, and leaned to one side to get a better look through the viewspider's thicket of legs. "He *is* doing something. Just not what you expected."

"He knows, doesn't he? He knows the slaves are to be killed?"

"He knows."

The image in the optical jelly was barely more than a shadow in a twilit mist. The shreeyam'tiz blocked the viewspider's image links along with the dhuryams' control; to maintain its view of Jacen Solo, it was forced to generate a shadow shape using the infrared-sensitive eyespots of the sessile polyps in the amphistaff grove.

"He just stands there," Nom Anor growled. He shifted his weight, glowering at the image. "How can he simply *stand*? The agony—!"

"Agony, yes. Suffering? Perhaps. He has learned much."

"Is he hiding? Is that it?"

Vergere shrugged again. "If so, he has picked the perfect spot."

The shadow of Jacen Solo stood at the heart of the amphistaff grove.

"And the polyps don't attack," Nom Anor muttered, gnawing absently on the edge of one knuckle. "They have slashed and slaughtered everyone within their reach for weeks: slave, warrior, and shaper alike. But this Solo—he's like one of those, what do you call them, trigger-birds, that sail along in perfect safety within the feeding tentacles of a Bespinese beldon."

"Perhaps he and the polyps have reached some ... understanding."

"I do not find the prospect reassuring."

"No? You should, Executor. It is for this that I have trained him, yes?"

Nom Anor pulled his knuckle away from his mouth and squinted at her. "For this?"

"Of course. Here, now, at the crisis point, at the Day of Decision, Jacen Solo does not stand with others of his kind. Despite the worst pain his nervous system can suffer, he has chosen to stand among the life-forms of an alien galaxy. *Our* galaxy, Executor. He has more in common with the masters than he does with the slaves, and he begins to recognize this."

"Are you sure?"

"He may have journeyed so far along the True Way already that the fate of slaves no longer concerns him."

"I don't believe it," Nom Anor growled. "I don't believe it for a nanoblip. You don't know these Jedi as I do."

"Perhaps not." Vergere's crest tanned a faintly self-amused green. "Does anyone?"

Abruptly, Nom Anor reached into a head-sized bubble-den in the wall near his knee and grabbed a villip. "There is a slave in the amphistaff grove," he said into it. "Pick him up. Bind him and return him to my coralcraft."

The villip whispered with the reply from the commander of Nom Anor's ooglith-masqued warriors. "*I hear and obey, Executor.*"

"As you value your father's bones, do not fail in this. This slave is a Jedi infiltrator who must not be allowed to disrupt the *tizo'pil Yun'tchilat*."

"*If he resists?*"

"I would prefer that he lives—but I do not *require*

it. Do not risk damage to the seedship. Minimize any disruption."

"*I hear and obey, Executor.*"

Nom Anor commanded the villip to revert to its original form. "So." He turned again to Vergere. "As you say: our Solo Project has progressed well. The Nursery has served its purpose. We'd have to remove him before the executions anyway; better to get it taken care of now, in case he still harbors any illusions of heroism. The ceremony must continue without any risk of interference. You should be planning the next phase of his training; you'll want to continue as soon as he's safely aboard my coralcraft."

"My people, Nom Anor," Vergere said meditatively, "have a proverb about counting glitterflies when all one has is maggots."

"What?" Nom Anor scowled. "What does that mean?"

"I believe—" She nodded toward the viewspider's image sac. "—that you are about to find out."

Jacen stands in the amphistaff grove, watching.

The slave seed shrieks flame through every nerve in his body: sizzling commands for him to run, to scramble and sprint for the coraltree basal only thirty meters away. He burns in this fire, but is not consumed.

The fire is an alembic that has distilled everything he is, has ever been, ever will be, into one eternal instant; like the white before it, the fire has washed away time.

All of Jacen's time has become one single *now*, and the fire inside him feeds his strength.

Out of the shadows, out in the blue-white glare of the Nursery's constant noon, four slaves suddenly step away from the nearest coraltree basal, letting its fronds drop from their hands. They do this casually, efficiently, without haste but with no wasted motion, and they glance toward the amphistaff grove, toward the deep shade where Jacen stands.

They don't seem to be in pain.

This, Jacen knows already, is because they're not really slaves.

He wonders fleetingly if Anakin had felt this way: calm. Ready. Looking at the price he was about to pay, and deciding he'd gotten a bargain.

Out in the blue-white noon, the four slaves press the sides of their noses, and the ooglith masquers they had worn peel apart, filaments unthreading from pores to leave smeared beads of blood like sweat. The masquers ripple and flow down the revealed warriors, then squirm away to vanish in the grass.

The warriors walk toward the amphistaff grove.

Jacen closes his eyes, and for one second he is among his family: his father's hand ruffles his hair, his mother's arm is warm around his shoulders, Jaina and Lowie groan and Em Teedee makes a sarcastic comment as Jacen tries one more time to tell a joke to Tenel Ka . . .

But Chewbacca is not there.

Neither is Anakin.

The four warriors stop just beyond the fringe of the grove. Juvenile amphistaffs whip the air threateningly, and the polyps' groundmouths gape wide, mutely anticipating a rain of blood and flesh. One warrior calls out in harsh, guttural Basic: "*Jeedai*-slave, come out!"

Jacen's only response is to open his eyes.

"*Jeedai*-slave! Come out from there!" They wear no armor; the only vonduun crabs within reach are the wild ones that infest the bog beyond the coraltree basal, coming out at night to feed on the polyps at the edges of the grove. Unarmored warriors could not survive even seconds within the hissing swirl of juvenile amphistaffs.

Jacen adjusts his stance, organizing his thoughts and his breathing into a Jedi meditation that reaches deep within himself, beyond the searing pain from the slave seed, into memories of what he has learned through his mental link with the dhuryam: memories so vivid they are like a waking dream.

Now the fully armed warriors who guard the shree-yam'tiz are taking notice. Some begin to move deliberately toward the amphistaff grove, and the warriors who ring the hive-pond shift uneasily and adjust their weapons.

"*Jeedai*-slave! If we must come in, it will go worse for you!"

Jacen is deep in the meditation now; he can feel the thrum of emotive hormones through the rudimentary brains of the amphistaff polyps around him. He can taste their blood hunger like a mouthful of raw meat.

The warrior turns and barks a command in the tongue of the Yuuzhan Vong. Two more false slaves step away from a coraltree basal and allow their ooglith masquers to slither down their legs. The newly revealed warriors grab a real slave; one holds him while the other crushes the slave's throat with a knife-hand strike. They step back and let the slave fall, watching dispassionately while he writhes in the dirt, choking to death.

"*Jeedai*-slave! Come out, or another will die. Then another, and another, until finally only you are left. Save their lives, *Jeedai*. Come out!"

Now Jacen's waking meditation dream interpenetrates with the memory of another dream, a real dream, a Force dream so vivid he can still smell the coralskipper buds, can still see the scarified faces of the warrior guards and the coral-maimed bodies of the slaves: a dream he had two years ago, on Belkadan.

A dream in which he freed slaves of the Yuuzhan Vong. How astonished he felt, how *bereft*, when that dream did not come true. When his attempt to fulfill its promise ended in disaster, in blood and death and torture, he felt as though the Force itself had betrayed him.

Now he sees that he had not been betrayed. He'd merely been impatient.

"*Jeedai*-slave! Come out!"

Jacen sighs, and surfaces from the meditation.

"All right," he says quietly, a little sadly. "If you insist."

His still shadow becomes a shade in motion, drifting noiselessly through the grove of blood-hungry polyps. He stops at the penumbra bordering the blue-white noon beyond. The amphistaffs whirl lethal halos at his back. "Here I am."

"Farther," the warrior commands. "Move beyond the reach of the grove."

Jacen opens his empty hands. "Make me."

The warrior turns his head fractionally toward his companions. "Kill another."

"You," Jacen says, "are no warrior."

The warrior's three companions jabber excitedly among themselves. The leader's head snaps around as though yanked by a tractor beam. "*What?*"

"*Warriors* win battles without murdering the weak." Jacen's voice drips acid contempt. "Like all Yuuzhan Vong, you make war only upon the helpless. You are a coward from a species of cowards."

The warrior stalks forward. His eyes glitter a crazed, feral yellow. "You call me coward? *You?* You simpering *Jeedai* brat? You shivering brenzlit, cowering in the shadow of your den? You *slave?*"

"This *Jeedai* brenzlit slave," Jacen says distinctly, clinically, "spits upon your grandfather's bones."

The warrior lunges, taloned fingers reaching to tear the eyes from Jacen's face. With an exhausted sigh, Jacen collapses before the warrior's rush, falling to his back—

while lightly taking the warrior's outstretched wrists and planting one foot in the pit of the warrior's stomach to make a fulcrum. Jacen rolls, kicking upward, and the warrior flails helplessly as he flips through the air into the blade-storm of the amphistaffs.

Jacen lies for a moment in the sudden rain of Yuuzhan Vong blood and gobbets of warrior flesh. He turns his head to watch the juvenile amphistaffs rake chunks of the warrior's corpse toward the salivating gape of the polyps' groundmouths.

Then he rises. He faces the remaining three. "Well?"

They exchange uncertain glances. At Jacen's back, the polyps slurp and gurgle, and the amphistaffs whirl hungrily.

The warriors stand their ground, calling out in their own tongue.

In answer to their call, two of the squads who guard the shreeyam'tiz lumber heavily forward bearing amphistaffs of their own, bandoliers of thud bugs and other less familiar weapons, and wearing full vonduun crab armor. The shell of a vonduun crab can stop a lightsaber; it can resist even the atomic-diameter edge of an amphistaff blade.

One of the three nearby shows Jacen his teeth: long and needle-sharp, curving inward like a predator's. *"Nal'tikkin Jeedai hr'zlat sor trizmek sh'makk,"* he spits. *"Tyrokk jan trizmek, Jeedai."*

Jacen doesn't need to speak their tongue to understand: no trick of wrestling will help a lone unarmed man against two squads of warriors, Jedi or not.

The warrior is advising him to prepare to die.

Jacen smiles. It's a sad smile: melancholy, resigned.

He nods.

In a part of his mind far from the pain and the blood

and the harsh blue-white glare, he can feel the dark satisfaction of the amphistaff polyps behind him as they swiftly, almost instantly digest the fallen warrior. He feels their glittering anticipation, and the shuddering release as they use the meal of warrior's flesh to give themselves the strength to reproduce.

Amphistaff polyps breed asexually; the amphistaffs themselves become a polyp's offspring, released from their nodules to squirm away in search of the proper ground to take root and begin their transformation into polyps themselves. Through his empathic connection, Jacen shows them the ground he recommends.

Trusting their friend, the amphistaffs take his advice.

He stretches forth his arms. The warriors can only stare in openmouthed awe as amphistaffs fall like leaves from the polyps at his back; as amphistaffs wriggle down the polyps' knobby leathern trunks and slither through the grass.

Amphistaffs twine about Jacen's ankles and climb his body like vines enveloping a forgotten jungle idol. They twist around his legs, his hips, his chest, coiling the length of his arms, shrouding his neck, curving up to embrace even his skull. The approaching squads of fully armed warriors slow uncertainly, not quite sure, now, how to attack.

Because the vonduun crab is not the only creature that can resist the cut of an amphistaff blade.

Jacen brings his hands together before him, and offers the warriors a solemn bow. When he parts his hands again, a mature amphistaff stretches between them, blade and spike, fully envenomed. As is every one of the seventeen amphistaffs that make up his armor.

Jacen says, "I'd like you all to meet some friends of mine."

* * *

Nom Anor hurled his sacworm across the chamber. It splattered against the wall, then slid to the floor, where it gave out a tiny whistling sigh, and died. Instantly Nom Anor mastered himself again, wiping his lipless mouth with the back of his wrist.

"So it is over," he muttered darkly. "We have failed. *You* have failed," he amended, wondering if he could get far enough away in his coralcraft to escape Tsavong Lah's anger at this new disaster, wondering if he could give himself up to the New Republic, if there was any way he could persuade the surviving Jedi not to slay him on sight. He still knew many secrets, *valuable* secrets . . .

Vergere interrupted his speculation. "Executor, let me go to him."

"Absolutely not. I can't have you running around in the middle of the *tizo'pil Yun'tchilat*, you foolish creature. Don't you remember that our Solo Project is *secret*? How secret will it be after you run through the Nursery trying to save his useless skin?"

"Hardly useless, Executor. As I said before, his education has proceeded very well indeed. Though I admit it could be going better right now."

"Could be *better*?" Nom Anor flicked his wrist at the viewspider's optical sac, where the dim silhouette of Jacen Solo armed himself. "He has learned *nothing*! He is about to throw his life away in a futile battle. Over mere *slaves*! He is as weak as any other Jedi—*weaker*!"

"He is not a Jedi," Vergere replied imperturbably. "And it is not *his* life that concerns me."

"Are you mad?" Nom Anor stomped furiously around the viewspider, which danced nervously to keep its delicate feet out from under the executor's human-style boots. "He cannot *possibly* win such a battle! How can he expect to fight two *squads*? Even if he goes back to hiding in the grove—"

"Winning," Vergere said, her crest fanning a solemn blasterbore gray, "is not the same as fighting. Watch."

The shadow suddenly vanished, and the image within the optical sac shifted and flickered liquidly as the viewspider sought new visual sources. "What's *happening*?" Nom Anor demanded uselessly. "Does he flee? Is he running away like the broken Jedi brat he has always been?"

"Executor." Her fingers wrapped his elbow, astonishingly strong. "Jacen Solo no longer has the Force, but that is not his only weapon. He is a warrior born: eldest son and heir to a long line of a warriors. He has trained since birth in the combat arts. He has been tested and tried, bloodied in battle, and he—"

"He's nothing but a *boy*." Nom Anor stared at her. "Have you lost your wits? I *know* this boy. Humans do not honor warrior lineage. His means nothing. *He* is nothing."

Vergere spoke without the faintest hint of irony. "I tell you this: though neither he nor they yet know it, he is the greatest of all the Jedi. Jacen Solo is the living Jedi dream. Even without the Force, he is more dangerous than you can possibly imagine. You must let me go to him. He must be stopped."

"Stopped from what? Soiling his robeskin as he runs away?"

"Stopped from destroying the *tizo'pil Yun'tchilat*. Stopped, very likely, from destroying the seedship itself."

Nom Anor's mouth came open, but from it came only a fading hiss. The calm certainty in Vergere's eye silenced him as effectively as a punch in the throat. He couldn't seem to get his breath. "Destroy the *ship*?" he was finally able to gasp.

"Don't you understand, Executor? He isn't running away."

She gestured at the viewspider's sac, where it had recovered enough image to show a lone shape sprinting headlong to meet the oncoming thunderclouds of warrior squads.

Vergere said, "He's *attacking*."

FIVE

SEEDFALL

Jacen Solo sprints into battle.

As he runs, he makes an image in his mind. The amphistaff he carries matches itself to this image, coiling more than half its length around his forearm. An internal pulse from its linked chain of power glands generates an energy field that rigidifies its semicrystalline cell structure, locking it in that form: a meter of it extends from his right fist, tipped with a double-handspan blade. The same field that rigidifies the amphistaff extends a fractional millimeter beyond the blade, giving it an edge no thicker than an atomic diameter.

So it is that when one of the unarmed warriors springs to bar Jacen's path, hands wide to grapple, the blade passes with only a whisper of resistance through flesh and bone. One arm spirals lazily through the air, showering droplets of blood; one leg topples sideways, twitching in the grass. Jacen does not even break stride.

The remaining two unarmored warriors decide they should leave him to their better-equipped comrades.

Thud bugs hum through the air around him, but the eyespots of the amphistaffs wrapped around Jacen's body are infrared—and motion-sensitive; he is able to integrate their empathic reactions into a full-surround field of perception that is not dissimilar to the Force itself—and he has trained for years to avoid weapons that he can only barely perceive. The greensward blossoms with scarlet detonations as he dodges, dives and rolls, comes to his feet, and keeps running.

Dozens more thud bugs curve toward him, homing like concussion missiles as he sprints straight at the oncoming squads of heavily armed warriors. The nearest warrior thrusts his amphistaff at Jacen like a force pike. Jacen dives beneath its point, rolling forward on his shoulder, stabbing upward; his blade enters the warrior's body at the joining of pelvis and thigh. The pursuing thud bugs denotate massively, scattering warriors like toy soldiers swiped away by the invisible hand of a giant child as Jacen's momentum completes the roll, bringing him to one knee and driving the blade upward through the warrior's groin and entrails and chest.

Only energy fields like its own can withstand the amphistaff's edge; the shells of vonduun crabs are intricately structured crystal, reinforced by a field generated by power glands very similar to those of the amphistaff itself. But that field protects only the shell; beneath their shells, vonduun crabs are soft, and when Jacen's blade slices through the crab's field-nerve cable from the inside, the armor might as well be made of bantha butter.

A multiple blast bug detonation slaps the warrior forward, and Jacen's blade shears through spine and armor alike to burst from the warrior's back in a fountain of gore—and slices as well through the warrior's blast bug bandolier. As Jacen rolls backward with the concussion and kicks free of the shuddering corpse, he grabs the severed bandolier. An instant later, he is up again, running, staggering, stumbling, deafened and half stunned by the explosions. Behind him, the warrior squads scramble and regroup. Jacen ignores them.

All his attention, all his concentration, all his will, is focused on the blast bug bandolier in his hand.

The bandolier is bleeding from its severed ends; dying, its sole wish is to release its children—the blast bugs locked in its linked belt of hexagonal germination chambers—so that they might fulfill their explosive destiny. Jacen can keenly feel its desire. In the emotional language of his empathic talent, he promises the ultimate satisfaction of this desire, if the bandolier will only wait for his signal.

Ahead, the remaining two squads draw themselves into a tight wedge, its point toward Jacen, its broad base covering the bacta-tank-sized tub that holds the shreeyam'tiz. As more blast bugs hum toward him from all directions, Jacen heaves the bandolier overhand like a proton grenade; it twists lazily, high through the stark noon.

With his empathic talent, he projects a pulse-hammer thrill of anticipation teetering over the brink to fulfillment, a shuddering surge of adrenaline that would roughly translate as—

Now!

The bandolier flares into a starshell over the base of the wedge at the same time as the blast bugs targeted on Jacen arrive in a thundering swarm, striking him and the ground and the warriors nearby indiscriminately, concussion bursts battering them all helplessly this way and that, ending with Jacen finally blown off his feet into a high spinning arc through the air.

As the inside-out world wheels around him in a darkening blood-tinged whirl, Jacen has time to feel the agony from his slave seed-web suddenly ease and to push an exhausted empathic invitation down through the slave seed. *All right, my friend. Now it's your turn.*

The blood-tinged darkness swallows him before he hits the ground.

* * *

"There, you see?" Nom Anor nodded contemptuously toward the suddenly vivid image in the viewspider's optical sac, showing Jacen lying unconscious, bleeding on the blast-shredded Nursery turf, still within his improvised armor of amphistaffs. "Your 'greatest of all the Jedi' has succeeded in killing a mere two or three warriors. A useless, weak fool—"

"You are not paying attention," Vergere chimed. "I ask you again: let me go to him before we are all lost."

"Don't be absurd. There cannot possibly be any danger. We'll watch the end of this little farce in full color. He is unconscious; the warriors will restrain him and deliver him as ordered."

Vergere's lips curved upward like a human's smile, and she opened her hands toward the sharp, detailed image, which showed Jacen stirring, shaking his head, struggling to rise. "Then why are they not doing so already?"

Nom Anor frowned. "I—I am not sure—"

"Perhaps the warriors have more pressing matters to attend to."

"More *pressing*," he said heavily, "than following my *orders*?"

"Executor, Executor," she chided. "You see, but you do not see."

In the viewspider's image sac, the quality of light had changed: the Nursery's stark blue-white noon now took on highlights of red, gold, yellow that danced and flickered and played over Jacen's hair and face and his tattered, blood-soaked robeskin. Nom Anor frowned at this, uncomprehending, until a thick twist of black, greasy-looking smoke drifted through the image.

The new colors came from fire.

His frown darkened into a scowl; his anger and disgust curdled into a ball of ice in his stomach. "What is going on?" he demanded. "Vergere, tell me what is happening in there!"

Now in the image sac, two crab-armored warriors staggered into view, scorched, bleeding from multiple wounds. One passed too close to Jacen's back, and one of the amphistaffs braided around the human's torso lashed out convulsively, spearing the warrior through the side of the knee. The other warrior kept running headlong, fleeing without a backward glance, and Nom Anor soon discovered what the warrior fled from: a limping, snarling, shouting mob, bearing a variety of improvised weapons, from spade rays to malledillos to writhing wild amphistaffs as much a danger to their wielder as to an enemy, which descended upon the hamstrung warrior to beat and chop him to death with savage triumph.

"Those are *slaves* . . ." Nom Anor breathed. "How can slaves have gotten so far out of control?"

Vergere's crest shifted to a brilliant orange, rippled with green. "Answer me this, Nom Anor: why is the viewspider's image so suddenly clear?"

He stared, drop-jawed and panting.

"The warriors were never his target," she said as though offering a hint to a puzzled child.

Finally, belatedly, he understood. The ball of ice inside his stomach sent freezing waves out to his fingertips. "He has killed the shreeyam'tiz!"

"Yes."

"How could he—why didn't you—he, I mean, you—"

"You will recall that I warned you."

"You—Vergere, you—I thought you were—"

Her black, fathomless eyes held his. "Have you not yet learned, Executor," she said expressionlessly, "that everything I tell you is the truth?"

* * *

The *tizo'pil Yun'tchilat* dissolved in slaughter.

Each dhuryam, severed from its telepathic links by the shreeyam'tiz, had been forced to wait, blind and deaf, sizzling in a rolling boil of stress hormones, burning with the desperate hope that the next sensation it would feel might be the awakening of sense and power and the pure clean knowledge that it, alone of all, had been chosen the *pazhkic Yuuzhan'tar al'tirrna*: the World Brain of God's Crèche.

But each had been secretly consumed by deep, gnawing terror: that instead it would feel only a slice of unstoppable blade, delivering the devouring fire of amphistaff venom to rip it out of life and into the eternal suffering the Gods inflict upon the unworthy.

And so when the blast bug bandolier had burst, sending dozens of the explosive creatures rocketing into the tank that held the shreeyam'tiz—where the fluid bath that supported and nourished the shreeyam'tiz had multiplied their concussive force, sending an immense gout of fluid and blood and shredded flesh reaching for the fusion spark that was the Nursery's sun—all but one of the dhuryams could not begin to guess what was going on.

All but one of the dhuryams were shocked, stunned, shattered to find their slave-based senses returning; all but one were more than shocked, more than stunned— minds blasted away by black panic—to find that their siblings had also recovered their senses and their slaves in a Nursery that echoed with explosions and reeked of fresh blood, filled with terrified, cowering shapers and heavily armed warriors shivering on the edge of combat frenzy.

The one dhuryam that knew what was going on was not shocked, or stunned, or panicked. It was simply desperate, and ruthless.

Dhuryams are fundamentally pragmatic creatures. They

do not understand trust, and so have no concept of betrayal. This particular dhuryam, like all the others, had long been aware that its life hung upon the outcome of the *tizo'pil Yun'tchilat*, and that its chances were no better than those of each of its dozen siblings.

That is: twelve to one. Against.

None of the dhuryams had ever liked those odds; this one had decided to do something about it.

It had made a deal with Jacen Solo.

When the telepathic interference from the shreeyam'tiz had suddenly vanished, the dhuryam not only knew exactly what had happened, it knew who had done it and why.

And it knew what to do next.

While echoes of the blast bug bandolier still rang within the Nursery, the dhuryam sent its slaves scrambling away from the coraltree basals, scattering toward a number of ooglith hummocks. A touch upon the nerve plexus that serves—in the shaped oogliths known as masquers—as the release caused these wild oogliths to retract similarly . . . but what these wild oogliths had enclosed was not their usual hollow skeleton frames of stone.

These oogliths had been coaxed to conceal stacks of crude, improvised weapons.

Certain tools had been stockpiled surreptitiously over some few days, concealed in the ooglith hummocks nearest the coraltree basals: mostly broad-bladed spade rays, long and heavy for the breaking of the ground, and armored malledillos as tall as a warrior, dense and tough enough to shatter stone with every blow.

The oogliths had also concealed a number of sacworms, filled to bursting with sparkbee honey; sparkbees were the wild baseline from which thud bugs and blast bugs had been shaped, uncounted years ago. Each sacworm's gut had also been injected with a tiny amount of a digestive enzyme from the stomachs of vonduun crabs. By swinging a spade ray like a catapult, a slave might hurl one of these sacworms a considerable distance.

Accuracy was not a consideration. The sacworms burst on impact, spraying gelatinous honey in every direction. The enzyme-activated sparkbee honey clung to whatever it struck; on contact with the Nursery's air, it burst into flame.

In seconds, fire was *everywhere*.

Warriors roasting to death within their useless armor were unable to protect themselves, and even less able to defend the shapers they had escorted. The shapers, having no experience or training for warfare, could only scramble for the nearest breath vein. Many died: splashed with flame, or crushed by blows from malledillos, or hacked by spade rays swung like vibro-axes. On the surface of the hive-lake, burning sparkbee honey spread like oil.

And all but one of the dhuryams shared a single thought: to gather to itself the slaves who were its eyes and hands. They had to pack their slaves onto the hive-island, to surround themselves with walls of flesh. None of them had any other hope of self-defense.

Except for one.

And so when all the slaves belonging to all the other dhuryams sprinted from throughout the Nursery, whipped onward by the coral seed-webs savaging their nerves, converging upon the hive-lake to drown the double ring of warrior-guards in waves of shuddering, clutching, bleeding bodies, the slaves belonging to one particular dhuryam did not.

Instead, they fanned out in teams of five. One team clustered around Jacen Solo, and waited while he dragged himself brokenly to his feet. Bleeding from a dozen wounds, he swayed as though faint or dizzy, then moved toward the lake with the five slaves around him. The other teams raced through the smoke and flames, skipping over corpses and slipping on spilled blood, until they reached the coraltree basals.

In seconds, the coraltree basals became towering columns of flame, fueled by sparkbee honey. The slaves did not wait to see if the flames would suffice, but went to work with spade rays and malledillos and captured amphistaffs, chopping and pounding and hacking each and every coraltree basal to death.

Nom Anor stared at the universe of bloody carnage within the viewspider's sac with numb, uncomprehending horror.

"What—?" he murmured blankly. "What—?"

"Executor. We're running out of time."

"Time? What time? This—this *disaster* . . . We are *dead*, don't you understand? Tsavong Lah will slaughter us."

"Ever the optimist," Vergere chirped. "You assume we'll live out the hour."

Nom Anor glared at her speechlessly.

Once again, that unexpectedly strong hand of hers clasped his arm. "Have the warriors outside this chamber escort me to the Nursery. And call your commander, if he still lives. I'll need someone with enough authority to get me through the guards, onto the hive-island— if any of the hive guards live that long."

"The hive-island?" Nom Anor blinked stupidly. He couldn't get any of this to make *sense*. "What are you talking about?"

Vergere opened a hand at the viewspider's optical sac. "Do you think he's finished, Nom Anor? Does our avatar of the Twin seek only confusion and slaughter—or does he produce confusion and slaughter as a *diversion*?"

"Diversion? To accomplish what?" Then his good eye bulged wide—in the viewspider's image sac he saw Jacen and the five slaves who accompanied him wade into the chest-deep murk of the hive-lake, hacking their way through the churning, struggling, bleeding tangle of slaves and warriors. One of Jacen's companions fell, speared through the throat by a warrior's amphistaff; another was dragged under the water by the clawing hands of unarmed slaves. The three remaining swung their spade rays wildly, trying not only to keep warriors and slaves at bay but also to splash a path through the flames that floated on the surface of the lake.

Jacen slogged grimly on, half swimming, without a glance at the slaves who defended him. Any warrior or attacking slave in his path fell to lightning slashes and stabs of the amphistaffs he wielded in both hands. He didn't even bother to wipe from his eyes the blood that flowed from a deep scalp wound.

All he did was walk, and kill.

He turned toward the center of the lake. Toward the hive-island. And kept walking.

Nom Anor breathed, "The *dhuryams* . . ."

"They are the brains of this ship, Executor. He has already shredded the *tizo'pil Yun'tchilat*, and he cannot hope to escape. What other target is worthy of his life?"

"You sound like you're *proud* of him!"

"More than proud," she replied serenely. "He surpasses my fondest hope."

"Without a World Brain to direct the separation and atmospheric insertion, the whole *ship* could be destroyed! He'll kill himself along with everyone else!"

Vergere shrugged and folded her arms, smiling. "Wurth Skidder."

Nom Anor's stomach roiled until he tasted blood. The Jedi Skidder had given his life to kill a single yammosk—and the dhuryams were vastly more valuable. Beyond valuable. Indispensable. "He *can't*," Nom Anor panted desperately. "He can't—the life-forms aboard this ship are *irreplaceable*—"

"Yes. All of them. Especially: he himself."

"He couldn't! I mean—could he? *Would* he?"

"Ah, Executor, what a happy place the universe would be if all our questions were so easily answered," she chimed, opening her hands toward the viewspider's image sac.

It showed Jacen Solo on the hive-island's shore, driving one of his blades through the chest of a maddened shaper while with the other he opened what might have been either a slave or a masqued warrior from collarbone to groin. Two of his escort survived; they had turned just at the waterline, where their blurring swipes of spade rays could not quite hold back a mob of suicidally fierce slaves. The two gave ground, forced backward up the beach, while Jacen scrambled up onto the nearest of the huge dhuryam chambers of calcified coral.

He paused there, hesitating, standing atop the waxy hexagonal plug that sealed the birth chamber's end, his amphistaffs raised, again swaying as though he might faint. Below, blunt edges of spade rays hacked into slave flesh, and Jacen flinched as though jolted by a near-miss blaster bolt, seemingly only now remembering where he was and what he had come here to do.

Then he drove his twin amphistaff blades downward through the plug.

"A less tractable question, as you see," Vergere said, "is, *Can we stop him?*"

Nom Anor staggered, fingers working uselessly as

though he thought he could reach through the view-spider's image sac and grab Jacen's throat. "Has he gone completely *mad*?"

Vergere's only reply was a steadily expectant stare.

He covered his face with his hands. "Go," he said, his voice weak, muffled. "Kill him if you must. Save the ship."

She gave a sprightly bow. "At your command, Executor."

He heard the hatch open, then close again, and instantly he dropped his hands. In his eyes shone the clear light of simple calculation. He stroked the villip, snapped orders, then let it fall. When he opened the hatch sphincter, a swift glance assured him the tubeway was empty.

Executor Nom Anor ran for his coralcraft as though pursued by krayt dragons.

He had not survived so much of this war by underestimating Jedi. Particularly the Solo family.

Killing dhuryams got easier after the first one.

The first one was murder.

Jacen could *feel* it.

Standing on the plug that sealed the mouth of the dhuryam's hexagonal birth chamber, the wax warm under his feet, almost alive, he felt the searing terror of the infant dhuryam trapped beneath him: smothering in panicked claustrophobia, nowhere to run, no hope to hide, screaming telepathically, begging bitterly, desperately. He could feel the life he was about to take: a mind as full of hopes and fears and dreams as his own, a mind he was about to rip out of existence with a slash of blade and caustic burn of amphistaff venom.

His every instinct rebelled: all his training, his Jedi ideals, his whole *life* absolutely forbid him to slay a helpless cowering creature.

He swayed, suddenly dizzy, suddenly aware how badly wounded he was—aware of the blood that poured down his face, aware of broken ribs stabbing every breath, aware of numb weakness spreading down his thigh from a slash he could not remember taking, aware that the concussion he'd suffered from the blast bugs had left his eyes unable to properly focus. He had fought his way to the island in something like the battle frenzy of a Yuuzhan Vong warrior, where pain and injury were as irrelevant as the color of the sky; he had taken lives of warriors and crazed shapers, perhaps of the very slaves he was fighting to save—

He looked down at the beach. Beside the shaper he had killed lay another corpse.

It looked human.

He didn't know, *couldn't* know, if that had been one of the masqued warriors. He'd never know. The only truth he had was that this corpse had once been a person who had stood against him with violence. A warrior? Or a slave—innocent, driven to attack Jacen against his will, helplessly maddened by the lash of seed-web agony?

Why did he feel like it didn't matter?

That feeling scared him more than dying did. *If that's who I've become, maybe it's right that I should die here.* Before he killed anyone else.

But each time the two slaves covering him, the ones trying to hold back the crush of slaves pressing up the beach, hacked into somebody's side or leg or head with a hard-swung spade ray, he felt those wounds, too.

Already, the inflowing tide of slaves had swamped the warriors guarding the hive-island; it would be only a matter of moments before the dhuryams turned their slaves against each other in a savage winner-take-all bloodbath. Dozens, maybe hundreds of slaves had been driven to their deaths already, thrown recklessly against the lethal ring of warriors. Once the dhuryams turned on each other, thousands more would die.

To the dhuryam beneath his feet, these people were only tools. Fusion cutters. Glow rods. The death of a slave brought no more emotion to this dhuryam than the absentminded curse Jacen's father would use if a hydrospanner broke while he struggled with the *Falcon*'s balky hyperdrive.

As though Vergere whispered in his ear, he remembered—

The gardener's choice.

He raised his twin amphistaffs over his head, then sank to one knee to drive them downward through the wax plug.

He felt the blades enter the flesh of the infant dhuryam below as though they sliced through his own belly; he felt the caustic snarl of venom spreading into the dhuryam's body as though it coursed his own veins.

He yanked the amphistaffs free and scrambled for the next birth chamber.

Killing the next one doubled the weight of his empathic pain, for the first one was still alive, still suffering, screeching telepathic terror and despair; killing the third buckled his knees and drew red-veined clouds across his vision.

And behind him, slaves who had been driven to suicidal madness by the relentless burn of seed-web pain now began to stop, gasping, blinking, to stand in stunned wonder, to turn to each other with hands out to ask for help or to offer it, rather than to wound and maim and kill. First the whole gang who had forced their way up the beach—then another gang, and another, as dhuryam after dhuryam thrashed, convulsed, death throes cracking birth chambers like eggshells.

Jacen kept moving.

A red haze closed in around him, a bloody mist that might have been real smoke and fog and copper-flavored fire, or might have been inside his head, or both. The hive-island became a nightmare mountain, all jagged rock and killing and an endless scramble toward a peak that he could never see. Figures rose up, indistinct blurs lurching at him through the red haze, swinging weapons, clutching, clawing. He cut at them, cut through them, killing and scrambling and killing, falling to hands and knees to drive blades again and again through one wax plug and another and another, casting aside amphistaffs with their venom glands exhausted, drawing new weapons out from his own armor, his armor that lived and saw and struck these red-blurred shapes with death-soaked accuracy.

Then he was up high, close to the top; he couldn't tell who might be around him or where he might be but he knew he was high up a mountain, cresting the uttermost peak of the galaxy, beyond the atmosphere, beyond the moons, taller than the stars. He raised his last amphistaff like a battle flag. Before he could plant it down through the blood-smeared plug beneath his torn and cut bare feet, a supernova flared inside his brain—

And burned down the universe. There was nothing left.

Nothing but white.

Hungry white: eating everything he was. But he had been in the white before. He knew its secrets, and it could not stop him.

Beneath this hexagonal lid was the source, the well-spring, the fountain of white. He could feel it down there: squirming alien tentacles bathed in slime and terror. He could cut off the agony. One stroke more would end it for everyone. Forever.

He lifted his amphistaff.

"Jacen, no! Don't do it!"

He whirled, staggering, white-blind and gasping.

The voice had been his brother's.

"Anakin—?"

"You can't kill this one, Jacen," Anakin's voice said from beyond the white. "This one's your *friend*."

Like a finger flick against a beaker of supersaturated solution, Anakin's voice triggered a phase change in Jacen's head: the white clouded, condensed, became crystalline, translucent, transparent—

Invisible.

The pain was still there, smoking through his veins, but it did not touch him: it passed through him unchanged like light through empty space.

He could see again.

Clearly.

Perfectly.

He saw the scarlet rags of meat that were the remains of three shapers caught before they could reach a breath vein on the far side of the Nursery beyond the sun. He saw the smoking ring of charred coraltree basals around the hive-lake. He saw the rivulets of blood trailing down his arms to drip from his knuckles.

Birth-chamber plugs all over the hive-island, pierced and leaking the blue milk of dhuryam blood—

Tangled corpses of warriors and slaves and shapers—

An inside-out world stuffed with terror, agony, slaughter—

He had done this.

All of it.

And: he saw Vergere.

Panting harshly, he watched her scramble up the last few meters of the dhuryam hive. Below, armored warriors struggled to hold off a mob of shouting, scrambling, bleeding slaves—slaves Jacen could *feel*, through his link with the dhuryam beneath his feet. He could feel it whipping them on, driving them upward.

He could feel it shrieking for them to kill him.

He heard a low, feral growling, like a wounded rancor cornered in its den. It came from his own throat.

"It was *you*," Jacen rasped.

Vergere looked up. She stopped, well away, out of amphistaff range.

"I heard him," he panted. His breath came hot and painful. "Anakin told me to stop. But it wasn't Anakin. It was you."

Vergere flattened her crest against her oblate skull, and there was no trace of cheer in her eyes. "Jacen," she said slowly, sadly, "in the story of your life, is this your best ending? Is this your dream?"

My dream . . .

He remembered hazily his hope of freeing the slaves; he remembered his deal with the dhuryam: it had agreed to spare the lives of the slaves, transport them safely planetside in the shipseeds, in exchange for Jacen's help in destroying its sibling-rivals. But in the slaughterhouse he had made of the Nursery, that memory seemed as indistinct as his dream on Belkadan: a ghost of self-delusion, a wisp of hope, lovely but intangible.

Unreal.

The savage chaos of blood and pain and death Jacen had spread throughout this inverted world—*that* was real. The bitterly clear light inside Jacen's head showed him all the stark shadows of reality: he saw what he had done, and he saw what he needed to do now.

He lifted his amphistaff over his head and let it swing to vertical, blade down.

"Jacen, stop!" Vergere took a step closer. "Would you kill your friend? Is that who you are?"

"This is no friend," Jacen said through his teeth. "It's an alien. A *monster*."

"And what does that make you? Did it betray *your* trust? Who is the monster here?"

"I can kill it right now. And when I kill it, I kill the Yuuzhan Vong homeworld." The amphistaff writhed in his hands. He tightened his grip until his hands burned. "Letting it live—that *would* be a betrayal. That would betray the New Republic. All the men and women the Yuuzhan Vong have murdered. All the fallen Jedi . . . even my . . . even . . ."

His voice trailed away; he could not say Anakin's name. Not now. But still he did not strike.

"And so you face a choice, Jacen Solo. You can betray your nation, or you can betray a friend."

"Betray a friend?" He lifted the amphistaff once more. "It doesn't even know what a *friend* is—"

"Perhaps not." Vergere's crest rippled, picking up scarlet highlights. She took another step forward. "But *you do*."

Jacen staggered as though she had punched him. Tears streamed from his eyes. "Then *you* tell me what to do!" he shouted. *"Tell me what I'm supposed to do!"*

"I would not presume," Vergere said calmly, taking another step toward him. "But I will tell you this: in killing this dhuryam, you kill yourself. And all the warriors, and shapers, and Shamed Ones on this ship—and *every one of these slaves*. Weren't you trying to *save* lives, Jacen Solo?"

"How do I—" Jacen shook his head sharply to clear tears from his eyes. "How do I know you're telling the truth?"

"You don't. But *if* what I say is true, would that change your mind?"

"I—I don't—" Snarling red rage welled up inside him.

They had put him through too much. He had passed beyond questions; all he wanted now was an answer.

An end.

"Everything—" Jacen forced words through his teeth. "Everything you tell me is a lie."

Vergere spread her hands. "Then choose, and act."

He chose.

He raised the amphistaff—but before he could bring it down, Vergere sprang forward into his way: to kill the dhuryam, he'd have to spear through her. He hesitated for an eyeblink, and in that instant she reached up and caressed his cheek, just as she had the very first time her touch had drawn him down out of the Embrace of Pain's blank white agony.

Her palm was wet.

Jacen said, "Wha—?"

He said no more, because his mouth had stopped working.

He had just enough time to think *Her tears—Vergere's tears*—before the paralytic contact poison they had become overwhelmed his brain, and the Nursery, the dhuryam, and Vergere herself all faded as he fell into a different personal universe, infinite and eternal.

This one was black.

There was a world that had once been the capital of the galaxy. It had been called Coruscant, and was a planet of a single global city, kilometers deep from pole to pole. It had been a cold world with four moons, far from its blue-white sun, orbited by mirrored platforms that focused the light of the distant sun to prevent the world from freezing.

Things had changed.

Closer now to its sun, warm, tropical, its kilometers-deep global city now kilometers-deep global rubble, with new seas forming where once there had been apartment towers and government offices. Three moons now wove an orbital ring into a rainbow bridge in the sky.

And above this world that had been a capital, this capital that had been a world, a shooting star flared: an immense globe of yorik coral entered the atmosphere at a steep angle, shedding a planetwide meteorite shower of bits and pieces and chunks of itself and blossomed with fire as they streaked to the surface.

Where they struck, they rooted, and began to grow.

The planet had ceased to be Coruscant; it had become Yuuzhan'tar.

But soon it would be, once again, the capital of the galaxy.

PART TWO

THE CAVE

SIX

HOME

Thousands of years passed before Jacen opened his eyes.

He spent those thousands of years in one endless claustrophobic nightmare: of being held, bound, cocooned, unable to move, to speak. He couldn't see, because his eyes would not open. He couldn't swallow. He could not breathe.

For a millennium he smothered, helpless.

Then he felt a muscle twitch in the middle of his back. It took a century, but he found that muscle, and he found he could make it contract, and he could make it relax again. As decades grew into another century, he found he could work surrounding muscles in his back as well. Then he could clench his thighs, and bunch the muscles in his upper arm—and his nightmare had become a dream, filled with possibility rather than dread.

And throughout the dream he kept expecting, somehow, that his chrysalis would crack, and he would at last be able to spread his new wings, and hear his wingflutes piping in harmony as he soared into the four-mooned sky . . .

When he finally opened his eyes and realized that this had been only a dream, a tremendous wash of relief flooded through him: he thought, for a moment, that it had *all* been a dream, the Nursery, the Embrace of Pain, the voxyn queen, Anakin . . .

Duro. Belkadan. All the way back to Sernpidal.

Either that had been all a dream, or he was still dreaming, because he didn't hurt anymore.

He lay on something soft, rounded, insanely comfortable, like an acceleration couch upholstered in living scarlet moss that smelled of flowers and ripe fruit. Insects buzzed nearby, invisible, screened by gently waving ferns twice Jacen's height; through these ferns wove vines like garlands of flowers, blooming with brilliant yellow and blue and vivid orange in fantastic and delicate array. The far distance echoed with a long, mournful pack hunter's howl. Somewhere above, an unseen creature lifted its voice in a song as thrillingly lovely as that of a manullian bird calling its mate in the Mother Jungle of Ithor.

Ithor, he thought, dully bitter. He remembered what the Yuuzhan Vong had done to Ithor.

Where in all nine Corellian hells am I?

The sunlight that trickled through the ferns around him had a familiar color: the way the shadows' penumbrae were rimmed in faded red . . . mmm, that was it. This sunlight was exactly the same color as the fusion spark that had lit the Nursery.

"Oh," he murmured numbly. "Oh, I get it, now."

It only made sense: the Yuuzhan Vong would of course have tuned their artificial sun to the same spectrum as the natural one that would light the world where they wanted the seedship's life-forms to grow.

He was on Yuuzhan'tar.

Still, there was something about the color of this light that twisted his stomach. The light in the Nursery hadn't affected him the same way, perhaps because of the thick mists that had always swirled through the interior—or maybe it was the deep purple-blue of this sky . . .

No two planets have skies exactly the same color; sky

color is a function of complex interactions between the solar spectrum and a world's atmospheric composition, and he couldn't help feeling that he'd seen this one before. Or one very like it. The color was close enough to spark his memory, but not so exact that he could recall which planet it reminded him of.

He sat up, and had to stifle a groan; he was sore, bruised from head to foot, and though his ribs had been expertly bound, moving gave him a stabbing pain in his side that slowly—agonizingly slowly—faded to a dull ache that throbbed all the way up into his neck.

Okay. This isn't a dream.

Slowly, more cautiously now, he swung his legs off his moss couch; it hurt, but he didn't feel dizzy or nauseated. After a couple of seconds, he stood up. A robeskin lay nearby, neatly folded. Whoever had bound his ribs had also fashioned him a sort of breechclout, sufficient to protect his modesty. He left the robeskin where it lay.

Beyond the ferns that had screened his bower he found a short cliff stretching up two or three times his height, thickly carpeted with variegated mosses. Some kind of epiphyte clung to the cliff with knurled woody finger-claws, draping long sprays of roots so fine they looked like wigs hung from hooks. Jacen dug his hands into the mosses and tugged, to see if they might support his weight so he could climb up and get a look around, but the moss pulled free almost without resistance, leaking purplish sap that smelled like tea and stained his fingers.

And the surface it had clung to—

Even cracked and stained with juices of unfamiliar plants, he could not mistake this stuff: this was what his whole world had been built from.

Duracrete.

This wasn't a cliff. It was a wall.

"Oh . . ." He stepped back, hands dropping nervelessly to his sides. As though his dream closed in on him again, he couldn't seem to breathe. "Oh, no, not really . . ."

He followed the wall a few meters to his left, where he saw clear sky through another screen of ferns. He parted the ferns, stepped through—

And found an alien world spread beneath him.

He stood on a ledge, one stride from a sheer drop that plunged more than a kilometer to a dazzlingly multi-colored jungle of ferns similar to the ones that screened his bower. Patches of brilliant scarlet darkened to crimson, joined other patches of shimmering black or gap-spark blue, all shot through with curving streaks of shimmer like rivers of precious metals, and it all *moved*: shifting, rippling, rolling through a rainbow spectrum and back again as leaves and fronds and branches and vines all twisted in some wind he could not feel. Flying crea-tures flitted from point to point far below him, hunting just above the forest canopy, too distant for his eyes— unaccustomed to such vast spaces—to make out their details.

This jungle curved away over a topography too random, too jagged, too *young* to be real; valleys were bottom-less chasms, shrouded in mist, joined by razorback ridges that intersected and parted again and doubled upon each other with no pattern any known geology could produce. Immense mountains rose in the distance: sharp spires, flat-sided and needle-topped, as though there had never come wind or rain to erode them. Some of these moun-tains had sides too steep even for this tenacious jungle of mosses and ferns. Where their bones were exposed, Jacen could pick out oddly regular patterns: squares, rectangles, all arranged rank upon rank, metric arrays in lines both horizontal and vertical. He squinted, frown-ing: those patterns were far too regular to be natural;

they were mathematically precise. He had seen something like this before—

Thinking, he happened to glance upward ... and forgot everything else, because that was his first sight of the Bridge.

From a razor-sharp, needle-pointed arc above the distant horizon, a mind-bending river of color swelled overhead. Following it, Jacen craned his neck back, and back, and back: a titanic spectrum, cascades of azure and incarnadine, of argent and viridian braided into an impossibly complex, impossibly vivid rainbow that filled a third of the sky before narrowing again to another knife-edged curve that vanished into the purple sky above the opposite horizon.

Jacen knew what it was; more than a few worlds in the New Republic sported planetary rings. And he also knew that none of those worlds had rings like this one. This would have been famous, legendary; for this view alone, such a world would have been renowned throughout the galaxy as a tourist destination. And if it was this vivid—this *huge*—even now, when its color must be washed out by the light of day and the purple of the sky, what must it look like after dark? He could barely imagine.

Looking upon it, he felt he understood something about the Yuuzhan Vong that had always puzzled him before. It was not uncommon for primitive species on ringed worlds to mistake the rings in their sky for magical bridges built by gods; even for Jacen, who was well aware of the physics behind what he saw, the sight produced a faint shudder of sympathetic awe. He could imagine all too clearly being one of a species that had evolved under such a sight: to them, such a Bridge could only be the work of gods. It would be impossible to doubt the gods' existence with the highway from their deific home to the world hanging forever overhead—so obviously magical, as well, that a creature could follow its curve all the way around the world and never reach either end. It would be only too easy to imagine gods patrolling their Bridge, looking down upon their creation.

With the gods so close at hand . . .

If the world is full of violence, savagery, and torture, this must be how they *want* it.

Lots of things about the Yuuzhan Vong made sense to him now.

"Magnificent, isn't it?"

Vergere's voice came from just behind his shoulder; though he hadn't heard her approach, he was too lost in wonder and new comprehension to be startled. And he had known somehow already that she would be here. He had felt her shadow upon his thousand-year dream.

He had known, somehow, that she was still part of his life.

"You know," Jacen murmured, still gazing up into the sky, "that's exactly what you said when you brought me into the Nursery. Those same words. Just like that."

"Truly?" Her wind-chime laughter tinkled around him. "You recall all that I say to you?"

"Every word," Jacen answered grimly.

"Such a clever child. Is it any wonder that I love you so?"

Slowly, painfully, Jacen lowered himself to sit with his legs over the edge, his feet dangling free a kilometer above the rugged jungle canopy. "I guess I was pretty messed up. Pretty battered," he said, laying one hand along the bandages that bound his sprung ribs in place. "You patched me up. You and those tears of yours."

"Yes."

He nodded: not thanks, just acknowledgment. "I didn't expect to live through it."

"Of course not. How could you, and achieve what you did?" she said kindly. "You found the power that arises of acting without hope . . . and also without *fear*. I was—I am—very proud of you."

Jacen met her eyes. He could see his own reflection, dark and distorted, in their glossy black surface. "Proud? All the people up there who died because of me—"

"All the people down here who *live* because of you," she countered, interrupting. She briefly told him how the shapers had been forced to give the dhuryam immediate control of the seedship, and how it had begun the breakup into individual shipseeds so quickly that there had been no time to round up the rampaging slaves. The dhuryam itself had used their slave seeds to herd them to safety, fulfilling its side of the bargain it had made with Jacen. "Yes, hundreds died in the battle—but thousands of slaves were able to ride the shipseeds to the surface: slaves who were to have been executed at the climax of the *tizo'pil Yun'tchilat*. You were magnificent, Jacen Solo. A true hero."

"I don't feel much like a hero."

"No?" Her crest splayed orange. "How does a hero feel?"

Jacen looked away, shaking his head silently. She settled in beside him, swinging her legs over the void below them, kicking her heels aimlessly like a little girl in a chair too high for her.

After a moment, Jacen sighed, and shook his head again, and shrugged. "I guess heroes feel like they've *accomplished* something."

"And you haven't? Several thousand slaves might disagree."

"You don't understand." In his mind, he saw again the body on the hive-island's beach: the one who might have been a slave, who might have been a warrior, who had bled out his life next to the corpse of a shaper who'd had no clue in combat: a shaper who'd only thought to put his own body between the infant dhuryams and the killing machine Jacen had become. "In the Nursery—once I started killing," he said softly, "I didn't want to stop. That must be—I can only think that's how the dark side must feel. I didn't *ever* want to stop."

"But you did."

"Only because you stopped me."

"Who's stopping you now?"

He stared at her.

She turned her quadrifid palm upward as though offering him a sweet. "You want to kill? There is nothing around you but life, Jacen Solo. Take it as you please. Even mine. My species has a particularly vulnerable neck; merely take my head in your hands, and with one quick twist, *thus*—" She jerked her head up and back as though an invisible fist had punched her in the mouth. "—you can satisfy this dark desire."

"I don't want to kill you, Vergere." He hunched into himself, resting his elbows on his thighs as though huddled against a chill. "I don't want to kill anybody. Just the opposite. I'm *grateful*. You saved me. I was out of control—"

"You were *not*," she said sharply. "Don't make excuses."

"What?"

"*Out of control* is just code for 'I don't want to admit I'm the kind of person who would do such things.' It's a lie."

He offered her half a smile. "Everything I tell you is a lie."

She accepted his mockery with an expressionless nod.

"But everything you tell *yourself* should be the truth—or as close to it as you can come. You did what you did because you are who you are. Self-control, or its lack, had nothing to do with it."

"Self-control has *everything* to do with it—that's what being a Jedi is."

"You," she said, "are not a Jedi."

He looked away. Remembering what she had done to him kindled a spark within his chest that grew into a scorching flame around his heart. His fingers dug into the lush moss that carpeted the ledge, and he made fists, tearing up a double handful, and a large part of him wanted that moss to be her neck. But years of Jedi training had armored him against rage. When he opened his fists and let those shreds fall into the wind, he let his anger fall with them.

"Being a Jedi isn't just about using the Force." His voice was stronger now; he was on sure ground. "It's a commitment to a certain way of doing things—a certain way of looking at things. It's about *valuing* life, not destroying it."

"So is gardening."

He hung his head, numb with memory. "But I wasn't trying to save anybody. Sure, it started out that way—that's what I *planned* for—but by the time you caught up with me on the hive-island, saving lives was the farthest thing from my mind. All I wanted was a club big enough to smack the Yuuzhan Vong all the way out of the galaxy. All I wanted was to *hurt* them."

She blinked. "And this is wrong?"

"It is for me. That's the dark side. It's the *definition* of the dark side. That's what you saved me from."

"I saved your life, Jacen Solo. That's all. Your ethics are your own affair."

Jacen just shook his head. His family history was itself the ultimate argument that the dark side is *everybody's* affair, but he wasn't about to get into that. "You don't understand."

"Perhaps I don't," she agreed cheerfully. "You seem to be telling me that *what you do* is irrelevant; all that matters is *why* you do it."

"That's not it at all—"

"No? Then tell me, Jacen Solo, if you had pursued the noble goal of saving those thousands of slaves in the manner of a true Jedi, what would you have done differently? Anything? Or would you only feel differently about what you have done?"

Jacen frowned. "I—that's not what I mean—"

"Does killing a dhuryam for a noble goal make it any less dead? Do you think it matters to these dead dhuryams whether you killed them in a frenzy of rage or with calm, cool Jedi detachment?"

"It matters to *me*," Jacen said solidly.

"Ah, I see. You can do whatever you want, so long as you maintain your Jedi calm? So long as you can tell yourself you're *valuing life*? You can kill and kill and kill and kill, so long as you don't lose your *temper*?" She shook her head, blinking astonishment. "Isn't that a little sick?"

"None of those questions are new, Vergere. Jedi have asked themselves all of them ever since the fall of the Empire."

"Longer than that. Believe me."

"We don't have a very good answer—"

"You'll never have an answer, Jacen Solo." She leaned toward him, her hand on his shoulder. Though her touch was warm and friendly, her eyes might have been viewports into infinite space. "But you can *be* an answer."

He frowned. "That doesn't make any sense."

She turned her palms upward in a gesture of helpless surrender. "What does?"

"Oh, well, yeah," he sighed. "I've wondered that myself."

"Look around you," she said. "Look at this world: at the patterns of the fern forest, at the rugged curves of terrain, the braided colors of the rings overhead. It is very beautiful, yes?"

"I've never seen anything like it," Jacen said truthfully.

"That is 'sense' of a kind, yes?"

"Yes. Yes, it is. Sometimes when I look out at the stars, or across a wild landscape, I get the feeling that it does make sense—no, more like what you said: that it *is* sense. Like it is its own reason."

"Do you know what I see, when I look at this world? I see *you*."

Jacen stiffened. "Me?"

"What you see around you is the fruit of your rage, Jacen Solo. You made this happen."

"That's ridiculous."

"You stole the decision of the *tizo'pil Yun'tchilat* from the shapers on the seedship. *You* chose the dhuryam that has become the *pazhkic Yuuzhan'tar al'tirrna*: the World Brain. You destroyed its rivals. You gave it the overlordship of this planet. This planet takes its shape from your dhuryam friend's intention, its personality—and its personality has been shaped by your friendship. All this beauty exists, in this form, because of you."

He shook his head. "That wasn't what I planned—"

"But it is what you did. I thought we had agreed that *why* you did it is of concern only to Jedi."

"I—you always twist everything around," he said. "You make it way more complicated than it really is."

"On the contrary: I make it simpler. What you see

around you, Jacen Solo, is a reflection of yourself: an artificial construct of the New Republic, remade by the Yuuzhan Vong into something new—something more beautiful than has existed in the galaxy before."

"What do you mean, an artificial construct?" The sick dread that had curdled in his stomach when he found duracrete beneath the moss slammed back into him. "Where *are* we?"

"Yuuzhan'tar," she said. "Did you not understand this?"

"No, I mean: what world was this *before*?"

She sighed. "You see, but you do not see. You know, but you do not let yourself know. Look, and your question is answered."

He frowned at the fern forest below, where mountain shadows stretched away from the setting sun. Those flying creatures were out in greater force now, in the twilight, and they circled higher and higher through the shadows as though in pursuit of nocturnal insects. Their wings were broad, leathery, their bodies long and tapered, ending in a sinuous reptilian tail—

Then one swooped straight up in front of Jacen and soared above into the darkening sky, and he could no longer ignore what they were.

Hawk-bats.

He said, "Oh."

Those strange metric designs on the distant mountains—he knew what they were, now. And the impossibly complex topography of the jungle, that made sense, too.

Jacen said, fainter now, "Oh. Oh, no."

The designs were viewports. The mountains were buildings. This place was a nightmare image of Yavin 4: the valleys and ridges were patterns of rubble carpeted by alien life. Far more than just an ancient temple complex like one on the gas giant's moon—what Jacen looked upon here was the shape of a single planetwide city, shattered into ruins, buried beneath a jungle.

And all he could say was, "Oh."

Long after Yuuzhan'tar had turned this face away from its sun, Jacen still sat on the mossy ledge above the jungle, now shrouded in night. Flashes of bioluminescence chased each other through the shadowed canopy in jagged streaks of blue-green and vivid yellow. The Bridge was impossibly bright, impossibly close, as though he could reach up, grab on, and swing from one of its braided cascades of color. The colors themselves shimmered and shifted as individual fragments in the orbital ring spun in their own rotations. It cast a glow over the nightscape brighter, softer, more diffuse, than any conjunction of Coruscant's moons ever had. This was the most beautiful place Jacen had ever seen.

He hated it.

He hated every bit of it.

Even closing his eyes didn't help, because just knowing it was out there made him shiver with rage. He wanted to burn the whole planet.

He knew, now, that somewhere deep in his heart, none of the war had ever seemed quite real; none of it since Sernpidal. He'd been nursing a secret certainty, concealed even from himself, that somehow everything would be all right again someday—that everything could be the way it used to be. That Chewbacca's death had been some kind of mistake. That Jaina could never fall into the dark. That his parents' marriage was strong and sure. That Uncle Luke would always show up just in time and everyone could have a laugh together at how afraid they'd been . . .

That the Anakin he'd seen die had been—oh, he didn't

know, a clone, maybe. Or a human-guised droid, and the real Anakin was off on the far side of the galaxy somewhere with Chewbacca, and someday they'd find their way home and the whole family could be together again.

That's why he hated this world spread before him.

Because it could never be home again.

Even if the New Republic somehow, impossibly, turned the tide. Even if some miracle happened and they retook Coruscant—what they won wouldn't be the same planet they had lost.

The Yuuzhan Vong had come, and they were never going to go away.

Even if Jacen *had* found a club big enough to knock the whole species back beyond the galactic horizon, nothing could ever erase the scars they would leave behind.

Nothing could ever heal his broken heart.

Nothing could remake him into the Jacen Solo he remembered: the cheerfully reckless Jacen, chasing Zekk into the downlevels; the exasperated Jacen, trying one more time to make Tenel Ka crack a smile; the Jedi apprentice Jacen, born to the Force, but still awed not only by the legend of Uncle Luke but by the power his uncle's teaching could draw out of him; the teenage Jacen who could wilt under his mother's stern glare, but still exchange roguish winks with his father and his sister the instant Mother turned away.

I spent so much time wanting to grow up. Trying to grow up. Trying to act like an adult . . . Now all I want is to be a kid again. Just for a little while. Just a day.

Just an hour.

Jacen reflected bitterly that a large part of growing up seemed to involve watching everything change, and discovering that all changes are permanent. That nothing ever changes *back*.

That you can't go home again.

This was what the alien beauty of Yuuzhan'tar whispered constantly in the back of his head: *Nothing lasts forever. The only permanence is death.*

Brooding, he sat through the long slow roll of the night.

Some unknown time later—by the wheel of the stars, constellations still mockingly familiar over this bitterly foreign landscape, many hours had passed unmarked—he asked, "What now?"

Vergere answered him from the darkness within the bower of ferns. Though no words had been exchanged between them since twilight, her voice was clear, chiming, fresh as always. "I have been wondering the same."

Jacen shook his head. "Don't you ever sleep?"

"Perhaps I will when you do."

He nodded. This was as much of an answer as he had learned to expect. He swung his legs back onto the ledge, wrapping his elbows around knees drawn up to his chest. "So, what next?"

"You tell me."

"No games, Vergere. Not anymore. And no more shadowmoth stories, huh?"

"Is what has happened such a mystery to you?"

"I'm not an idiot. You're training me." He made an irritated gesture, a flick of the wrist as though tossing away something nasty. "That's what you've been doing from the beginning. I'm learning more tricks than a monkey-lizard. I just don't know what you're training me to *do*."

"You are free to do, or not do, what you will. Do you understand the difference between training and teaching? Between learning to *do* and learning to *be*?"

"So we're back to the shadowmoth story after all."

"Is there another story you like better?"

"I just want to know what you're *after*, all right?

What you want from me. I want to know what to expect."

"I want nothing from you. I want only *for* you. 'Expecting' is distraction. Pay attention to *now*."

"Why can't you just explain what you're trying to teach me?"

"Is it what the teacher teaches—" The darkness itself seemed to smile. "—or what the student learns?"

He remembered the first time she had asked him that. He remembered being broken with pain. He remembered how she had guided him to a state of mind where he could mend himself; like a healed bone, he'd become stronger at the break.

He nodded slowly, more to himself than to her. He rose, and went over to the moss-covered couch at the edge of the black shadows cast by the broken walls and the screen of gently weaving ferns. He picked up the neatly folded robeskin, and looked at it for a long moment, then shrugged and slipped it on over his head. "How long before the Yuuzhan Vong arrive?"

"Look around you. They are already here."

"I mean, how long before something happens? How long can we stay here?"

"That depends." A soft chuckle came from the darkness. "How thirsty are you?"

"I don't understand."

"I'm told that a human can live three standard days without water—four or five, with careful conservation. Would it be too forward of me to suggest that we might leave in search of some, before you are too weak to move?"

Jacen stared into the darkness. "You're saying it's up to me?"

"Here, look at this."

Out from the shadows flew a pale, irregular object

half the size of Jacen's fist; it curved through a slow arc, gently tossed. Jacen caught it instinctively.

In the clear light reflected by the Bridge, he found the object to be rough-textured and lumpy, like a rounded hunk of limestone. It had several flattened nubs, sticky with a black, puttylike secretion, that might have been stumps where pieces had been broken off. The object as a whole seemed to be the yellowish white color of bleached bone, but all its cracks and crevices were crusted with something flaky, dark, brownish—

Blood. Dried blood.

"What *is* this thing?" A hard fist clenched the bottom of his throat, because he already knew.

It was a slave seed. A mature slave seed.

His slave seed.

This was why he hadn't been in pain.

He should throw it off the precipice: hurl it into the jungle of ferns a kilometer below. He should set it on the floor beside him and smash it flat with a hunk of duracrete: crush it into paste. He should *hate* it.

But he didn't.

He stared at it, aching, astonished at the empty whistling loss that suddenly gaped inside him.

Without thinking, he hiked up his robeskin and peeled back the strips that bound his chest, peering beneath them. On the spot where she had stabbed him so many weeks ago, he now bore a wider scar, as long as his finger, a scar the bright pink of newly healed flesh; she must have healed him with her tears, almost like bacta.

He found he had to sit down. He sank in place with a sigh like an overloaded landing strut. "You cut it out of me . . ."

"While you slept. You were unconscious for quite a while." Vergere moved slowly out of the shadows, and crouched at his side. "Are you all right?"

"I—I'm—" Jacen shook his head blankly. "I mean, thank you. I guess."

"Did you not want it removed?"

"Of course I . . . I mean, I did. I just—I don't know." He held it up into the softly shifting light. "It's dead, isn't it?"

Vergere nodded solemnly. "Once a slave seed has extended its tendrils throughout a host's nervous system, it is no longer an independent organism. This one died within a minute of its removal."

"Yeah." Jacen's voice was barely more than a whisper. "I just feel—I don't know. I hated it. I wanted it out of me. I *wanted* it dead—but, you know, while it was in me . . . it made me *part* of something. Like in the Nursery. During the fight, it was almost like having the Force again. Now—"

"You feel empty," Vergere supplied. "You feel alone. Lonely. Almost frightened, but also strong, yes?"

He stared at her. "How? . . ."

"The name for what you are feeling," Vergere said through a slow, gentle smile, "is *freedom*."

Jacen snorted. "Some freedom."

"How did you expect it to feel? You are free, Jacen Solo, and that can be lonely, and empty, and frightening. But it is also powerful."

"You call this freedom? Sure, I'm free—on a ruined planet occupied by the enemy. No friends, no ship, no weapons. Without even the Force." He couldn't help thinking, *Without even the slave seed.* He glowered out into the gaudy shimmer of the Bridge. "What good does *freedom* do me?"

Vergere settled into feline repose, arms and legs folded beneath her. "Well," she said at length. "That's a question worth considering, yes?"

"Oh . . ." Jacen's breath caught in his throat. "That's what you meant just now? When I asked you *what next*?"

"You are free," she repeated. "Go where you will. Do what you will. Be what you will."

"And what are *you* going to do?"

Her smile shifted infinitesimally. "What I will."

"So I can go? Just go? Walk off? Do whatever I want—and nobody will stop me?"

"I make no promises."

"How am I supposed to know what to do?"

"Ah—" Her smile expanded, and her eyes drifted closed. "—now we return to epistomology."

Jacen lowered his head. He'd lost what taste he'd ever had for playful banter.

He realized, sitting there with Vergere reclining by his side, that this ledge, high up the side of a ruined building, was in its own way kind of like the Embrace of Pain. He could sit here until he rotted, wallowing in misery—or he could *do* something.

But what?

Nothing seemed to matter. On this shattered planet, each direction was as good as any other. There was nothing *useful* he could do—nothing within his reach that would make a difference to anyone but himself.

On the other hand, who says I have to be useful?

And, sitting on that ledge, he discovered that there was one direction that still meant something to him.

He got up.

Vergere opened her eyes.

He parted the ferns, moving back into the night shadow beneath them, and found his way to the moss-covered wall. Starting at one rear corner, he walked the wall's length, scraping a long strip of the moss aside with his hand. It came off easily, revealing blank duracrete beneath. He glanced over his shoulder at Vergere, who watched him silently through the screen of ferns.

Shrugging, he went back to the corner and started along the adjoining wall.

Three paces from the corner, his scraping fingers revealed a vertical crack, straight as a laser, bordered with metal strips; beyond the crack, the wall became durasteel, instead. Jacen felt around on the wall at about waist height until his fingers closed on a manual release. He turned it, pushed, and the durasteel door slid aside with an exhausted groan.

"What are you doing?"

Jacen didn't answer.

Beyond lay a hallway that smelled of mildew, dimly lit by bulbous growths of phosphorescent lichen, its floor patched with ratty, insect-eaten carpeting. It had been years since he had prowled the lower levels with Jaina and Lowie, Tenel Ka and Zekk, but the smell was unmistakable. The hallway was lined with numbered doors: this had been one of the old midlevel apartment blocks. At the far end of the hall, an open arch led to emergency stairs.

Jacen nodded to himself, and headed for the stairs without so much as a glance at Vergere.

Her voice echoed along the hall. "Where are you going?"

He didn't owe her any answers. Silently, he started down the stairs. The stairwell was walled with age-clouded transparent fiberplast, netted with reinforcing wire. Dimly through the webs of scratches, cracks, and wire, he could see a walkway, far below, leading into the blank black-stained wall of a neighboring building.

Halfway down the first flight, he paused, sighing.

"You coming, or what?"

"Of course." Vergere appeared at the stairtop behind him, smiling broadly in the Bridgelight. "I was only waiting for you to ask."

SEVEN

THE CRATER

"This is *Jacen Solo*?" The master shaper, Ch'Gang Hool, stared in open horror at the image in the dwarf viewspider's sac of optical jelly. A cluster of long, delicate tentacles implanted at the corner of his mouth twitched, knotting and unknotting itself, before reaching sinuous feelers upward to continue its jittery, nervously obsessive preening of the master shaper's starburst headdress. "This—this is the Jacen Solo of Duro? The slayer of the voxyn queen? The *Jeedai* sought by *Tsavong Lah*?"

"It is."

"And this is the same *Jeedai* who sparked the slave revolt that came within a *crizt* of destroying the seedship? The slave revolt that killed *hundreds* of our holy caste? The slave revolt that spat vicious infidel scum across *my pristine planet*?"

"*Your* planet, Master Shaper?"

"The shaping of this world is my honor, and my task!" Ch'Gang Hool snarled. "Until that work is done, every living thing in this stellar system answers to my will— even the fleet! Even the *World Brain*! If I choose to call this planet mine, who dares argue? Who? *You*?"

"Oh, not I." A long forefinger tipped with curved talon tickled the dwarf viewspider on its control node, enlarging the image of Jacen Solo until the Jedi's head filled the optical sac. "For argument, I think you'd have to try *him*."

"How did he come to be here? How has he survived? It has been *weeks* since seedfall! This dangerous *Jeedai* has been running loose all this time? Where has he been? Why have I not been *informed*?"

On the far side of the dwarf viewspider, Executor Nom Anor brandished his imperturbable needle-toothed smile. "The warmaster orders that you bend all available resources toward his apprehension."

"Orders, does he?" Ch'Gang Hool's headdress bristled aggressively. "Until he comes to take possession of this world, *I* am the ultimate authority here! We'll see about his orders!"

"Call it a suggestion, if you like." Nom Anor leaned forward, opening his hands, the perfect image of friendly reasonability. "Nonetheless you are, as you say, responsible for the shaping of Yuuzhan'tar. I now have brought to your official attention that loose upon this planet's surface is this exceptionally dangerous Jedi; a Jedi who singlehandedly—what was your phrase? Ah, yes—came within a *crizt* of destroying the seedship." Nom Anor settled back upon the pod beast, enjoying the ripple of its muscle beneath him as it adjusted its shape to support his new posture. Really, these shapers had it good—too good for their own good, he thought. Perhaps that was why he found it such a pleasure to spin this one up. "How you meet this *clear and immediate threat* is—of course—entirely up to you."

Ch'Gang Hool scowled. "I have never yet heard adequately explained how this dangerous *Jeedai* came to be aboard the seedship in the first place—"

"Direct all inquiries to the warmaster," Nom Anor advised airily. "I am certain he'll be *happy* to take time out of *fighting the war* to answer your slightest, silliest concerns."

"Is it slight, that the *Jeedai* who slew our voxyn queen is at large upon our *homeworld*?" Ch'Gang Hool shook his eight-fingered master's fist at the executor. "Is it *silly*, to be alarmed to find we have been infiltrated by the *single most dangerous enemy of our entire people*?"

"Just between you and me and the viewspider, here," Nom Anor said agreeably, "what's slight is your niggling about some imaginary *insult* to your *authority*. What's silly is worrying about how Jacen Solo *got* here; you should be vastly more worried about *what he is doing right now*."

Rising blood pressure blued the master shaper's face. "Where is he? You know, don't you?"

"Of course." Again, Nom Anor displayed his needle-pointed smile. "I was only waiting for you to ask."

There was something wrong about this crater.

Jacen backed up along the notch in the crater's rim wall, frowning. Vergere, a few paces beyond, stopped when she sensed Jacen was no longer following, and she looked a question back at him.

He shook his head. "I have a bad feeling about this."

The outer slope of the crater was a scree of rubble, spilling off exposed structural members of what had once been government offices; this section of the crater's rim had been a weight-bearing wall several kilometers high. The multicolored ferns and mosses covered it as though it were natural ground, but their roots were too shallow to bind the rubble solidly in place. They'd had to climb slowly, with Vergere in the lead. Jacen couldn't know if his next step might fall on a loose chunk of duracrete and trigger an avalanche, or send him tumbling through a crust of fibertile into some semi-intact room below. Vergere never explained how she was always able to find the safest path; Jacen assumed she was using some kind of Force-sense.

The notch had once been part of a vehicle accessway, possibly an air taxi stand; three meters or so of its reinforced sidewalls had survived the destruction of the surrounding building. Jacen settled into their shade, just deep enough that he could see down the crater's inner slope, and sat on a speeder-sized hunk of lichen-crusted wreckage.

This crater—

It was big enough to swallow a Star Destroyer without a trace. Big enough to lose the seedship in. It dropped forever away from them in a flattening curve, its bottom lost in black shadow: shadow cast by a billowing column of cloud that stretched up to a flat anvil top.

The cloud darkened as it descended, reaching deep into the crater, licking itself with forked tongues of lightning. Thunder rumbled up from below, and the air crackled with negative ions.

Jacen swallowed. "I have a bad feeling about this," he repeated.

"And well you should." Vergere hopped back to him, and settled onto the lichen beside him. "No place on this planet is more dangerous."

"Dangerous . . ." he echoed. "How do you know?"

"I can feel it in the Force." She laced her fingers together into a bridge upon which she rested her chin, and smiled up at him. "The question is, how did *you* know?"

He squinted at her, then turned his head to frown back out into the crater. How *did* he know? He sat in the shade of the ruined accessway wall, and thought about it.

Weeks of trekking had thinned and hardened his body, carving him into knotted rope and tanned leather. His hair had grown out in unruly curls, now streaked with blond by the harsh ultraviolet of the blue-white sun. His thin, itchy teenager's beard had filled in, wiry, darker than his hair. He could have dug up some depilatory creme from an abandoned refresher along the way, or even a blade sharp enough to shave with, but he hadn't bothered. The beard protected his cheeks and jaw from sunburn.

He could have picked up clothing, too, if he'd wanted it—he wore a pair of tough boots he'd found—but no regular clothing could be as durable, or as useful, as the robeskin. Warm at night, cool during the day, self-cleaning, it even healed itself when it ripped. Beneath the robeskin, he wore the breechclout Vergere had fashioned for him. After he'd found the boots, he'd plaited strips torn from the robeskin to make himself a pair of self-cleaning socks that never wore out.

The robeskin had proven useful in other ways, as well: across his back he wore a sizable knapsack, similarly plaited. The strips had healed in place, making a living pack that never broke or wore out; like a muscle, the knapsack seemed to get stronger the more he used it. He carried it stuffed with as much food as would fit. One three-day stretch where they had been unable to scrounge a meal had cured him of any trust in his luck.

Food was available, if one looked hard enough: mostly breadmeal, sugar-yeast preserves, and the freeze-dried protein squares that had been staples of the downlevel dwellers. Maybe it didn't taste good, but none of that stuff ever spoiled. Unlike during the planet's former life as Coruscant, water was plentiful; hardly a day passed without a rain squall, and fresh pools were easy to find among the rubble and wreckage.

Sometimes they had wandered deep in the gloom of the lower levels, creeping along rickety walkways or down corridors slick with granite slug trails, as though this were still the planet on which he'd grown up; sometimes those lower levels opened unexpectedly upon immense open swaths where gargantuan buildings had collapsed, becoming vast valleys that teemed with alien life, and they were forced to pick their way across a dangerously chaotic surface of Vonglife-covered rubble.

Though the Yuuzhan Vong had altered the planet's orbit—the sun, formerly a searing pinpoint, was now close enough that it showed a clear disc nearly the size of Jacen's fingernail at arm's length—they seemed to have left the planet's rotation alone, as near as he could tell; his own circadian rhythms, conditioned by a lifetime in Galactic City, seemed to match the day–night cycle of Yuuzhan'tar well enough.

Vergere had seemed perfectly content to let Jacen set the pace and direct the journey. She never again so much as asked where they were going. They ate when he was hungry, and rested when he was tired, when he was neither, they walked. If Vergere ever slept, Jacen didn't see her do it. She would seem to settle into herself from time to time, and was capable of remaining immobile for hours; but whenever he would move or speak she was alert as though she'd been standing continuous watch.

Also in his knapsack he carried a few useful items they'd scrounged: a glow rod, a pair of electrobinoculars, a handful of power cells and his prize, an MDS personal datapad. Though it was ancient—a 500 series, hopelessly obsolete—and most of what it was loaded with seemed to be instructional games, simplified image generators, and other kid stuff, there was one useful program: an interactive holomap of Coruscant.

Every few days, he'd managed to find an intact PDD terminal—buried deep within the midlevels of a half-ruined building, or sheltered under a slab of fallen wall, once even hanging by its access cable on a twisted steel walkway that led to empty air, the building to which it had connected having collapsed entirely. Public Data Display terminals are extremely durable, designed to absorb a lot of abuse—they have to—and some of the PDDs he found still worked, or could be kicked to life after jacking in one of his spare power cells. Then he could upload the PDD's location into the YOU ARE HERE function of the datapad's holomap, tracking his progress.

What he would do when he arrived, he didn't know. There probably wasn't anything left but a vast mound of wreckage like the ones across which they scrambled every day. He didn't even really know why he was going. He had no plan, only a destination.

A destination was enough.

He pulled the electrobinoculars out of his knapsack and powered them up. Something about the Vonglife down in the crater bothered him. He wasn't sure what it was, couldn't be sure; even after weeks in the Nursery and weeks more on Yuuzhan'tar, he was far from an expert.

He'd avoided contact with the Vonglife whenever possible; much of it had unpleasant properties—the tea-smelling purple sap that had bled from the duracrete moss, for example, had turned his hands into masses of blistered welts for three days. Over the weeks of the trek, he'd found that the Vonglife had a certain pattern: it grew in vast patches, surrounded by rings of starkly bare rubble. Near the center of each patch, he could usually spot one of the ecogenerating biomachines that the shipseeds had scattered across the planet, churning out spores or seeds or sometimes even living creatures.

He and Vergere had once spent most of a day watching hundreds of unnamable herd beasts stumble out into the light from the cavernlike mouth of one of these bio-machines. Slow-moving bovine sexapeds, they would blink stupidly at the unfamiliar sun, gathering themselves instinctively into herd groups before shuffling off to begin cropping vegetation. No sooner had they begun to eat than they began to grow—so quickly that Jacen had been able to watch them mature over the course of the day. And for every fifty or hundred of the sexapeds, the biomachine had produced a predator, from huge bipedal lizardlike creatures with knife-tipped facial tentacles instead of teeth, to groups of fierce insectile pack hunters no larger than Gupin.

He and Vergere had seen the Yuuzhan Vong themselves now and again, and not only shapers tending their new planet. Warriors patrolled even the midlevels, armed, shivering with disgust at the machines through which they were forced to march. For a time, Jacen had wondered if they might be searching for him personally, but as their trek lengthened they began to come across signs that he wasn't the only fugitive lurking in the deep shadows below the zone of destruction: fresh tracks in the dust, caches of food recently picked over, wreckage cunningly arranged to look random while it concealed hiding places within. Three or four times, he even caught glimpses of other humans, darting furtively from cover to cover, always at night, always cautious about exposing themselves even to the light of the Bridge. They could have been refugees, people left behind and forgotten in the chaos of the evacuation; they could have been lifelong midlevel dwellers, avoiding contact with the upper world by instinct; they could have been slaves escaped from the seedship. Jacen didn't know. He never planned to find out. He avoided them.

They were attracting the attention of the Yuuzhan Vong.

He didn't know if the Yuuzhan Vong had any use for slaves on their new homeworld, or if whatever people they caught were executed on the spot. This was something else he planned never to find out.

The Vonglife that clung to the inner curve of the crater looked different from any he'd encountered so far. He twiddled the autozoom on his electrobinoculars, to flip the enhanced image back and forth between a wide-angle overview and tightly focused close-ups of individual plants. The foliage was patchy and strange, and its coverage was unexpectedly poor; everywhere he directed the electrobinoculars, he found streaks of rusting durasteel and hunks of rubble, as though the Vonglife struggled here with an environment too hostile for it to flourish. The mosses, so brilliantly colored everywhere else, here were nondescript grays and browns and murky greens; the ferns that elsewhere formed towering jungle canopies were here stunted, twisted, curling randomly, fronds dull and streaked as though coated with dust.

Dialing back the magnification, he swept the vertical tower of the thunderhead that rose from the crater's midpoint. Its gray-black base looked as flat as its dazzling white anvil, and the whole column twisted as it rotated slowly, as though the cloud couldn't quite decide if it might want to become a massive Coriolis storm.

All this looked plenty threatening, he allowed, but not enough to explain the smothering dread that crushed his chest when he so much as thought about going down there. "All right, I give up. What is it about this place? What makes it so dangerous?"

Vergere touched his arm, and with a gesture directed his attention toward a thicket of what looked like coniferous shrubs—though the electrobinoculars' range and azimuth display indicated the smallest of them stood more than ten meters tall. On the slope around the thicket, a small herd of agile hoofed reptilelike creatures sprang from rock to rock, cropping nervously at the sparse moss. An instant later he found out what had been making them so nervous: one of those massive bipedal tentacle-faced predators lunged out of the shrub thicket with astonishing speed. It seized the nearest of the hoofed reptilians in powerful prehensile forepaws, its blade-tipped mouth-tentacles stabbing and sawing to swiftly slay and disjoint the captured animal, carving it into bite-sized hunks. As the rest of the herd bounded away, the predator settled down in the slanting sunlight to devour its kill.

"*That* is why this place is so dangerous," Vergere said with a hint of a challenging smile. "It is filled with what you would call the dark side. I should say: the dark side is very, very powerful here, more powerful than anywhere else on this planet. As powerful, perhaps, as it is anywhere in the galaxy."

Jacen lowered the electrobinoculars, blinking. "That's not the dark side," he said. "A predator hunts to feed itself and its family. That's just nature."

"And the dark side isn't? I thought the danger of the dark side was that it *is* natural: that's why it's easier than the light, yes?"

"Well, yes, but—"

"Is what you have seen not the exemplar of the dark side? Is this not what you fear so much: aggression, violence, passion?"

"You want to know what the real dark side would look like? If that predator had slaughtered the entire herd, just for the fun of it. For the joy of killing."

"Do you think this predator takes no joy in its successful kill?"

Jacen looked again through the electrobinoculars,

watching for a moment as the predator seemed to shiver with delight in its meal. He didn't answer.

"Kill one, it's nature, kill them all, it's the dark side?" Vergere went on. "Is the line between nature and dark side only one of degree? Is it the dark side if that predator kills only half the herd? A quarter?"

He lowered the electrobinoculars once more. "It's the dark side if it kills more than it needs to feed itself and its family," he said, heating up. "That's the line. Killing when you don't need to kill."

Vergere cocked her head. "And how do you define *need*? Are we talking about the line of starvation, or simple malnutrition? Is it the dark side if they only eat half the slain animal? Does a predator partake of the dark side if its family is a few kilos *overweight*?"

"It's not about that—"

"Then what is it about? Are we back to *why*? Does intention always trump action? It's not the dark side for that predator, say, to slaughter the entire herd and leave them to rot, so long as it *thinks* it needs them for food?"

"It's not that *simple*," Jacen insisted. "And it's not always easy to describe—"

"But you know it when you see it, yes?"

He lowered his head stubbornly. "Yes."

Vergere uncoiled her fingers toward the blood-smeared predator on the slope below. "You didn't *this* time . . ."

Jacen's answer was interrupted by a shattering thunderburst that sounded like the whole sky had exploded.

He yelped and threw himself against the wall at his back. Rubble slid and shifted in the crater wall above; an avalanche of duracrete hunks and twisted support beams poured over the lip of the wall to slam the notch's floor centimeters from Jacen's knees. Another crash blasted through the sky, and another; he turned sideways to the wall and tucked his head, hands doubled to protect the back of his neck against the pounding of debris. More blasts sounded, but the crater no longer shook, and Jacen risked a glance upward.

"What was *that*?"

Vergere pointed into the limitless purple above the arch of the Bridge. "There."

"I don't see anything—"

"Jacen—" She waved a hand at the electrobinoculars that hung, forgotten, around his neck.

He yanked them to his eyes, aiming where she had pointed. The autofocus sharpened an image, and one of his father's Corellian curses snuck through his lips. Those explosions hadn't been explosions, and they hadn't been thunder.

They'd been sonic booms.

Yorik coral vessels the size of the *Millennium Falcon* whipped through broad looping arcs around the crater, tracing an impossibly complex rosette. And all of them spat bulbous objects like seedpods, colored the same purple as the sky, in a continuous stream.

Now the shell of one seedpod began to peel back like an Ithorian starflower opening toward the sun, revealing tangled wads of white filaments like silkweed. The silk unraveled swiftly, releasing its seeds to the wind, trailing long, long streamers of white fibers. Jacen spun the zoom wheel on the electrobinoculars, and one of those seeds snapped into focus, and it wasn't a seed.

It was a Yuuzhan Vong warrior.

The white silk strands trailing above it snapped open into a parachute canopy. Soon all the seedpods had blossomed, dropping a round dozen warriors apiece— hundreds—*thousands*—

"Great." Jacen lowered the electrobinoculars. "We've stumbled into their airborne infantry training camp.

Could have been worse, huh? Could have been an artillery range—"

"Jacen."

There was a hard, cold darkness in Vergere's voice that he'd never heard before. He went suddenly still, watching: an animal catching wind of a larger, faster predator.

She said, "This is no training exercise. They are hunting for you."

Jacen swallowed. "I'm not going back," he said hoarsely. "I've had enough of the Embrace of Pain for *three* lifetimes—"

"Oh, no fear of *that*." Her usual sprightly cheer flowed back into her, straightening her back and curving her lips into a human-style grin. "They have no interest in your pain, Jacen Solo. These are the soldiers of the master shaper. If they catch you, they will kill you. Purely. Simply. On the spot."

He squinted back up into the sky with only his unaided eyes; he could now just barely make out the thousands upon thousands of tiny purplish specks.

"All this?" he murmured. "All this, just for *me*?"

"You now get the first hint of how important you are."

He met her gaze steadily. "Well, somebody thinks so, anyway. Any suggestions?"

Vergere nodded, turning away to gaze once more upward. "There seems to be an updraft from the crater; perhaps something to do with that strange storm. It's blowing the pod troopers outward, toward the rim of the crater, and beyond."

"So?"

"So: if you are to escape them, there is only one way you can go."

Again, she unfurled a hand toward the interior of the crater.

"Down."

EIGHT

INTO THE DARK

Lightning blazed overhead, and thunder slammed the crater floor hard enough to shake the ground. Shivering, Jacen pressed himself into a broken corner that had once been the interior of a fashionable refresher. Icy rain streamed down his spine, and pellets of hail stung his skin. He clenched his jaw so that his teeth wouldn't chatter.

The Yuuzhan Vong were coming.

Whole squads of warriors had come bounding over the crater's rim before Jacen and Vergere had made it even halfway down the inner slope. The warriors had leapt recklessly from slab to rock to rubble, gaining rapidly. Jacen could not possibly have matched their speed; in the service of the True Gods, injury or maiming—even death—is a warrior's fondest hope.

He didn't know how long he'd been waiting here, shivering in the icy rain. Vergere had told him to wait, had told him she could find an escape route, but she had to hunt for it and she could move faster alone. Though she had not said the words, had not asked him to, Jacen trusted her.

What choice did he have?

Oh yeah, sure, I'm free, he thought sourly. *Some freedom.*

The rain, the hail, the bitter wind, they were bad. The waiting was worse.

Worst of all was that he could *feel* the Yuuzhan Vong closing in.

The center of his chest was hollow: an empty space where the slave seed once had been. If he changed his breathing, if he closed his eyes, if he *thought* about that hollow—directed his attention into the emptiness at his center—somehow that brought another sense to life. He couldn't have described the feeling; there were no words, exactly, for how it felt. The slave seed had sent fibers throughout his body, had woven itself into his nervous system until those fibers were an inextricable part of who he was—but those fibers vibrated to a life foreign to this galaxy.

He just knew . . .

He could feel the Yuuzhan Vong swarming down the crater's slopes, could feel them slogging through the thunderstorm in the crater's center. He felt the sizzle of alien stress hormones coursing alien veins. He felt one's shortness of breath as a warrior slipped around a blind corner that might hide a fugitive Jedi; he felt one's black rage at the death of comrades in the Nursery, and his heart echoed with another's savage lust for vengeance. He felt the shocking, nauseating nonpain that slammed up a leg from an ankle broken by an unlucky shift of rubble, and he felt the frustration of a warrior ordered to remain behind to tend some clumsy brenzlit's broken ankle while he burned to leap forward, to hunt and find and slay. He felt them all.

Like he was all of them, and all of them were him. At the same time.

And more: he felt the crush of tender fronds under hard hot boot heels. He felt the primitive distress of moss when half a struggling colony was scraped off a broken door by the stumble of a warrior against it. He felt the blank terror of a small family of burrowing, roughly mammalian creatures, cringing at the groundborne impact vibrations of so many running feet.

Accepting the warriors' feelings, opening himself to their emotions, their sensations, he no longer felt the cold: Yuuzhan Vong metabolism, faster and hotter than human, turned the icy rain into a refreshingly astringent shower. The sting of hail became harshly intoxicating, like scratching an inflamed rash. And he was no longer afraid—

Not that he was afraid to die. He'd left fear of death behind on the worldship at Myrkr—but in the blasting thunderstorm, his body had cringed and shook, twisting away from imagined slashes of amphistaffs, bracing against impacts of imagined thud bugs, a biological reflex that took no account of his courage. But now—

Now, all he felt was a fierce rise of predatory joy as a warrior raised his amphistaff and crept toward a small white-robed human shivering in a corner at the meeting of two broken walls, and only when a tall shadow loomed through the curtain of rain right in front of him did Jacen realize that the small white-robed human who was about to die was himself.

Lightning blasted overhead as he twisted, and the amphistaff blade only scored his ribs before stabbing deep into the duracrete of the wall at his back. In the ringing darkness that followed the flash he let the knapsack drop off his shoulders, catching one strap as it fell; while the warrior yanked his amphistaff free, Jacen swung the knapsack two-handed and slammed fifteen kilos of cans and equipment into the warrior's face. The warrior staggered backward and Jacen pounced, swinging again, landing solidly, buckling the warrior's knees.

Jacen spun the knapsack overhand to smash the warrior straight down to the ground, but the warrior lifted his blade to parry, slashing the knapsack in half, scattering protein bars and canned synthmilk, shearing the electrobinoculars neatly in half and stabbing into the electronic guts of the datapad—which exploded into blue-white sparks that lit up the rain and scaled the length of the amphistaff to scorch the warrior's hands.

The warrior hacked a glottal curse as his hands spasmed involuntarily. Smoking, the amphistaff fell limp to the ground between them. Jacen grimaced as pain bit his own hands, chewing its way up his arms—but it wasn't his pain.

This was pain from the warrior's burns.

When the warrior leapt to attack unarmed, Jacen met his attack effortlessly, pivoting slightly so that the warrior's spiked boot missed him by a centimeter. The warrior skidded, caught himself, then twisted and fired a lightning punch overhand toward Jacen's temple. Jacen tilted his head a fraction, and the punch only ruffled his hair.

"If you don't stop," Jacen said, "I'll have to hurt us."

The warrior snarled and swung his knotted fists. Jacen flicked the first punch aside; the second, he parried with an open palm as he stepped forward, swinging his own doubled arm, so that the warrior's knuckles slammed into the point of Jacen's oncoming elbow. The warrior howled as his knuckles shattered, and a blaze of alien pain ignited in Jacen's arm: splintered bones stabbing through third-degree electrical burns.

"I can do this all day." He could: the warrior might as well have been a part of Jacen's own body. He could no more fail to meet an attack than one of his hands would miss the other in the dark. He would feel every scrap of whatever pain he inflicted, but so what? It was only pain.

And the rest—

He let himself go, moving light and easy, counters to

every attack as clear and obvious and predictable as a form he'd done a thousand times: like training with Jaina, when their Force talents and their twin bond had made them practically one person. More warriors sighted the fight—the dance—and thud bugs snapped through the air, and Jacen actually felt he should apologize as he gracefully faked the warrior off balance and then took his outstretched arm and spun him into their path. The thud bugs hit him like hammers. Vonduun crab armor saved his life, but transferred enough hydrostatic shock to snuff his consciousness like a switched-off glow rod.

Jacen felt that, too: an eyeflash of blackout that staggered him.

When his eyes cleared, three warriors had him boxed.

Knowing how they would attack wouldn't help; no one alive could move fast enough to dodge. The warriors slashed at him, amphistaffs lengthening with whipcrack speed. None of the blades even grazed him.

He had not moved.

To the nerve nodes that served as all three amphistaffs' primitive brains, Jacen suddenly appeared to be a— small, disturbingly misshapen, but still unmistakable— amphistaff polyp; uncounted millennia of natural selection had hardwired amphistaffs against cutting polyps.

Well, that worked okay, Jacen thought. *But once they drop them and come after me barehanded, I'm cooked.*

So he attacked.

He took three running steps for momentum toward the one on the left and sprang into the air. The warrior's instinctive reaction—to lift his amphistaff and spear Jacen through the guts—did him no good at all, because the amphistaff dropped limp between his hands and the warrior could only gape in astonishment as Jacen slammed both feet into his chest and flattened him as if he'd been hit by a speeder.

Jacen hit the ground running, and never looked back.

They came after him like hungry gundarks, snarling fury. He dashed blind through the storm, slipping, skidding, head down, navigating by the feeling in the middle of his chest: toward where the Yuuzhan Vong weren't. He could feel them spot him, could feel surges of rage and feral blood lust from all directions as hunters glimpsed him, vaguely, wraithlike through the rain and hail, and felt every flash of stark joy when they spotted him in the stuttering blue-white strobe of lightning. Thud bugs tracked him, blasting splinters off walls, scattering chunks of sodden moss. Shouts from all sides: harsh coughs with too many consonants, half smothered in rain, half buried in thunder. He didn't speak the language, but he could feel the meaning.

They had him surrounded, and were closing in.

This, he said to himself, *would be a really good time for Vergere to show up.*

As if summoned by his thought, an invisible hand shoved his shoulder, knocking his headlong dash into a diagonal stagger. Before he could recover his balance, an invisible rope hobbled his ankles and brought him crashing to the ground—

Which collapsed under him with the dull rip of rotten fibertile, and dumped him headfirst four meters down to a damp stone floor that he hit like a cargo sack. He lay there, half stunned, gasping, wind knocked completely out of him, staring at the sudden constellations that wheeled around his head but shed no light into the surrounding gloom.

A section of wall slid aside, revealing another room beyond, dimly lit by glow globes in conservation mode. The light from the far room haloed a small, slim avian silhouette in the doorway. "Jacen Solo. It is time to come in from the storm."

He looked up at the Jacen-sized hole in this room's ceiling, and let the icy rain that poured in on him wash the stars out of his head. "Vergere? . . ."

"Yes."

He felt the confusion of the hunters above: as far as they could tell, he had simply vanished. "Uh, thanks, I guess—"

"You're welcome."

"But—"

"Yes?"

Slowly, he pulled himself up. No bones seemed to be broken, but his whole body ached. "You couldn't have just, maybe, said 'Hey, Jacen! Run this way!'?"

Her head canted a centimeter, and her crest seemed to glow a deep burnt orange. She extended a hand toward him.

"Hey, Jacen," she said. "Run this way."

After one last glance through the hole above at the black, lightning-lashed clouds, he did.

Deep into the planet, deep into the darkness—
Running.

Glow globes dead, or pulsing feebly; flashes of rooms, bare and sterile, the only life flattened cartoons of foliage spidering across walls in mosaic tiles; hard clap of boots on stone, harsh breath rasping through dust-filled throat, over lips and teeth coated with sand—
Running.

Sweat burned in Jacen's eyes, blurring Vergere's back; she streaked ahead, turning corners, ducking through doorways, diving down stairwells, leaping into abandoned turbolifts to slide the guardrails, and he followed desperately—

Deeper into the planet. Deeper into the darkness.
Running.

That calm open hollow at his center evaporated some-where along the way; he didn't feel the Yuuzhan Vong anymore. Gasping, losing Vergere and catching sight of her again, his sprint dipping into a stagger, he couldn't know if the Yuuzhan Vong were gaining, falling behind, circling ahead. His imagination crowded the corridors at his back with fierce sprinting warriors, but to look be-hind risked losing Vergere forever.

Daggers of fire stabbed into his lungs with every step. Ragged black blots danced in his vision, growing, blending, twisting until they suddenly billowed and swal-lowed him whole.

Deep in the darkness . . .

He awoke on the floor. Warm rain trickled down his cheeks as he sat up. The palm of one hand was skinned raw. A drop of that warm rain touched his lips, and he tasted blood.

Vergere crouched nearby, half shadowed in the weak amber light from a single glow globe well down the cor-ridor. She watched him with feline patience.

"Until your head becomes as hard as these flagstones, I'd suggest you avoid knocking it into them," she said.

"I . . ." Jacen's eyes drifted closed, and opening them again cost him tremendous effort. His head thundered like the storm above. The corridor swirled around him, and darkness pressed in on his brain. "I can't . . . get my breath . . ."

"No?"

"I—can't keep up, Vergere. I can't—draw on the Force like you do, I can't get . . . strength . . ."

"Why not?"

"You *know* why not!" Black fury ignited his heart, blood steaming in his head, spinning him to his feet. Two strides put him above her. "You *did* it to me! I am *sick* of your questions—sick of your *training*—"

He pulled her to her feet, then off her feet, holding her dangling above the floor so close that his teeth might as well have been clenched in her flesh. "And most of all," he growled, low, murderous, "I am sick of *you*."

"Jacen—" Her voice sounded oddly thick, oddly tight, and her arms fell limp to her sides—

And Jacen discovered that his hands were locked around her throat.

Her voice trailed to a fading hiss. "That . . . twisssst—"

My species has a particularly vulnerable neck—

His hands sprang open, and he took a step back, and another, and another until his back came hard against the sweating stone of the wall. He covered his face with his hands, blood from his palms painting his face, blood and sweat from his face stinging his skinned palm. His chest heaved but he couldn't quite breathe; he never had managed a really good breath; his strength fled along with his rage and his knees turned to cloth, and he sank down to huddle against the wall, eyes squeezed shut behind his fingers.

"What? . . ." he murmured, but he couldn't finish. *What is happening to me?*

Vergere's voice was warm as a kiss. "I told you: here, the dark side is very, very strong."

"The dark side?" Jacen lifted his head. His hands shook, so he clasped them together and pinned them between his knees. "I, ah—Vergere, I'm sorry—"

"For what?"

"I wanted to *kill* you. I almost *did*."

"But you didn't."

Waves of trembling rippled through him. He ventured a shaky laugh. "You should have left me behind. I probably have less to fear from the Yuuzhan Vong than I do from the dark side."

"Oh?"

"All the Yuuzhan Vong can do is kill me. But the dark side . . ."

"Why is it so to be feared?"

He turned his face away. "My grandfather was a Lord of the Sith."

"What? Of the *Sith*?"

He turned back to find Vergere staring at him in blank astonishment. She tilted her head one way, then another, as though she suspected he might change appearance when viewed from a different angle. "I had thought," she said carefully, "that you were of *Skywalker* blood."

"I am." He hugged himself against the shaking. Why couldn't he *breathe*? "My grandfather was Anakin Skywalker. He became Darth Vader, the last Sith Lord—"

"Anakin?" She settled back into herself, openly stunned—and clearly, astonishingly, saddened. "Little *Anakin*? A Lord of the Sith? Oh . . . oh, could it not have been otherwise? What a tragedy . . . What a *waste*."

Jacen stared at her in turn, his mouth hanging open. "You say that like you knew him . . ."

She shook her head. "Knew *of* him, more. Such promise . . . Do you know, I met him once, not five hundred meters above where we now sit? He couldn't have been more than twelve, perhaps thirteen standard years old. He was—so *alive*. He burned . . ."

"What—what would Darth Va—I mean, my grandfather—what was he doing on *Coruscant*? What were *you* doing on Coruscant? Five hundred meters *above* us? What was this place?"

"Do you not know? Has this been lost, as well?" She rose, and extended a hand to help him to his feet. She touched the wall nearby, her fingers skittering through a complex pattern on a sweating rectangular slab, which slowly swung wide, opening a doorway into a gloom-filled chamber beyond.

"This way." The chamber threw back a dark resonance, as though she spoke beside a drum. Her gaze was steady once more, and expressionless as the stone of the walls. Lost in wonder, Jacen stepped past her into the darkness.

"This was our tower of guard: our fortress watch upon the dark," she said. The doorway narrowed into a dim yellow stripe of globe-glow, then vanished. "This was the Jedi Temple."

"This—?" Awe squeezed his chest, and he floundered in the dark; he had to gasp harshly in order to speak. "You—you *are* a Jedi!"

"No, I am not. Nor am I Sith."

"What *are* you, then?"

"I am Vergere. What are you?"

In the darkness her voice seemed to come from everywhere at once. He turned, seeking her blindly. "No more games, Vergere."

"This has never been a game, Jacen Solo."

"Tell me the truth—"

"I tell you nothing but truth."

She sounded so close by that Jacen reached for her in the dark. "I thought everything you tell me is a *lie*—"

"Yes. And the truth."

"What kind of truth is that?"

"Is there more than one? Why even ask? You will find no truth in me."

This time her voice came from behind him; he whirled, extending his hands, but found nothing he could grasp. "No *games*," he insisted.

"There is nothing that is *not* a game. A serious game, to be sure: a permanent game. A lethal game. A game so grave that it can be well played only with joyous abandon."

"But you said—"

"Yes. It has never been a game. And it always has. Either way, or both: you had better play to win."

"How can I play if you won't even tell me the *rules*—?"

"There are no rules."

A scamper of footsteps to his right; Jacen moved toward them silently.

"But the game does have a name," she said from the opposite side of the room. "We are playing the same game we have been playing ever since Myrkr: we are playing 'Who is Jacen Solo?' "

He thought with longing of the glow rod, lost with his sliced-open knapsack in the crater above. Thinking of the glow rod, of bright golden light springing from his fist, made him suddenly ache for his lightsaber: he thought of that clean green glow filling the room, cutting through all shadows, making everything clear again. His hands burned to hold it one more time. In building that lightsaber, he had built himself an identity. He had built himself a destiny.

He had built himself.

"If that's the game," he said, "I can end it right now. I *know* who I am, Vergere. No matter what you do to me. No matter what new torture you put me through. If I never touch the Force again. It doesn't matter. I *know*."

"Do you?"

"Yes," he said solidly into the darkness. "I'm a Jedi."

A long, long silence, in which he seemed to hear the entire room drawing a slow, slow breath.

"Indeed?" She sounded sad. Disappointed. Resigned to a melancholy fate. "Then the game *is* over."

"Really?" he said warily. "It is?"

"Yes," she sighed. "And you lose."

The room burst to light; after so long in the dark, Jacen felt like he was being jabbed in the eye with a piece of the sun. He flinched, shading his eyes with an upraised arm. Slowly his eyes cleared; the room was larger than he had thought—a ten-meter ceiling, walls decorated with the same floral mosaics, lit by blazing glow globes the size of the *Falcon*'s cockpit, hanging suspended by tripled chains of verdigris-caked bronze that swung gently above its tiled floor—

And it was full of Yuuzhan Vong.

He turned to Vergere. Beyond a ring of warriors, she stood companionably beside a medium-sized male who wore a long, loose-fitting robeskin of black.

They spoke, but Jacen could not hear them. His ears roared like a forest fire. The Yuuzhan Vong male spoke again, more sharply, but Jacen did not understand. Could not understand. Had no need to understand.

Jacen had seen this male before.

He had seen this male on Duro, with Leia's lightsaber behind his belt. He had seen this male on the worldship at Myrkr. He knew this male's name, and he tried to say it.

Tried to say—

But before he could even open his mouth—

A hot tidal surge of red billowed through him, and washed away the world.

Jacen did not swim in the red tide, he floated: drifting, spinning in the eddies, tumbling in the surf. The red tide ebbed, waves washing out, and he bobbed to the surface. The red tide drained from his head, leaving him gasping on the floor.

His hands hurt.

He looked at them, but he couldn't quite see them, or he couldn't quite make sense of what he saw; his eyes

wouldn't quite focus. He let his right hand fall to the
chilly mosaic tile of the floor, wondering blankly that the
outwash of the red tide had left the floor so cold, and so
dry. A savor of scorched meat hung in the air, as though
his father had jury-rigged the autochef again. But Dad
couldn't have jury-rigged the autochef. There was no autochef. And Dad wasn't here, couldn't be here, would never
be here—and the *smell* . . . Nothing made sense. How
had he fallen to this floor? What caused this roil of smoke
and dust? A curving wall of rubble choked off three-
quarters of the chamber—where had *that* come from?

Answers were beyond him.

But his hands still hurt. He raised his left hand and
frowned his vision clear.

A circle in the middle of his palm—a disk about the
size of a power cell—was blackened, cracked, oozing
thick dark blood. Wisps of smoke coiled upward from
the cracks.

Oh, he thought. *I guess that explains the smell.*

"How . . . how does it feel, Jacen Solo—" The voice
was thin, ragged and harsh, rasping, broken by coughs.
The voice was familiar. The voice was Vergere's. "—to
once more . . . touch the Force?"

She lay crumpled on the floor a few meters away,
just within a ragged archway lipped with jagged stone,
as though some incomprehensibly powerful creature
had trampled her as it crashed through the wall. Broken
stone littered the floor. Her clothing was shredded, smoldering, red embers sliding along torn edges, and burned
flesh beneath it still smoked.

"Vergere!" He was at her side without knowing
how he got there. "How—what *happened*?" A sickening
conviction clotted in his guts. "Did *I*—?" His voice
trailed off.

He remembered—

Through a fever-dream haze, red-soaked images leaked back into him: the room filled with Yuuzhan Vong warriors, Vergere standing beside Nom Anor as though the two knew each other, as though they were coworkers. Comrades. Friends. Nom Anor had said something to her, and she something to him, but betrayal had hammered any hope of meaning from his brain. He remembered a long gathering breath: inhaling a galaxy of hatred and rage—

And he remembered channeling that whole galaxy of rage down his arms and hurling it at Vergere.

He remembered watching her writhe in the electric arcs of his hatred: remembered the sizzle of his own hands burning as lightning burst through them: remembered how that pain had only fed his anger.

And he remembered how *good* it had felt.

Clean.

Pure.

No more wrestling with right and wrong, good and evil. Every knotty problem of Jedi ethics had dissolved in one brain-blasting surge; once he had surrendered complexity, he'd found that *everything* was simple. His hatred became the only law of the universe. Anger alone had meaning, and the only answer to anger was pain. Someone else's pain.

Anyone else's pain.

Even now, awake, alert, choking on horror, he could feel the sweet echo of that clean, pure rage. He could hear it calling to him. It coiled inside him: a malignant parasite chewing at the bottom of his mind.

What have I become?

Vergere lay on the floor like a broken doll; her eyes were dull, glazed, empty, and her crest showed only dirty gray.

"Vergere—" he murmured. It had been so easy to hurt her. So *simple*. Tears spilled onto his cheeks. "I warned you, didn't I? I *warned* you. The dark side—"

"Don't . . . make excuses . . ." Her voice was even fainter now, breathier, more ragged.

"I wouldn't dare," he whispered. There was no possible excuse. No one knew the dangers of the dark side better than he; those dangers had haunted the depths below his entire life—

Yet he had fallen so easily.

He had fallen so *far*—

The wall of rubble closed off most of the chamber: tumbled hunks of duracrete, fallen in a steep slope from uncountable floors above. The only light in the much-reduced chamber was leakover from glow globes in the ruined hallway outside. The ceiling had collapsed, he remembered that much, remembered the roar, the pounding, the dust and flying splinters of stone. No, wait, it hadn't collapsed . . .

He had pulled it down.

He remembered swirling within the red tide, remembered feeling Vergere lose consciousness, remembered reaching for a new target, a new *victim*, reaching for Nom Anor with the lightning that had felled Vergere—

And being unable to find him.

He could *see* the Yuuzhan Vong executor, could *hear* him shouting orders to the warriors around them all, but he could not touch him with the lightning. There had been a circuit missing: the lightning would ground harmlessly into the floor or the walls or arc back to make Vergere's unconscious body spasm in convulsions. The lightning of his rage could only span gaps between poles of the Force—neither Nom Anor nor his warriors could conduct that current. Frustration had compounded Jacen's fury; he had thrown himself outward seeking power to do these creatures harm—

And the storm above the crater had answered.

He remembered the wild joy of release as the power of

the storm had roared into him and through him and became a mad vortex within the underground chamber, lifting stone and brick and chunks of duracrete to whirl and batter and slash the Yuuzhan Vong, pounding the warriors with pieces of the planet that had once been Jacen's home. A shrug of wind had crushed the Yuuzhan Vong into one corner of the chamber, and he remembered bubbling laughter exploding with malice into a shout of victory as he had reached up his hand and brought down the building around them.

He rocked back on his ankles, hands going to his face. Was it possible? He had buried them alive. All of them. And he didn't care.

No: he *did* care. That's what made it even worse.

He had buried them alive, and he was *happy* about it.

The dark side called to him: a shadow worm whispering promises of ecstasy as it ate into his heart. It murmured infinite release, humming a song of the eternity that lies beyond all shadows of doubt and remorse.

He shook himself violently and lurched to his feet. "I have to get out of here."

"Jacen . . ." She lifted a hand as though to stay him, as though to ask for his help.

"No, Vergere. No. I have to go—I have to go *right now*. I'm sorry I hurt you, I'm so sorry, I *am*—" *Liar,* the shadow worm snickered inside him. *Just wait, and watch, and she'll give us an excuse to do it again.*

Vergere's eyes seemed to clear then, and a hint of a smile curved her lips. "The dark side? . . ."

"It's—it's too *strong* for me here. I warned you. I *warned* you what could happen—"

She raised her hand once more, reaching for his leg; he took a hasty step back to avoid her touch, and she let her arm fall limp to the floor. "You see . . ." she whispered, ". . . but you do not see. Jacen . . . why would the Jedi

Council . . . build its Temple upon . . . a nexus of the dark side?"

"Vergere, I—" He shook his head helplessly. "I have to go. I have to go before—before I . . ." *hurt you again,* he finished silently. He couldn't say it out loud. Not here. "I don't have time for guessing games."

"No guessing . . ." she said. "The answer is . . . simple. They wouldn't."

He went very, very still. "What do you mean? I can *feel* the dark side here. I *touched* the dark side, and it, and it, it touched *me*—"

"No. What you feel is the *Force.*" Slowly, painfully, she lifted herself onto her elbows, and she met his blankly astonished stare. "This is the shameful secret of the Jedi: *There is no dark side.*"

How could she lie here with smoke still rising from the shreds of her clothing, and expect him to believe this? "Vergere, I *know* better. What do you think just happened here?"

"The Force is *one*, Jacen Solo. The Force is everything, and everything is the Force. I've told you already: the Force does not take sides. The Force does not even *have* sides."

"That's not *true*! It *isn't*—" The red tide surged into his chest, reaching for his heart. *Everything I tell you is a lie.* This was only another of her lies. It *had* to be. If it wasn't—

He couldn't let himself think it. He shook his head hard enough to make his ears ring. "It's a *lie*—"

"No. Search your feelings. You know this to be true. The Force is one."

But he could *feel* the dark side: he was drowning in it.

"Light and dark are no more than nomenclature: words that describe how little we understand." She seemed to draw strength from his weakness, slowly managing to sit up. "What you call the *dark side* is the raw, unrestrained Force itself: you call the *dark side* what you find when you give yourself over wholly to the Force. To be a Jedi is to control your passion . . . but Jedi control limits your power. Greatness—true greatness of any kind—requires the *surrender* of control. Passion that is *guided*, not walled away. Leave your limits behind."

"But—but the dark side—"

She rose, her smoldering garments wreathing her in coils of smoke. "If your surrender leads to slaughter, that is not because the Force has darkness in it. It is because *you* do."

"Me?" The red tide turned black, poisonous, strangling, burning through his ribs from the inside. "No—no, you don't understand—the dark side is, it's, it's, don't you see it? It's the *dark side*," he insisted desperately, hopelessly. There were no words for the truth inside him; nor were there words for the horror that rolled into him, because he could feel the Force again.

He could feel that she was right.

But that would make me—does make me . . . His knees buckled, and he staggered to maintain his balance, stumbling, reaching for the wall, something stone, anything solid, anything *certain*, anything that he could lean on that wouldn't become smoke and mist and let him fall forever. He whispered, "The dark side . . ."

She paced toward him, relentless, inexorable. "The only dark side *you* need fear, Jacen Solo, is the one in your own heart."

And in her eyes, he found that certainty, that solidity: the permanent, immutable truth he hoped would keep him upright—

His reflection.

Distorted. Leering. Misshapen. An illusion of light,

floating on a glossy curve of surface . . . above depths of infinite black.

They say the truth hurts. A gasp of lunatic laughter bubbled wildly through his lips. *They have no idea . . .* The Embrace of Pain had been nothing but a scratch, the slave seed only a toothache—

His laughter choked itself to a smothered sob. He threw himself past Vergere into the hallway, and fled.

Running.

Every time Nom Anor glanced back toward the wall of rubble that so easily could have become his tomb, a spectral hand reached into his chest to twist his heart apart. "You *assured* me there would be no danger!" he said for the fourth time.

He spoke Basic—it would not do for the warriors to hear him complain—and he gritted his teeth, clenching arms and legs, because the warriors must not see him tremble.

"Nom Anor," Vergere said with the patience that grows of wounds and exhaustion, "you are alive, and uninjured save for bumps and bruises." She wept a continuous rain, mopping away her burns with tears. "What have you to complain of?"

Nom Anor looked once more at the wall of rubble; he could still feel the strangling panic of being so easily, casually, almost negligently shoved aside—and then the rumble of the ceiling's collapse, and the howl of the maelstrom within the chamber, and the boil of dust, and the absolute night that had swallowed him . . . "You should have *warned* me how dangerous and erratic this 'Dark Jedi' power can be," he insisted.

"Look around you. A dozen warriors, and you. And me. All *living*. If, instead of wielding this 'dangerous power' about which you whine, Jacen Solo had been calm, centered, and armed with his lightsaber . . ." One arm rippled in a shrug more eloquent than any words. "You saw what he did in the Nursery. There might have been survivors, but you and I would not be among them."

Nom Anor only grunted. "I do not understand the purpose of this Jedi babble of the 'dark side,' either. What was the use of sparking this crisis? Here I am, at your insistence, lying to the Shaper Lord, manipulating his troops, lurking in this hideous place—not to mention placing my life at *considerable risk*—to trigger this . . . what? What has any of this to do with converting Jacen Solo to the True Way?"

Vergere looked up from tending her wounds. "Before one can learn truth, one must unlearn lies."

"You mean, *our* truth. The True Way." Nom Anor squinted at her. "Don't you?"

"Our truth, Executor?" Her eyes seemed to expand into vast pools of unreadable darkness; in them he could see only his reflection. "Is there any other?"

NINE

THE BELLY
OF THE BEAST

Ever deeper, ever darker, farther and farther below even the memory of light—

Jacen staggered out from a downlevel stairwell onto some forgotten catwalk, gasping. Had he been running for hours? For days? His legs refused another step, and there was no reason to force them.

No matter how far or fast he fled, he could never outrun himself.

The ancient duracrete floor of the catwalk, rotten with age and neglect, collapsed beneath his weight; a frantic grab onto a lichen-crusted rail left him hanging by one hand over a hundred-meter drop. This shaft might once have been a dump for wrecked air taxis: twisted, rust-eaten metal tangled together below, a heap of curving knife edges and torn jagged points.

He hung there for a moment, imagining a long, long plunge, a slicing, ripping impact, a flash of colorless fire . . .

Maybe he should just let go. Maybe this was his only answer to the darkness inside him. Maybe he wouldn't even scream on the way down.

There was only one way to find out.

His fingers loosened.

"Jacen! Hey, *Jacen!* Over here!" He knew the voice. He could not remember ever *not* knowing this voice; it was as familiar as his own. The voice was a trick—he knew it was a trick, it had to be, he'd been tricked this way before—but he could not make himself ignore it. With the deliberate caution of an experienced climber in a tricky traverse, he reached up and grabbed the rail with his free hand, so that he had enough strength to hold on while he turned his head to look.

On a smog-blackened balcony jutting just below the far end of the gangway, stood Anakin.

Jacen muttered, "You're not real."

"Come on, Jacen!" Anakin waved, and beckoned. "This way! Come on! You'll be safe here!"

Jacen closed his eyes. There was no such thing as *safe*. "You're not real."

When he opened them again, Anakin was still there, still beckoning, wearing a loose-fitting tunic and pants in the Corellian style, lightsaber hung loosely at his belt. He waved Jacen on, jittering with urgency. "Jacen, come *on*! What's the matter with you? Let's go, big brother, let's *go*!"

"I saw you die," Jacen said. He opened himself to the throb of the Force around him; the red tide swelled within his chest, but he pushed it down, focusing tightly, reaching out with his feelings . . .

Uncle Luke had told, sometimes, of getting guidance from his dead Master, the legendary Obi-Wan Kenobi. He had told of seeing his Master, hearing his voice, feeling him in the Force, long after Kenobi's death—

Jacen could see Anakin. Could hear his voice. But when he reached toward his brother through the Force, he felt nothing. Nothing at all.

"Two out of three," Jacen said through his teeth. The red tide roared into his ears. He clenched his teeth together to lock his voice in the back of his throat. "Two out of three makes you *Vong*."

"Jacen! What are you waiting for? Come on!"

He could put up with a lot. *Had* put up with a lot. More than anyone should ever have to. But to have some Yuuzhan Vong masque himself as *Anakin*—

The red tide gathered in a wave of power that spun him into an effortless rising somersault, flipping high above the crumbled catwalk. He landed balanced upon the rope-thin rail, his feet rock-steady, his arms loose, nerveless at his sides. His power would not let him fall.

The shadow worm in the center of his chest shouted for blood.

Two out of three makes you dead.

"All right," the shadow worm rasped through Jacen's mouth. "Wait there. I'm on my way."

He ran along the rail lightly, swiftly, a drumbeat of murder in his heart drowning any thought of the long fall below; he was at the catwalk's end in seconds, but Anakin had already darted through the balcony door into the building. Jacen spread his arms and let his rage uphold him as he fell forward, kicking off the rail, gliding over the hundred-meter drop onto the balcony.

He landed in a crouch, skidding, left hand splaying onto a smooth cold layer of slime that coated the balcony. Hawk-bats burst out of the doorway, shrieking and clawing, a wheeling cloud of leather and fur and talon.

Jacen made a fist: an instant gale howled around him, sending the hawk-bats scattering, tumbling helplessly away into the darkness. He sprang forward, eating ground like a sand panther running down a paralope, bounding through the ink-black interior of the building with the Force to guide him around and over obstacles. A flash of booted feet disappearing through a doorway into a globe-lit corridor drew him onward. He reached the doorway in one long Force-boosted leap.

Impossibly, Anakin was already a hundred meters away,

at the far end of the corridor, looking back over his shoulder. "Come *on*, Jacen! You have to *run*! Follow me!"

"Count on it." Jacen burst into a sprint; the Force lent wings to his heels, driving him inhumanly fast, and faster, and faster still. He covered the hundred meters in an eyeblink, and found Anakin still well ahead, still looking back, beckoning, urging him onward.

Jacen ran.

The pursuit became a dream of flight, of effortless leaps, feet only skimming the floors beneath. The Force rolled through him, a crimson river sweeping him onward, beyond the sterile precincts below the crater. The river not only fed him strength, it spoke the structure of the buildings through which he raced directly into his mind: he could feel twists and turns and doorways ahead and behind, could feel where his path might be blocked with rubble or where the floor might not support his weight. It whispered girders and beams, transparisteel and duracrete beneath the Vonglife that thickened around him, Vonglife growing to a riot of shapes and colors, fibrous and fleshy, that clung to walls and ceilings and sprang from floors, Vonglife he could see and smell and touch, but that still wasn't real, couldn't be real, not to Jacen, not now, because it didn't shape the flow of the crimson river. It didn't exist in the Force, and so for Jacen it didn't exist at all.

Right up until he ran into a corridor that snapped closed behind him like the maw of a space slug.

He skidded to a stop. The floor and walls were warm, body temperature, ridged with cartilaginous rings that glowed a sickly bioluminescent green. The ends of the corridor *felt* open—in the Force, there was nothing around him save wide-open space—but to his eyes, the corridor was closed at both ends by flaps of striated flesh like muscular valves.

Anakin was nowhere to be seen.

Panting dry rage, Jacen turned his mind toward that void in the center of his chest where the slave seed had once been. The Force faded from his consciousness; the structure of the broken buildings around him faded into the same nonexistence from which the Vonglife now emerged—but even as the nature of this corridor leaked into his mind, he found he still couldn't feel Anakin.

Maybe it wasn't just in the Force that he didn't exist, Jacen thought.

Hawk-bats had scattered in panic when he'd leapt to the balcony . . . why hadn't they reacted to Anakin? In the cold smooth slime that had coated the balcony's surface, there had been no footprints.

Suckered.

He'd let the red tide drown his brains.

I've been had.

With a crackle of deforming cartilage, the ring closest to the mouth of the corridor squeezed shut, then the next and the next and the next. Jacen frowned, struggling to correlate this with what he sensed through the remnants of the slave seed-web. no malice, no blood lust, nothing aggressive at all, only a kind of pleasurable contentment, a happy relish pulsing around him—then the contraction of the rings reached him, crushing him off his feet, squeezing him along the corridor like a glop of vegitein in a null-g foodpaste tube, and he understood.

The contraction of the rings wasn't an attack, it was a peristaltic wave. This wasn't a corridor.

It was a throat.

Jacen knelt, shuddering, eyes squeezed shut, hands splayed on the flesh-warm floor. After the valve at the end of the corridor had dilated to let him squirt through, it had sealed itself behind him with a wet, meaty slap.

He tried not to listen to the screaming.

—please somebody please please somebody HELP ME—

The screaming was another trick.

Probably.

—please oh PLEASE help me I don't want to do this I don't want to DO this can't you HELP ME PLEEEEEEASE—

It had to be a trick.

The floor had the grainy smoothness of water-worn limestone, all grays and browns, pocked and pimpled with mineral deposits dissolved in the fluids dripping from overhead along down-reaching irregular nipple-cones like stalactites. Some of them wore the iridescent sheen of travertine. Scattered clots of bioluminescent growths shed a soft yellow-green glow—these could have been some kind of cave moss, or phosphorescent fungus. To the eye, this place was a typical cavern of porous limestone, hollowed by the erosion of a vanished underground river.

That's why Jacen had his eyes closed. Because he knew it wasn't.

It was a stomach.

It was the belly of the beast that had swallowed him.

With his eyes open, the dissonance between what he saw and what he felt had spun his brain into dizzy retching nausea; even with his eyes closed, even driving his consciousness down into the hollow center of his chest, the shimmering discord was twisting his mind inside out.

He could feel the beast as though he *were* the beast—throat and stomach and chilly semisentient satisfaction at having lured another victim—but he could still feel his own body, still feel the bruises left by the cartilage rings of the throat, the sting of one elbow where he had skinned it skidding through the beast's pyloric valve, the ache in his swelling knee that he did not remember twisting while he'd chased the phantom Anakin, the hot rasp of his own breathing, and the cold empty fullness in his stomach, which was inside the belly of the beast, which *was* the belly of the beast, because the beast and he were one.

He had swallowed himself.

—*please oh PLEASE why why WHYYYY please I don't want to die like this you have to help me HELP me you have to HELP MEEEEEE*—

The voice sounded human. Female. Raw, ragged, sobbing with exhausted terror. It sounded absolutely real.

As real as Anakin had looked.

He wouldn't fall for it again.

Many kinds of Vonglife used forms of telepathy, from yammosks to villips—even coralskippers reportedly had a mental bond with their pilots. It was obvious to Jacen now: this great cavern beast was a sessile Vonglife predator that had developed a specialized variety of telepathy to lure victims into its mouth. The hallucination of Anakin was only a side effect: any victim would see someone or something they'd instinctively trust to lead them to safety. They would follow blindly, trusting, and be consumed.

The irony was bitter: the shadow worm that coiled through his chest had defended him from that false trust, while the rage that fed the worm had sent him headlong into the cavern beast's mouth anyway.

This, Jacen reflected in his first clear thought since falling into the dark, *is going to be an ugly way to die.*

But that was okay. Dying was okay; he didn't mind. Better to die than to live with the darkness inside him. At least it would be *over*. He could just kneel here and wait to die—

If only it were *quiet.*

—*please help me please aaaaAAAAAA*—

The phase transition of terror into raw agony jolted Jacen's eyes open, and he lurched to his feet. He couldn't listen to this, trick or not. He knew too much about pain.

"Shut up," he growled, low in the back of his throat. "Shut up shut up shut up."

The screams echoed through a puckered gallery mouth that yawned a few meters to his left: a tunnel beyond led down, dropping away into the yellow-green gloom. Jacen stumbled drunkenly on the slope. The screams continued: wordless now, bleak, animal, edged with despair.

The tunnel led deeper and deeper, turning upon itself in a long loose spiral, opening at last into another cavern vastly larger than the first, a cavern dank, dim, the bio-glow that had lit the throat and the chamber above only shimmering faintly through the mouths of other tunnels that opened around the walls. White swirls of mist curled through the air—no, not mist, Jacen discovered as he entered the cavern, but smoke: eye-burning, chokingly harsh, tasting of acid. The floor of this cavern was ruggedly uneven, dimpled as though it were only a thin skin over bowls big enough to swim in; the bowls tapered steeply downward, bottoming in upcrumpled hummocks of stony flesh like lips of refresher-sized mouths.

He coughed, batting smoke away from his face, and staggered toward the screams, following a winding course balanced on the thin curving rims where the bowls met edge to edge.

Deep in the cavern, one of those mouths had pursed around a girl.

Jacen paused above her, balanced on the warm stone bowl rim. She looked as real as Anakin had: real from her tangled, matted hair to the tear-streaked dirt that smeared her face. Only her head and one arm protruded from the tight-sealed lips that held her, and when she saw him above she reached for him, fingers straining help-lessly, eyes white with pain and fear.

"Please whoever you are PLEASE you have to HELP ME please it's EATING me, it's, it's, it's eating me ALIVE—"

He knew what those puckered lips were, now. The cavern above was actually only a crop, or a gizzard; the real stomachs were behind those mouths at the bottoms of the bowls below. That's why the cavern beast was showing him a girl down there.

She was bait.

"Shut up," Jacen whispered. "You're not real. Shut up."

All he wanted was a quiet place to die. Was that too much to ask? Hadn't he *earned* that? Why did everything have to be so *hideous*, so gruesome, so just plain *rotten all the time*? Couldn't he even die in peace?

Did the whole universe *hate* him?

There's only one answer when the universe hates you, whispered the shadow worm from the base of his skull. *Hate it back.*

So he did.

It was easy.

He hated the universe. Hated everything about it: all the pointless suffering and empty death and all the stupid mindless mechanical useless laws and all the squirm-ing blood-smeared ignorant life, hated the stony flesh under his feet and the air that he breathed, hated him-self, hated even the hate he felt and suddenly he wasn't tired anymore, he wasn't confused anymore, everything was simple, everything was easy, everything made sense because hate was everything and everything was hate, and he didn't want to die anymore.

All he wanted was to *hurt* someone.

He looked down at the screaming girl. He hated her.

She wasn't even real. Like a dream. He could do whatever he wanted. Anything. His heart thundered, and his breath came short and hot.

Anything.

Power raged through him as though a dam had burst in his chest. He smiled, and stretched forth his hand, and made a fist.

The Force stifled her screams to a shocked choke. Through the Force he could feel her terror, feel the savage burning of digestive acids slowly dissolving her skin; in the Force he could feel power, real power, power enough to crack her skull like a pterosaur egg, power enough to—

Wait, begged his last shred of sanity. *Wait*—

He could *feel* her—in the *Force*?

"Oh—" he whispered. His knees buckled. "Oh, oh no, oh *please* no—"

His hatred and his strength failed together. He pitched forward, his boots losing purchase on the rim, and he tumbled down the inner curve of the bowl to splay bonelessly beside the stomach-mouth. He might have just lain there, just let himself pass out, let himself sleep until the mouth beside opened again to close around him, instead, but a hand, a girl's hand, a *real* hand belonging to a *real* girl, clutched desperately at his robeskin, yanking him awake, and her shriek scorched his ears. *"HELP me you have to HELP ME you have to help me*—"

"Sorry," Jacen mumbled, blinking rapidly, trying to make his eyes focus, struggling weakly to rise. "I'm sorry, I'm so sorry, I didn't *know*—"

His vision cleared, and he saw her, really *saw* her, for the first time. He saw that her hair had once been long and flowing and golden blond under its coating of greasy dirt; he saw that her eyes were blue, and her face a delicate oval; he saw that—

She's barely even my age.

And if I don't do something RIGHT NOW, *she won't get any older.*

He couldn't trust his legs to support him; he swung himself around to brace his feet against the crumple of stomach-lips, and took her wrist in both hands. He pulled hard, hard as he could, hard enough to make her begging turn to a yelp of pain—

"You're breaking my ARM *please you have to get up, you have to pull me UP—"*

Get up? He didn't have the strength to stand. He didn't have the strength to save her. He had only strength enough to hurt her even more.

And to torture her final minutes with empty hope.

He could barely imagine what she must have gone through, to miss the evacuation of Coruscant, to survive the bombardment, and the invasion of the Yuuzhan Vong. To have lived through the shattering transformation of her world into theirs: the tearing of a whole planet from its orbit. To have hidden in constant terror all these weeks and months in the downlevel shadows, desperately avoiding the conquerors. And when the cavern beast had led her down its throat . . .

Her heart must have been bursting with relief and joy. She had finally found sanctuary—

Then she had found that the only real sanctuary is death.

And how she would come to that death: eaten alive, digested while still awake and aware.

And when she had looked up to see him on the rim above her, an explosion of sudden hope—

Because she couldn't know that the man who had come to her rescue was a broken ex-Jedi, tainted with darkness, half mad with suicidal despair.

How had he ended up so *useless*?

The simple unfairness of it made him angry.

Why should *he* be the one who has to watch this girl die? He'd never asked to be a hero. He'd never asked for power. From the very day he was born, the whole galaxy had been watching him, waiting for him to do something great, something that would live up to the legend of his illustrious parents, of his legendary uncle.

He couldn't even live up to his *own* legend. Such as it was.

And there had been plenty of people who had enjoyed that, hadn't there? There had been plenty of dirty sniggering people who got plenty of dirty sniggering satisfaction out of calling him a coward behind his back, and not one of those nasty vicious sniggering creeps had even once had to feel what it was like to hang in the Embrace of Pain, or toil hopelessly to save a few lives in the Nursery, or be forced to face the black-hearted indifference that was the real truth of the universe—

Anger blossomed within him, surged and swept him away in the familiar red tide, but this time he didn't fight it, didn't struggle and thrash and drown himself in its current. He welcomed it.

In the red rising tide, he found all the power he needed.

TEN

HOME FREE

Home.

The Solo apartments, not far from the ruined hulk of the Imperial Senate, still stood nearly intact.

Home was where Jacen had been heading ever since he'd woken up under the Bridge. Where else did he have to go?

Is anything better than finally finding your way home?

One thing he'd never asked himself: once he got home, what then?

He'd been half expecting, all these weeks, that reaching the place where he'd grown up would mean something: that he'd find some kind of safety there. Some kind of answers. As though if he could only lie down for a nap in his own bed, he'd wake up to find that the nightmare he'd lived—losing his family, his youth, his faith—had been only a hypnoid fantasy sparked by teenage hormones and an undigested dinner.

Is anything worse than finally reaching home, and finding that you're still lost?

He'd been lost at home for hours by the time Anakin walked in.

Jacen sat in his place, in the chair he'd always used at the dining table on those rare occasions when the whole family had been together: to the left of his mother's chair, next to Jaina, who'd always sat at his father's right.

Across the table, Anakin always used to sit next to the specially designed Wookiee-sized chair for Chewbacca.

Jacen tried to summon memories of those happy family times—tried to hear Chewbacca's half-howled laughter, tried to see his mother's struggle to maintain a disapproving glare at one of his father's slightly risqué stories, tried to feel Jaina's elbow in his ribs or a surreptitious glop of orange protato flipped at him by Anakin when their parents weren't looking—but he couldn't. He couldn't fit those images into this dining room.

The dining room was different now.

A slickly glistening blue glob of puffballs—some sort of fungus colony—had enveloped Chewbacca's chair and a quarter of the dining table; pale yellow tendrils rooted it to the leafy purple underbrush that had sprouted from the floor. The table itself had cracked in the middle, buckling beneath some kind of bloodred taproot the size of a Hutt that had broken through the ceiling and seemed determined to drill its way through the floor as well. The walls were draped with multicolored creepers that served as habitat for a variety of hand-sized creatures resembling scaled, warm-blooded spiders.

Jacen was pretty sure they were warm-blooded; at least, their clawed seven-toed feet felt warm as they ran down his arms, up his chest, and across the back of his shoulders. He'd blink once in a while, when one would scamper over his face, but that was his only motion.

He could have moved, if he wanted. He just couldn't come up with a reason to.

The arachnoid creatures spat some kind of mucuslike secretion, globs of thick glassy saliva that stuck tenaciously to whatever it touched, with the sole exception of the arachnoids themselves. While it was still wet, their prehensile feet stretched and spun and drew the saliva out into thick glistening ropes that tightened and turned translucent as they dried, filling half the Solo dining room with a frosted fibrous web.

Jacen was pretty sure that this web was intended to bind him to this chair—that these arachnoids had some vague presentient plan to eventually eat him. He could have broken free without much effort, earlier, before the web had grown strong. He hadn't. Even now, a shrug of his anger could scatter the arachnoids and flashburn their web into nonexistence.

But he couldn't think of a reason why he should bother.

Anakin walked through the web strands as though they didn't exist. He wore a dark vest over a loose tunic, and close-fitting breeches in the Corellian style. He hooked his thumbs behind a wide leather belt, his right near an empty clip where his lightsaber should have been, and gave Jacen a crooked smile so much like Han's it brought tears to his eyes.

whatcha doin', big brother?

One of the arachnoids scampered along a strand that passed through Anakin's chest at an angle from shoulder to floating rib. Neither paid the slightest attention to the other.

Jacen looked at Anakin for a long time, then sighed. "What are you this time?"

this time?

Jacen closed his eyes. "You remember Uncle Luke talking about his Master? About how he could feel Master Obi-Wan in the Force sometimes, even after he'd seen Darth Vader . . . seen *our grandfather*—kill him on the first Death Star? How he could hear Master Obi-Wan's voice giving him advice, and a couple of times even see him?"

sure. everybody knows those stories.

"I guess I kept expecting you to help *me* like that. I

mean, I know: you're not my Master. And I saw your
body. I saw—what they did to you. But still . . . I guess I
kept hoping, you know? I just—I just wanted to hear
your voice again. One more time. See you grin. Smack
you one on the top of the head for doing something as
stupid as get yourself killed."

not that you ever needed all that much of a reason, huh?

Jacen's closed eyes filled with tears. "Yeah. One last
time, you know?"

sure.

"That's why I fell for it. Both times."

both times?

Jacen tilted his head in a sketch of a shrug. "Back in
the Nursery, when Vergere stopped me from killing the
last dhuryam. She used the Force to fake your voice,
and I—"

how do you know?

Jacen opened his eyes, frowning. "What?"

you sure it was a fake? Anakin's grin was as playfully
lopsided as it had ever been. *she was using the force,
right? how do you know the force wasn't using her?*

"I guess I don't," Jacen admitted slowly. "But it doesn't
really make any difference."

if you say so.

"The last time, you had nothing to do with the Force.
You were telepathic bait."

maybe i was. are you sure that's all i was?

Jacen frowned without answering.

*what would have happened if you hadn't seen me
there on the balcony?*

He lowered his head. "I—I don't know. I might have
let myself—" *fall,* he finished silently. He couldn't say it.

He *had* let himself fall. He had fallen faster and farther
than any mere drop to his death.

so seeing me there saved your life, huh?

"Yeah. I guess. But what you led me to—I mean, what *it*, the telepathic projection, what it led me to—"

it, me, whatever. Anakin waved a dismissive hand. *don't get hung up on meaningless distinctions.*

"But down there—down inside the cavern beast—" Bitter acid slid up the back of Jacen's throat. He couldn't go on.

you saved the girl, didn't you?

"Oh, sure. Saved her. I sure did." Jacen coughed, gagging on the memory. "But the *others*—"

There had been other people in the belly of the beast: a lot of people, fifty or more, nearly all human. They had come crowding to the mouths of the stomach chamber gullet-tunnels only a moment after Jacen had freed the girl.

None of them was happy.

With raw Force rolling through him in dark waves, he had been able to seize his own hands telekinetically, using them like tools to peel back the clamped-shut lips of the stomach-mouth. He could feel every centimeter of the girl in the Force, could feel her terror and hope and the agony of her acid-scorched skin, and with the Force he'd lifted her effortlessly, setting her safely on the bowl rim above. A Force-assisted leap had carried him neatly to her side, then he'd lifted her in his physical arms and leapt to the gullet-tunnel down which he'd come. Her clothing had hung in tatters, her skin reddened, peeling, seeping fluid, cooking in the slow heat of the acids that still coated her; Jacen had swiftly stripped off the remnants of her clothing, replacing them with his own robeskin.

It's all right. You'll be all right, he had told her. *The robeskin will take care of you.* It would not only absorb and eliminate the leftover acids, but also eat necrotic skin on her burns and probably save her from serious infection, even gangrene.

He hadn't told her that, of course; despite the darkening thunder of the Force rolling through him, he hadn't been thoughtlessly cruel enough to tell her—after what she'd been through—that the clothing he had given her was already eating parts of her flesh.

And then, clad only in his breechclout, he had looked up and seen the others. The cavern-beast people, fifty-odd of them. Some of them had blasters.

Some of the blasters had been pointed at him.

"It was so—so *sick*. I couldn't believe it." Jacen shook his head. "I didn't *want* to believe it."

Anakin stared at him patiently.

"Worse than Peace Brigaders. Worse than anything I can think of." Jacen shut his eyes against the memory. "They were *living* in there."

The cavern beast was a conservative predator: if its telepathic bait captured more animals than it needed for food, captured survivors could live for a considerable while inside. The moisture that had dripped continuously from the "stalactites" was actually an internal food reserve, analogous to a human's stored fats and glycogen, that could both hydrate and nourish creatures in the cavern beast's multiple crops. The cavern beast processed waste matter ultra-efficiently, extracting nutrition from its captives' feces and water from its captives' urine, and the body heat given off by captives helped the cavern beast regulate its internal temperature. When it needed the extra nutrition of a living body, it could squeeze one of its inhabited crops, forcing captives down the gullet to the stomach chamber.

"They were mostly downlevel refugees who'd missed the evacuation—but some of them were escaped slaves, from the seedship. The Yuuzhan Vong are familiar with cavern beasts, and they avoid them; it wouldn't surprise me if these were the original unshaped baseline from which they bred their worldships, like the one where you . . . the one at Myrkr." He coughed, obscurely embarrassed. "Sorry."

it's okay, jace. Anakin's grin was easy, friendly. *don't worry about me. i'm not sensitive.*

Jacen nodded. "I guess I am, though."

you always were. go on.

Jacen sighed sadly, but anger began to trickle through his guts again. "So it makes a perfect hiding place from the Yuuzhan Vong patrols. The cavern beast hides them, gives them shelter, water, food—sometimes it lures in animals that can be killed and eaten, or traps a refugee who's carrying a stash of protein squares or whatever. There's only one problem. Every once in a while it gets hungry. Sometimes there's an animal or two that can be thrown to the stomachs."

Jacen swallowed and looked at the ceiling. Brilliant green fingers of moss had crept in through the crack forced open by the immense taproot. "And sometimes—" His voice came out thick, hoarse with remembered fury. "—sometimes there isn't."

Anakin nodded gravely. *the girl.*

"Yeah, the girl. They had a rule: last to arrive is first to go. First to go . . . *in.* The girl had gotten there only a few hours before me. But some of them—the ones who did that to her—" His breath went hot, and his vision began to haze subtly red. "Some of them had been in there for weeks. *Weeks,* do you understand? Do you understand what they were *doing*? How many—how many people—" He had to stop, panting, until he could force the rage back down below his throat.

Anakin watched him expressionlessly.

Finally, he could go on. "They didn't even kill her, just knocked her on the head and threw her in." Muscle bulged at the corners of his jaw. His voice dripped loathing. "I guess they didn't kill her because they didn't want her *murder* on their *consciences*."

Anakin shrugged. *people are capable of rationalizing just about anything.*

"But she woke up before the stomach closed over her, and almost got out. Made it halfway. Far enough to scream." Jacen's voice dropped to just above a whisper. "That's where I came in."

so what happened?

"I sure wasn't about to let them put her back in. I wasn't about to let them put *anyone* in—but all the stomachs were opening, and the crops were forcing everyone down the gullets. The cavern beast wanted to be fed, and if they didn't take care of it, it'd just take care of itself."

and the last one in—

"Was me. Right."

they tried to feed you to the cavern beast?

Jacen said, "It never got that far."

no?

"I've *changed*, Anakin. I've . . . I can't excuse it. I can't even *explain* it. But you—you should know—"

it's okay, jace. no matter what happened—no matter what you've done, or what's been done to you—you're still my big brother, y'know? you always will be.

"Big brother," Jacen echoed tonelessly. His eyes ached. He leaned his elbows to his knees, and rested his face in his burned hands. "Funny—these past couple of years, I felt like *you're* the big brother."

that's kinda silly.

"Is it? You—Anakin, you were so *sure* of yourself. So sure of *everything*. So *strong*. I really—I looked up to you, Anakin. You always seemed to know what to do next. Things were so *easy* for you."

everything's easy when you have no doubts.

"But that's what I *wanted*. To be sure. That's what

I thought being a Jedi *was*." He lifted his face, and his eyes were wet. He laughed bitterly through his tears. "Don't you get it? You're exactly what I want to be when I grow up."

what, dead?

"You know what I mean."

i didn't question things because i was never the questioning kind of guy. i was never thoughtful, like you. i was more like uncle luke: a human weapon. point me at the bad guys and turn me loose, i knock 'em down and everybody cheers.

but things are different now. doing things the old way—my way, uncle luke's way—that's just getting people killed. look at what happened to me. what's happening to all of us.

"Better that than what's happening to me," Jacen whispered. "Better off dead."

you think so?

Regret welled up inside him, building a pressure of guilt and self-loathing that he could no longer lock away. He looked at his hands: at the burn-cracked flesh in the middle of his palms, roasted in the lightning of his rage. "Anakin, I went dark."

did you?

"Under the old Jedi Temple, when Vergere handed me over to Nom Anor—what I did was bad, but it wasn't *evil*. It was panic, and exhaustion, and suddenly finding the Force again when I thought it had been taken from me forever. Saving the girl . . . I'm not sorry for that. Anger was all I had left. And I didn't hurt anybody."

except yourself.

"But that's okay, isn't it? Isn't that part of being a Jedi, to sacrifice your own welfare to save others?"

Anakin turned one palm upward. *you tell me.*

Jacen looked away. Remembering hurt. Talking hurt

even more. But *not* talking about it—not admitting what he'd done, rationalizing it, *justifying* it—that he would not do.

I haven't fallen that *far,* he thought.

Yet.

He had used the darkness for strength, letting it course through his veins like blood to keep him upright and functioning while the cavern-beast people appeared, while he learned who they were and what they had done to survive. He might have been able to hold on to his temper, if it had only been that. What they had done—what they had become—sickened him, but he was not a judge. He was a Jedi. He might still have found some way to help them. Even as the stomach-mouths gaped around them, fogging the chamber with their acidic gases, and the cavern-beast people had closed in around him, blasters leveled, coldly murderous while faking regret, he might still have resisted his dark lust to do them harm.

The final ounce of pressure on Jacen's trigger had come from the girl.

He's the last, he's the last! she had shouted. *Take him—him! He's the last!*

"She turned on me," Jacen said quietly.

do you blame her?

He shook his head. "How can I? She's just a girl. A girl who knows what it feels like to be digested alive. A girl who knew that if it wasn't me, it'd be her. Again."

i guess i mean, did *you blame her?*

"That's different." Jacen's face was bleak as a sandstone cliff on Kirdo III. "I blamed all of them. I hated them. And I set out to hurt them."

really?

"I *knew* what I was doing; I knew exactly what it meant. I reached into the dark. I *wanted* it. I reveled in it. I remember laughing. I remember telling them how much trouble they were in. I remember feeling them through the Force as their fake regret turned to real fear. I remember *liking* it."

They had fired on him, blaster bolts streaking scarlet through the greenish acid-fog. Laughing, Jacen had caught their blaster bolts with the palm of his right hand, effortlessly channeling away the destructive energies before they could do him harm. Flicks of his wrist had seized those blasters with the Force and tossed them negligently aside.

how many of them did you kill?

"All of them." Jacen looked down at his trembling hands. He clenched them until his burns leaked blood onto his palms. "None of them. What's the difference?"

While the Force had roared through his head, he'd reached down into the hollow center of his chest, into the void where the slave seed had been, and there he had found the dim semiconsciousness of the cavern beast. With the Force for power, he'd created a delusion: a simple conviction so deeply rooted in the cavern beast's murky mind that no evidence to the contrary could ever shake it.

Humans are poisonous.

So is every other sentient species of the New Republic.

The cavern beast had had no resistance against this kind of trick; it lacked even the rudimentary ability to say to itself, *But none of the ones I've already eaten have made me sick* . . . All it'd had was a defensive reflex.

It vomited.

A massive surge of reverse peristalsis had swept up the people, the girl, Jacen, and every other foreign object throughout the cavern beast's immense interior and washed them all out through the luminescent cartilage-lined throat down which Jacen had entered. He remembered their anger, and their growing panic as the pile of people outside the cavern beast's mouth had disentangled itself into individuals again, and they'd found the teeth of their sanctuary locked against them. No longer could they pay for safety from the Yuuzhan Vong with the lives of others. *You've killed us,* someone had sobbed. *You've killed us all.*

Jacen had stared at them, icy with power. *Not yet.*

These soft, weak, contemptibly treacherous creatures— he could imagine nothing more loathsome. He'd turned his back on them. Walked away.

He'd left them to the Yuuzhan Vong, and to each other.

but you did help them. better death than life bought with innocent blood.

"Is that supposed to make it all right? I wasn't trying to help them. I wanted them to *suffer.* I can't even blame it on the dark side—I know that now. The dark side didn't make me do anything."

i know. that's not the way it works.

"It was all *me,* Anakin. I gave in to my *own* darkness. I let my dark side run wild—"

you could have killed them all. you had the power. and you could have killed the cavern beast. you had power enough for that, too, i bet. just like you could have killed vergere, and nom anor. but you didn't kill anybody. instead you used the power you'd found to serve life. your dark side ain't all that dark, big brother.

"It doesn't matter. You can't fight the dark with the dark."

that's uncle luke talking. fighting the dark was his job. the yuuzhan vong aren't dark. they're alien.

"And I can't seem to make myself fight them."

who says you have to?

Jacen's head snapped up. "You do. *Everyone* does. What other answer is there?"

why are you asking me? Anakin had lost his playful

crooked smile, and he'd moved close enough that Jacen could reach out and touch him—

If he could make himself move his hand.

If there had been anything there to touch.

The despair that pinned him to his seat swelled into a black hole of hopelessness that sucked air from his chest. "Who else can I ask? What can I do? *What am I supposed to do now?*" He sagged, shaking. "I've completely lost it, haven't I? Here I am, arguing with a *hallucination*. You don't even exist!"

does it matter? you're not that easy to get through to, big brother. i have to take any means available.

"*How can it not matter?*" Jacen suddenly shouted. "I need—I *need*—I don't know what to *believe*! I don't know what's *real* anymore!"

on the seedship, i was a force projection. then i was telepathic bait. now i'm a hallucination. that doesn't mean I'm not me. why does everything have to be one or the other?

"Because it *does*! Because things are either one thing, or something *else*! That's the way it *is*! You can't be fake and real at the *same time*!"

why not?

"Because—because you *can't*, that's all!"

the force is one, jacen. it encompasses all opposites. truth and lies, life and death, new republic and yuuzhan vong. light and dark and good and evil. they're all each other, because each thing and everything is the same thing. the force is one.

"That's a *lie*!"

yes. and it's the truth.

"You're not Anakin!" Jacen shouted. "You're *not*! Anakin would never talk like that! Anakin would never *believe* that! You're just a hallucination!"

okay. i'm a hallucination. that means you're talking to yourself.

that means what i'm saying is what you *believe.*

Jacen wanted to howl, to rage, to leap from his chair and *fight*—something. Anything. But the black hole ate his breath, his strength, his anger; it swallowed even the universe of hate, and ended up emptier than it had begun. Where all his hope, all his love, all his certainty had ever been now gaped a cold void, filled only with the blank inanimate hunger of vacuum, and Jacen collapsed.

He didn't even have the strength to cry.

He fell into the black hole.

Eons passed, or nanoseconds.

Within the black hole, there was no difference between the two.

Stars condensed from intergalactic hydrogen, ignited, fused, burned heavy metals, shrank to white dwarfs that faded to brown, all between one breath and the next.

Eternity within the dark.

Information infell across the event horizon: a voice.

He knew the voice, knew he should not listen—but he was not just in the black hole, he *was* the black hole, capturing everything, holding it forever.

"What is real? What is illusion? Where is the line between truth and lie? Between right and wrong? It's a cold and lonely place, Jacen Solo: the void of *not knowing*."

He didn't answer. A black hole can't reply. An event horizon is the ultimate valve: anything at all can pass through in one direction, nothing at all in the other.

But the infalling voice triggered this black hole into quantum decay. His personal event horizon shrank in an instant to a point mass in the middle of his chest—

And Jacen opened his eyes.

"Vergere," he said dully. "How did you find me?"

She had settled felinelike upon the Solo dining table, arms and legs folded beneath her. She stared at him with interstellar eyes. "I do not share our masters' prejudice against technology. Portions of the planetary database survive in memory cores. Discovering the home address of the former Chief of State was no great trick."

"But how did you know? How did you know I'd come home?"

"It is an instinct of all pack animals: the mortally wounded crawl back to their own dens to die."

"Wounded?"

"With the greatest wound a Jedi can suffer: freedom."

Another riddle. He had no strength for riddles. "I don't understand."

"When you always know what is right, where is freedom? No one *chooses* the wrong, Jacen Solo. Uncertainty sets you free."

Jacen thought about that for a long time. "Die at home," he murmured. "Some home. Have you *seen* this place? Jaina's room is full of some kind of plant that tried to *eat* me. The kitchen looks like a coral reef. My collection—" He could only shake his head. "This isn't my home."

"Neither are you going to die," she said cheerfully. "Have you forgotten? You're dead already. You have been these many months; you have nearly completed your passage through the lands of the dead. Now is time not for death, but for new life. You are *healed*, Jacen Solo. Arise and walk!"

Jacen sank lower in the chair, staring blindly up through the tangle of arachnoid cables. "Why should I?"

"Because you can, of course. Why else would anyone bother to get up?"

"I don't know." He closed his eyes again. "It doesn't

matter whether I get up or sit here until I starve. Nothing matters. Nothing *means* anything."

"Not even your brother's death?"

He shrugged listlessly. Life, death—all was one. One with the Force. He said, "The Force doesn't care."

"Don't *you* care?"

He opened his eyes. Her gaze had the peculiar, almost humorous intensity he'd seen in the Embrace chamber, in the Nursery, at the crater. But he was too tired, too broken, to puzzle through whatever she might want him to discover. "Whether I care doesn't matter, either."

Corners of her mouth tricked up and down. "Does it matter to *you*?"

He stared at his hands.

After a long, long silence, he sighed. "Yes. Yes, it does." It never occurred to him to lie to her. "But so what? Sure, *I* care—but who am I?"

She gave a shrug so subtle it was almost a shiver. "That's always been the question, yes?"

"But you never have an *answer*—"

"I do have an answer," she said kindly. "But it's *my* answer, not yours. You will find no truth in me."

"You keep telling me that." Bitter ashes rasped in the back of his throat. "Or in anybody else, either, I guess."

She said, "Exactly."

A high buzzing whine rose in his ears, skirling around his head like an angry sparkbee trapped inside his skull. "Then where is the truth supposed to be?" he asked blurrily. "Where? Tell me. Please." He could barely hear his own voice over the buzz in his ears. It grew to a roar.

She leaned forward, smiling, and the roar drowned what she said, but he could read the words from her lips.

Ask yourself where else can one look.

"What?" he gasped faintly. "What?"

As the roar became a storm inside his head, pounding

away all words, all hope of sense, she gathered her four opposable fingers into a point and lightly tapped his chest—right on the center, right over the void left by the slave seed, right over the point mass of his own personal event horizon—as though knocking on a door.

Down in that void, there was quiet. There was calm: the eye of the storm inside him. He threw his mind into the calm, quiet void, let the quiet calm swell to envelop everything he was.

The storm blew away.

The black hole swallowed itself.

He was not alone in the quiet calm. Here was the Force: the living connection that bound him to everything that is, that ever has been, that ever will be. Here too was the Vonglife: from the dim satisfaction of the blue puffball basking in the warmth of his and Vergere's body heat, to the industrious concentration of the arachnoids that skittered through their growing web . . . to the balanced readiness for instant violence of twelve Yuuzhan Vong warriors who now filed into the room—

And the breathless anticipation of triumph that shone through Nom Anor, as he entered behind them.

Yuuzhan Vong warriors. Twelve of them. Armed.

And Nom Anor.

The warriors spread out in a shallow arc.

Jacen regarded them steadily, without alarm. Here in the quiet calm of his center, there was no such thing as surprise, no such thing as danger. There was only him, and all of them, and the universe, of which each was a small interlocking component.

He looked at Vergere in wonder. He understood now, where he never could have before. She had not said *Ask yourself where else can one look.*

She had said: *Ask yourself. Where else can one look?*

Nom Anor paced forward, hands clasped to each

other within the voluminous sleeves of a floor-length robeskin so black it gleamed. Jacen could see his own reflection distorted in its glossy surface.

Nom Anor, Jacen thought, *is standing in our dining room.*

"The meaninglessness and despair from which you suffer," Nom Anor said silkily, "is the inevitable result of your bankrupt religion. This Force of yours, it has no *purpose.* It merely is what it is: corrupt with the rot that infects this whole galaxy. Full of lies and illusions, petty jealousies and betrayal. But there *is* purpose in the universe. There is a *reason to get up,* and you can find it. I can share it with you."

He's been listening, Jacen thought. *Of course. Vergere would have led him here.*

"Now is the time," Nom Anor continued, "for you to leave behind your useless Force. Now is the time to leave behind your life's darkness and delusion. Now is the time to take your place in the pure light of Truth."

Jacen's voice seemed to echo around him, as though the calm, quiet void from which he spoke was a vast cavern. "Whose truth?"

"*Your* truth, Jacen Solo," Nom Anor said with a flourish. "The truth of the *God you are*!"

"The God I am . . . ?"

From within one of those voluminous sleeves, Nom Anor produced a lightsaber. All twelve of the warriors tensed, their faces twisted into masks of loathing, as he triggered the blade and stepped forward. Brilliant purple energy sliced through the arachnoid webs; Jacen watched without expression as Nom Anor swiftly and efficiently carved away the spit cables that had webbed him into the chair.

The executor released the activation plate and knelt at Jacen's feet. He lowered his head in obeisance, and offered up the deactivated lightsaber to Jacen on outstretched palms.

Jacen recognized the handgrip's design.

It was Anakin's.

He looked at Vergere.

She returned his gaze steadily. "Choose, and act."

Jacen saw with preternatural clarity the choice he was being offered. The opportunity.

Anakin's lightsaber. Anakin had made it. Anakin had used it. It had changed him, and he had transformed it. Its crystal was not like those of other lightsabers, but was a living Vonglife gem.

Part Jedi. Part Yuuzhan Vong, he thought. *Almost like me.*

They were offering him Anakin's life: his spirit, his skill, his courage.

His violence.

Jacen had first used a lightsaber in combat at the age of three. He was a natural.

And now he could feel the Yuuzhan Vong. And the Force was with him.

He could follow Anakin's path. He could be pure warrior. He could be even greater than his brother had been: with the dark power he could command, he could surpass any living Jedi, even Uncle Luke. Surpass even the Jedi Knights of old.

He could be the greatest sword of the Force who had ever lived.

More: He could avenge his brother with the weapon his brother had forged.

I could pick that up, he thought, *and kill them all.*

Is that who I am?

Is that who I want to be?

He looked at Nom Anor.

The executor said, "Take up the blasphemous weapon

and slay—or choose life. Choose to learn the Truth. Choose to *teach* the Truth: to share Truth with your people. Let me teach you the truth you can share: the truth of the God you are!"

Jacen reached for the lightsaber, but not with his hand.

The handgrip seemed to levitate, bobbling in the air above Nom Anor's palms—then it flipped away, hurtling toward Vergere. She caught it neatly, and set it on the table at her side.

He stared at her, and not at her—he gazed at his own reflection on the glossy black curves of her bottomless eyes. He gazed silently, expressionlessly, until he felt himself reflect the reflection: he became pure surface, gleaming over an infinite well of darkness.

A mirror for every image of night.

He filled himself with stillness; when he was so still that he could feel the universe wheel around the axis he had become, he stood up.

Nom Anor hissed soft triumph. "You will become a star, a sun, *the* Sun—and you will fill the galaxy with the Light of the True Way."

"All right," Jacen said. A cold, still surface, flawless: unrippled by weakness, or conscience, or humanity.

"Why not?"

PART THREE

THE GATES OF DEATH

ELEVEN

TRAITOR

For the sake of argument, suppose the conquest of Coruscant has caused casualties on an unimaginable scale.

Suppose ten *billion* people died in the Yuuzhan Vong bombardment—

Suppose *twenty* billion more were killed in the ground-quakes that accompanied the alteration of the planet's orbit—

Suppose another *thirty* billion have since starved to death, or been killed by Yuuzhan Vong search-and-destroy teams, or have been poisoned, or eaten, or otherwise died from contact with Vongformed life—

Suppose an additional *forty* billion have been enslaved, or interred, or otherwise held captive by the Yuuzhan Vong.

These supposed numbers are exactly that: pure supposition. Imaginary. Even when Coruscant's planetary database had been intact, the global census had been mostly guesswork. In the wake of the conquest, there was no practical way to number the missing and the dead. One hundred billion is an unreasonably high figure—probably outrageously inflated—but even so—

Subtract these casualties from the preconquest population of Coruscant.

There are nine hundred billion people left over.

Nine.
Hundred.
Billion.
Survivors can be a weapon, too.

The camp ships had been popping out of hyperspace for months now. No one could predict when, or in what star system, the next would arrive. The camp ships were kilometers thick, roughly globular, vast random glued-together masses of hexagonal chambers that ranged from the size of a footlocker to the size of a carrier's flight deck. The ships might have been some kind of plant, a vegetal species specially bred by the Yuuzhan Vong; they might have been agglomerate exoskeletons abandoned by gargantuan interplanetary animals.

Analysis of sensor data showed clear indications of dovin basal–like gravity fields around the hyperspace exsertion points; and mere seconds after each ship's appearance, there would follow a new gravity-distorting burst. Some New Republic analysts thought these secondary bursts were dovin basals collapsing into self-generated point masses. Others claimed that the secondary bursts were the signatures of whatever dovin basal–like creatures had served as the engines of the camp ships, vanishing back into hyperspace to return to their starting point.

This much was certain: these ships came at random, infalling through inhabited star systems. These ships had no food supplies, life support, or usable engines. All these ships had was people.

Millions of people.

Hundreds of millions: survivors from the conquest of Coruscant.

Each populated system that unexpectedly found itself the custodian of a camp ship faced a stark choice: it could further strain its war-burdened resources to house and feed the refugees, or it could let them die: smother, or starve, die of thirst, freeze, or slowly cook in their own waste heat. The ships could be simply ignored—left to drift between planets, frozen mausoleums eternally commemorating that stellar system's callous, lethal neglect of a hundred million lives.

No world of the New Republic could face collective guilt on that scale; if they could, they never would have been admitted to the Republic in the first place.

No one knew if any camp ships had been jumped to uninhabited systems. No one wanted to think about that. Some Jedi explored, feeling with the Force through vast dust-swept reaches; but there had never been many Jedi in the first place, and the few who remained had little time to spare from the war. Planetary and system-wide governments mounted no searches. They couldn't afford to. They didn't have the resources to support the refugees who had ended up in their laps already; to search for others would be not only useless, but insane.

Despite painful shortages of both raw materials and technical expertise, the New Republic systems did what they could.

To construct cities big enough to shelter hundreds of millions of people was clearly impossible in the wartime economy, but there was another option. The ships were roomy, and held air against the vacuum of space. So the refugees were kept where they were, while the host systems did their best to supply the overcrowded ships with waste and water recycling, atmosphere scrubbing and replenishment, light, and food.

They became orbital refugee camps. Hence the name.

Life in the camp ships was hard.

Even in the wealthiest systems, every camp ship's food

had to be rationed at the brink of starvation; even the best recyclers couldn't remove from the water the growing taste of having been *used*, again and again. Cramped, dirty, stinking: atmosphere plants overloaded with sweat and breath and other variously noxious effluents of a thousand species, atmosphere saturated with enough carbon dioxide to give the entire population continuous thudding headaches—those species, at least, that had heads. Even photosynthetics suffered, despite the oversupply of carbon dioxide, since they were forced to rely on dim, intermittent artificial light.

Everyone suffered, and very, very few were allowed to leave.

No one talked about the real reason the refugees were sequestered aboard the camp ships.

It was this: interplanetary space was the ideal sanitary cordon. Many worlds had received, courtesy of the Yuuzhan Vong, unpleasant surprises along with refugees allowed dirtside. All refugee populations included unguessable numbers of spies, saboteurs, Peace Brigaders, collaborators of all sorts—

And sometimes worse.

Ganner Rhysode had spent weeks chasing the rumor.

He'd heard it from a tramp navigator in a tavern on Teyr, who'd gotten it from a dock steward at the spaceyard on Rothana, who'd been talking to a freighter pilot on the Sisar Run, who'd heard a casual mention from a customs inspector in the Sevarcos system, or maybe it was the Mantooine, or Almania; the inspector had heard it from a friend in the fleet whose cousin was a civilian volunteer on the camp ship at Bothawui.

Ganner had laboriously backtracked each link, chasing across what was left of the New Republic, through weeks in hyperspace and day after day after day of playing "Have

you seen—?" with bored clerks and hostile freight load-
ers, suspicious bureaucrats and sarcastic corridor kids.

By the time he reached the numbered curtain that passed
for an apartment door inside the million-celled honeycomb of the camp ship, he was so tired he couldn't even
remember what system he was in.

The number on the curtain was in three parts, giving
the coordinates of the chamber's location as measured
from the center of the rough globe of the camp ship; in a
ship lacking anything that resembled decks—or even
straight lines—three-dimensional coordinates were the
only practical addresses these chambers could have. This
particular chamber was remote, nearly at the hull, on the
side opposite that which the tide-locked ship turned
toward the world it orbited.

It was—as Ganner had wryly reflected when he had
learned the chamber's coordinates—on the dark side.

Ganner didn't look much like Ganner these days: gone
was the flashy blouse and tight leather trousers, the gleam
of gold piping, the tall, immaculately polished boots. Instead, he wore a shapeless tunic of nondescript brown
fabric over baggy gray leggings that hid his boots—now
scuffed, and bearing the dirt of dozens of worlds. Gone,
too, was the devastating smile and the dashing glint in his
clear blue eyes; he'd even let a scruffily curling beard
muddy the clean sharp lines of his classic jaw.

This wasn't exactly a disguise. He'd made no secret of
his identity; on the contrary, he wielded his identity as a
weapon, to cut through tangled kilometers of bureau-
cratic red tape that would have kept him off the camp
ships. But he was different as he could get from the
Ganner he had always been.

Being that old Ganner had done him far too much
damage.

Here, for example, outside the chamber: the old Ganner would have swept aside the curtain with a flourish and posed, dramatically backlit, in the doorway. He would have coolly announced himself and askēd his questions, counting on his imposing height and intimidating glare, his reputation, and his sheer gutsy *dash* to bully out the answers he needed.

Now, instead, he leaned back against the pebbly wall beside the door and let himself slide down. He settled in, sitting, as though he were just another refugee, taking a nap at the side of a corridor.

He let his head drift forward and his eyes fall closed while he reached into the Force, seeking feelings from the chamber beyond. This could be a trap, and he was done with taking foolish chances. Caution was his byword, now, and unobtrusiveness his best defense.

He felt humans inside the chamber, with enough Force presence that there might have been five of them—as he'd been told there would be, by the harried data clerk who'd accessed their file on the temporary, obsolete, and overloaded central server that held the sketchy records compiled by this camp ship's volunteer administrators—but Ganner couldn't quite resolve the Force sensation into distinct individuals.

He frowned, squeezing his eyes more tightly shut, concentrating.

It was almost as though inside this chamber there was one person with five different personalities . . . or that all five of them participated in some kind of group consciousness. That would be rare in humanity, but hardly impossible. The galaxy had spawned dozens, if not hundreds, of minor variations on the human theme; Ganner knew he hadn't seen them all.

And the unknown, he had learned through bitter experience, was always dangerous. Often deadly. His little half joke about this chamber being on the dark side didn't seem funny anymore.

He had a feeling he was about to get himself killed.

He sighed, and got up.

From the moment he had begun chasing this rumor, he had sort of, somehow, half known he would end up like this: alone, no backup, no one even knowing enough about where he was to mount a search for him when he did not return. It'd taken him two days just to walk this deeply into the camp ship.

No one would ever know what had happened to him.

Well, one person would be able to guess . . . but he didn't think she'd care.

He remembered the dark flame in Jaina's eyes when he'd told her of the rumor.

"Another stupid lie," she'd said. "And you're an idiot for believing it."

He'd tried to explain that he didn't actually believe the tale; he just thought it should be checked out. He'd tried to tell her how important this could be to the morale of the whole New Republic. "Don't you get it? He's a *hero*. It'd be like—like he rose from the *dead*, Jaina! It'd be *magical*—it'd be a miracle! It'd give us *hope* again."

"We don't need hope," Jaina had told him. A grim set had hardened the once soft curve of her jaw ever since Myrkr. "We need more ships. We need better weapons. And we need Jedi. We need to keep on *fighting*. We don't need you wasting everybody's time on *fantasies*."

Ganner had persisted. "But what if it's *not* a fantasy? Your mother still claims he's alive—"

"My *mother*," Jaina had said, a slow, ancient weight on her words, a weight too vast, too old for a teenage girl, "lost both her sons *on the same day*. She hasn't gotten over it. She probably never will."

"She has a right to know—"

"I'm not arguing with you, Ganner. I'm telling you. Keep your fat yap shut. I don't want anything about this getting back to Mom. To raise her hopes and then crush them again would break her. If you do, I'll break *you*."

"But, but Jaina—"

She had leaned close to him then, and that dark flame in her eyes had burned so hot that Ganner took a step back. "Don't think I won't, Ganner. And don't think I can't."

He didn't answer. He believed her.

She said, "The Vong kept Jacen alive after they captured him. For a long time. They kept him alive so they could *hurt* him. I could *feel* it. I never even told Mom and Dad what they put him through. What happened to Anakin . . . that was better. That was clean."

Tears had sparked in her eyes, but her voice was hard enough to cut transparisteel. "I felt Jacen die. In one instant, he was—he was just *gone*. Blasted out of existence like he'd never existed at all. I *felt* it. If he were alive, I wouldn't need *you* to come and *tell* me about it! I'd *know*!"

Her hands had clenched to fists, white-knuckled, pressed against her sides, and her lips drew back over her teeth. "Don't talk to me about this—this *garbage* ever again. And don't talk to anyone else, either. *Anyone*. If I find out you've so much as looked in a mirror and told *yourself*, I will hurt you. I will teach you things about pain that no one should ever have to learn."

Ganner had stood and stared, gaping, dumbstruck at the hurt and the pure black rage that beat against him through the Force. What had happened to her? There had been some rumors—

"Hey, Jaina, it's okay," he'd said. "I won't tell anybody, I promise. Don't get mad—"

"I'm not mad. You haven't *seen* mad. You better hope

you never do." She had folded her arms and turned her back to him. "Get out of my sight."

Ganner had walked unsteadily away, shaken. Jaina had always held herself so together, had always been so competent, so in control, that it had been easy to forget that she'd lost both her brothers that day, too.

Had lost her twin: the brother who'd been half of all she was.

Later—much later—he reflected: *Well, y'know, I only promised I wouldn't talk about it. I never promised I wouldn't look into it.*

That was when he had set out. Alone.

The old Ganner might have done the same, he occasionally thought with a certain melancholy resignation. It would have made a great story, a story about the kind of Jedi Ganner had always wanted to be: the lone hero, searching the vast reaches of the galaxy on a quest he cannot share, braving unimaginable dangers and facing incalculable odds.

That had been Ganner's fantasy self: the cool, calm, dangerous hero, the kind people trade stories about in voices hushed with awe, and all that adolescent crap.

Vanity, that's what it was: pure vanity. Vanity had always been Ganner's fatal weakness. Nothing wrong with being a hero—look at Han Solo, or Corran Horn. Nothing wrong with *wanting* to be a hero: Luke Skywalker often talked about his youthful dreams of adventure, and look how he turned out.

But when you start *trying* to be a hero, you're in a whole galaxy of trouble. Lust for glory can become a sickness: a disease that bacta cannot cure. In its final stages, it's all you can think about. At the end, you don't even care about actually *being* a hero.

You just want people to *think* you are.

The old Ganner Rhysode had suffered from that style-over-substance disease. He'd had as bad a case as any he'd ever seen. It had nearly killed him.

Worse: it had nearly driven him dark.

In unguarded moments he still found himself drifting back to those dangerous dreams. Just thinking about it could give him the shudders. He had worked very hard to squeeze his lust for the admiration of others into a small, quiet voice, and he hoped one day to silence it forever.

So he had set about his quest quietly. Inconspicuously. Anonymously. Making sure the tale did not spread. He had to be sure he was doing this for the right reasons. He had to be sure he wasn't suffering a relapse into the glory sickness. He had to be sure he chased this rumor only because it was the right thing to do. Because the New Republic desperately needed any glimmer of hope.

Because Jaina did.

Every time he remembered that dark flame in what had once been soft brown eyes, he felt another blow on a spike driving into his chest. Flirting with the dark—sure, lots of the Jedi had, since the war's beginning. Some had even claimed it was the galaxy's only hope. At the Myrkr worldship, the strike team had discussed it seriously, as an option.

But it was one thing for, say, a Kyp Durron to talk about the dark: he was a creature of tangled hostility and self-loathing, always had been—the incredible brutality of his childhood, and the unimaginable crimes it had driven him to commit, had twisted him to where holding on to the light was a struggle for him every single day. It was another thing for young Jedi, in a desperate situation, to debate using dark side power.

For Jaina Solo to look in his eye and threaten his life was something entirely different.

It hurt him. Hurt him worse than he would have ever guessed it could.

The Solo kids were supposed to be invulnerable. They were the galaxy's new generation of legends: the clean, pure hope of the Jedi. Doing the right thing came *naturally* for them. It always had. They had been, were *supposed* to be, Happy Warriors of the Force: all three of them had already, without even trying, been exactly the kind of heroes Ganner had nearly killed himself trying to imitate.

They'd been born for it.

But now Anakin and Jacen were dead, and Jaina—

Jaina was making Ganner frighteningly aware that she was the granddaughter of Darth Vader.

What hurt him the worst: there was nothing he could do about it.

Well, no, that's not entirely true, Ganner thought as he slowly heaved himself to his feet in the camp ship corridor. *There is one thing I can do.*

Maybe—just barely possibly—she had lost only one brother. Jacen could be alive. Maybe Ganner could prove it. Maybe he could even *find* him; it might not save her, but it would have to help. And if he failed . . . well, no harm done.

She had no hopes left to crush.

Ganner nodded to himself, then leaned close to the curtain that served as the chamber's door. "Excuse me?" he called softly. "Hello? Does anybody here speak Basic?"

"Go away." The voice that answered from beyond the curtain sounded oddly—vaguely, just barely—familiar. "There is nothing for you here."

The feeling he'd had, that he was about to get himself killed, swelled into an overwhelming premonition of doom. Ganner's knees went weak, and a very large part of him wanted to bolt down the corridor and get away—

but though he hadn't been much of a hero, the one virtue he'd never had to fake was courage.

He took another deep breath. The hand he lifted to pull aside the curtain trembled, just a little, and he stared at it until it stilled. Then he gently tugged a gap between the curtain and the wall. "I'm sorry to intrude," he said. "I won't bother you for long. I just have a question for you. One question, that's all, and then I'll leave you alone."

From inside, a middle-aged, heavyset human stared at him stonily. "Go away."

"In a moment, I will," Ganner said apologetically. "But I understand that someone who lives here claims he saw Jacen Solo alive, on Coruscant, after the invasion. Can I talk to whomever that might be?"

From what little he could see beyond the curtain, there seemed to be only one or two small rooms beyond, and almost no possessions of any kind. The man who blocked his path wore only a long, shapeless white tunic, almost like a loose robe; the others within—all men—wore identical garments. *Some kind of religious thing?* Ganner wondered, because they all had some kind of aura in common, a similar way of carrying themselves, similar posture or some such, that you sometimes see among members of fanatic cults. *Or maybe it's just poverty and desperation.* "I can pay," he offered.

"There's nothing for you here," the man repeated.

One of the others moved up behind the man's left shoulder, and gestured toward the lightsaber that hung from Ganner's belt. He grumbled something in a guttural tongue that Ganner couldn't understand.

"Not everyone who carries that weapon is a Jedi," the man replied without shifting his blankly hostile stare from Ganner's face. "Be silent."

Again Ganner was struck by some weirdly familiar resonance in the voice, though he knew he'd never seen this man before. Somehow he thought this voice should be higher, fresher, more cheerful. He shook his head. He'd worry about that later. He might not be the best sabacc player in the galaxy, but he knew when to turn his cards face-up. "I am a Jedi," he said quietly. "My name is Ganner Rhysode. I have come to inquire about Jacen Solo. Which one of you saw him alive?"

"You are mistaken. No one here saw anything. You had better go."

One of the others stepped forward and said something that sounded like *Shinn'l fekk Jeedai trizmek*.

"Silence!" the man snapped over his shoulder.

Hairs prickled up the back of Ganner's neck, but his expression remained only politely curious. "Please," he said, "tell me what you know." He reached out through the Force to nudge a little cooperation out of this man—

And awoke to find himself jogging away down the passage, with no memory of having turned aside, no idea how he'd gotten here.

What? he thought blankly. *What?*

Dizzily, blurrily, he worked it out: that guy back there could use the Force—could use it as well as the most powerful of Jedi. That middle-aged, average-looking man had brushed aside Ganner's probe and blasted back with a Force compulsion so strong that even though Ganner knew what it was, it continued to drive his legs in a staggering lope away from the chamber.

He wrenched himself to a stop, gasping, leaning on the pebble-textured wall. The dread he'd felt had vanished; it must have been a Force projection as well: subtle, undetectable. Now, too late, he wished he had broken his promise to Jaina and brought along a dozen Jedi for backup—because now he felt from the chamber behind him only one presence in the Force.

One alone.

Of the other four in there, he felt nothing at all.

His lightsaber appeared in his hand and its blade snapped to life. *You're not the only one who can play games with the Force,* he thought, grinning, feeling for a moment the old rush, the familiar buzz of happy anticipation with which he'd always faced sudden danger.

In the old days.

Leave that Ganner behind, he told himself. He released the activation plate and his blade vanished. *I'm not like that. I'm cautious. Cautious and unobtrusive.*

Slowly, gradually, he began to withdraw from the Force: shutting down his Force presence as though he were still moving away. This left him Force-blind—but also Force-invisible.

He crept back toward the chamber, moving silently along the passage wall.

A powerful Force-user in the camp ship—along with what were very probably masqued Yuuzhan Vong. And this Force-user had knowingly blown his cover when he'd put the compulsion on Ganner; in mere minutes, he could disappear forever into the anonymous millions who crowded the immense ship. Ganner had heard the stories from Yavin 4: he knew that the Yuuzhan Vong had been trying to turn Jedi to their service. If they had finally succeeded, the consequences would be literally incalculable.

He was in over his head. Way over his head.

But what else could he do?

This guy's stronger than I am. Cold dread prickled up his arms, and this time it wasn't any Force projection. It was the real thing. *And there are five of them.*

I really am going to get myself killed.

But he kept moving, creeping along the wall, silent lightsaber loose in his tingling hand. How could he not?

He could imagine all too well trying to explain to Skywalker: *Well, um, actually—I didn't do anything about the Jedi traitor and the Yuuzhan Vong infiltrators because of, well, I mean, because of how, uh—well, I'd be really embarrassed if people thought I got killed because I was playing hero again—*

He choked off the thought; he was at the chamber door, and his Force trick wouldn't fool this guy for more than another second or two. No time to plan. Barely time to act.

No killing, he told himself. *Not until I'm sure they're Vong.*

With a sigh he relaxed the mental tension that had held him outside the Force. Perception flooded him, and in its surge he felt the Force-user within the chamber blaze like a homing beacon in an asteroid belt.

Ganner flowed into action without thinking, just moving, his blade sizzling to life, slashing away the curtain's fastenings, gathering it as it fell, bagging the head of the nearest white-robe while he kicked a second aside. He faked another low-line kick and leapt high, whipping an overhand right to crash the handle of his lightsaber onto the top of a third's head hard enough to drive him to his knees, then used him like a pommel horse, vaulting his legs high for a double kick that flattened the fourth like he'd been shot with a bowcaster. He whirled back to the first just as the white-robe managed to claw the curtain off his head, and dropped him with an elbow across the jaw.

He felt motion behind him and sprang into a Force-assisted back flip that spun him high and wide and ended with him in a perfectly balanced stance one arm's length from the middle-aged man, the tip of his lightsaber's blade half a centimeter from the hollow of the man's throat.

"Nobody's dead and nobody's hurt," Ganner said

coolly, voice as even as his lightsaber's hum, "but that can change. Anytime. It's your call."

The four Force-invisible white-robes, scattered around the small chamber off balance or off their feet entirely, hesitated. The middle-aged man stood motionless.

Ganner couldn't restrain the hint of a smile. *Not only am I good at this,* he thought reflexively, *I do it with style.* He squashed the thought the instant it registered, exasperated with himself. *Just when I think I'm making progress—*

He gathered his caution in layers like body armor. "All right," he said, calm, quiet, and slow. He held the eye of the middle-aged man and twitched the lightsaber; within the red-rimmed shadows cast upward on his face by the blade's yellow glow, the man's stare was as stony as ever. "Back up. Toward the door."

The man's stare softened into something like resignation, and he shook his head in sad refusal.

"I'm not bluffing," Ganner said. "You and I are going to have a talk in the corridor. As long as nobody does something stupid, there's no reason why we shouldn't all live through this. Now *move.*"

Another twitch of the lightsaber, enough to shave a micrometer of skin off the man's collarbone—and the man only sighed. "Ganner, you dope."

Ganner licked his lips. *He says that like he knows me.* "You don't seem to understand—"

"You're the one who doesn't understand," the man said tiredly. "We're being watched. Right now. If I so much as step outside this chamber, a Yuuzhan Vong pilot watching us will trigger a dovin basal concealed not very far from here. It will take all of ten seconds for this whole ship to collapse into a quantum black hole. A hundred million people will die."

Ganner's mouth dropped open. "What—how—I mean, why, why would—"

"Because they don't trust me yet," he said sadly. "You shouldn't have come back, Ganner. Now you can't leave this room alive."

"I got *in* easily enough—"

"Getting out is different. And even if you do get away, knowing only what you know already—"

"*If* I get away? Who's holding the lightsaber here?"

"It's not a bluff, Ganner. I only wish it was."

Ganner could hear the conviction in his voice, and in the Force he felt truth behind his words. *But I already know he's stronger than me. He could be faking the truth I'm feeling, and I'd never know it.* And even if it *were* true, he couldn't get any of this to make *sense*—

He couldn't begin to guess what might actually be going on, or what he should be doing about it.

"I'm telling you this," the man went on, "because the same thing will happen if I am killed. In case my conscience tempts me to sacrifice myself. As I said, they don't trust me yet."

"But—but—" Ganner sputtered. That feeling of being in over his head thickened. He was drowning in it. Taking a two-handed grip on his lightsaber to keep the blade from trembling, he tried to recover control of the situation. "All I want," he said, almost plaintively, "is to hear what you know about Jacen Solo. Start talking, or I'll have to take the chance that you're bluffing."

The man looked at Ganner like he knew him, like he'd known him for years, like he saw through him with the melancholy perception of a disappointed parent. Again, he sighed. "Talking won't help."

"You don't have a choice."

"There's always a choice."

Slowly, deliberately, without any hint of a threatening speed, he lifted a hand. He pressed a spot on the side of his nose, and his face split in half.

Ganner took an involuntary step back.

The man's face peeled open like the rind of an Ithorian bloodfruit, thick meaty flaps pulling away from each other, taking with them his thinning lank hair, the defeated pouches under his eyes, the jowls that had thickened his jawline. A network of hair-thin filaments slowly retracted from the pores of the face revealed beneath, leaking blood.

Beneath the retracting masquer, the face Ganner saw was thin, chiseled, fringed with a raggedly scruffy beard, topped with blood-matted hair that might have been brown. Even through the streaks of blood and the distortion caused by the withdrawal of the masquer's feeder filaments, Ganner knew this face—though it was a face too old, too lined with privation and pain, set with eyes too sadly experienced, to be the face he knew it was.

Ganner's mouth dropped open. His fingers loosened as his hands fell to his sides; his lightsaber's blade vanished and the handle clattered on the floor.

When he could finally speak, the only word that could pass through his nerveless mouth was *"Jacen . . ."*

"Hi, Ganner," Jacen said tiredly. He reached into his sleeve and withdrew a small pouch, which he teased open, turning it inside out as he drew it over his hand like a mitten, revealing a small fabric pad that had been inside the pouch. He tossed it to Ganner. "Here, catch."

Ganner was too astonished to do anything other than catch it reflexively. The pad was damp to his touch, and warm with Jacen's body heat. "Jacen? What's going on?"

Numbness gathered in the center of his palm, and began to climb his wrist. He frowned down at the pad in his hand. "What is this?"

"The tears of a friend of mine," Jacen said. "They're a contact poison."

"What?" He stared. "You're kidding, right?"

"I don't have much sense of humor these days." Jacen peeled the pouch off his hand and tossed it aside. "You'll be unconscious in about fifteen seconds."

Ganner's hand was already dead, and his right arm hung limp; the numbness washed into his chest, and when it touched his heart it shot throughout his body. He pitched forward, unable even to lift an arm to break his fall—but Jacen caught him and lowered him gently to the floor.

"Wake the villip," Jacen said to one of the others—Yuuzhan Vong warriors, Ganner now knew they must be. "Tell Nom Anor that our trap has failed. Other Jedi will follow this one. We must return home."

Nom Anor? Return home? Ganner thought as darkness closed in around his mind. *They've done it. They got Jacen.*

They've turned him.

One of the warriors barked in their harsh tongue.

Jacen shook his head. "No. We'll take him with us."

Cough hack snarl—

"Because I say so," Jacen answered. "Do you dare dispute my word?"

With a final convulsion of his will, Ganner reached out through the Force and seized his lightsaber, lifting it with his mind, squeezing its activation plate to snap the blade to sizzling life. One of the warriors barked a warning in their guttural tongue.

Jacen gestured, and Ganner felt a stronger mind than his take hold of the lightsaber and wrench it from his control. The lightsaber's blade vanished.

The handgrip bobbed gently in the air between Jacen and the warriors.

"Do not soil yourself by touching the blasphemous weapon," Jacen said.

The last thing Ganner saw as darkness swallowed him was an amphistaff snaking out from Jacen Solo's sleeve, to slice the handle of Ganner's lightsaber neatly in half.

"We will take this pathetic excuse for a Jedi to Yuuzhan-'tar," Jacen Solo said. "*Then* we'll kill him."

Inside a camp ship, a chamber moved. This chamber had been grown specially, bred into this particular camp ship for this particular purpose. It had appeared to be just another chamber within the million-celled honeycomb—but now it cast itself loose and slid along under the camp ship's hull like a parasite digging its way out through an animal's skin.

This particular chamber enclosed a pod of yorik coral that had its own dovin basal. This dovin basal could have been used in either of two ways. With one command, it could have generated a gravity field intense enough to crush the entire camp ship into a point mass smaller than a grain of sand; but it had been given the other command, and so it would drive the chamber and its occupants across the galaxy.

The skin of the camp ship developed a small boil. This boil bulged on the ship's dark side. When it burst, it spat forth the chamber, which instantly streaked away, accelerating frantically into hyperspace, heading for Yuuzhan'tar.

Within that chamber were four warriors of the Yuuzhan Vong, one pilot within the coral pod, and two humans. One of the humans sat in silent meditation. The other lay paralyzed, unconscious, but even in the dark void where he seemed to float, he held on to one thought. He didn't know where he was being taken, he didn't know what would happen to him; he didn't even know, really, who he was. He knew only one thing.

This was the one lone thought to which he gave all his strength, to fix it forever in his memory:

Jacen Solo is a traitor.

TWELVE

THE LIGHT OF
THE TRUE WAY

On the surface of an alien planet, a Jedi Knight lies dreaming.

Organisms that are devices join with devices that are organisms to tend the needs of his body; glucose and saline circulate through his bloodstream, along with potent alkaloids that sink his consciousness deep beneath the surface of the dream. The planet that holds him is scarred with splotches of riotous jungle over a skeleton of ruined city, and its sky is bounded by a Bridge woven of rainbow.

The Jedi Knight dreams of aliens and Yuuzhan Vong. He dreams of traitors who are Jedi, and Jedi who are traitors. And sometimes, in the dream, the traitor turns to him and says, *If I'm not a Jedi, am I still a traitor? If I'm not a traitor, am I still a Jedi?*

Another figure in his dream: a skeletal Yuuzhan Vong whom he somehow understands is Nom Anor, the Prophet of Rhommamool. The Nom Anor of Duro.

Of Myrkr.

And there is one more figure in the dream: small, lithe and agile, a feather-crested alien of unknown species, a white fountain of the Force.

The Jedi Knight also dreams himself, lying motionless as though dead, tangled in a net of vines and woody limbs that is half hammock and half spiderweb. He watches from outside himself, floating, far, far above in some astral orbit, too far to hear voices though he somehow knows what they say, too far to see faces though he somehow knows how they look—

And he somehow knows that they are talking about killing him.

He no longer pays close attention; he has had this dream many, many times. It replays in his head like a corrupted data loop.

The dream always begins:

Not that I question the sincerity of your conversion, the Nom Anor figure murmurs slyly to the traitor, *but you must understand how this would look to, say, Warmaster Tsavong Lah. He might feel that if you were, in fact, devoted to the True Way, you would have slaughtered this pathetic Jedi without mercy back at the camp ship, rather than carting him all the way here.*

The traitor counters expressionlessly, *And deprive the True Gods of a full formal sacrifice?*

The feather-crested alien nods in fond approval, and soon the Prophet must agree. *Any Jedi is a worthwhile captive,* he allows. *We can sacrifice him this very day. In fact*— Here fleshless lips draw back to reveal a smile like a mouthful of needles. —*you can sacrifice him. To slaughter one of your former brethren will go far to ease . . . the, ah, warmaster's doubts.*

Of course. The traitor agrees with a nod, and here the Jedi Knight's dream always becomes a nightmare: trapped once more inside his motionless, helpless, silent body, as though a corpse already, drowning in horror. He tries to reach into the Force, to touch the traitor's cold and treacherous heart—and receives, to his astonishment, a distinct feeling of warmth and good cheer, as though the traitor has given him a wink and a friendly squeeze on the arm. *But we can do better. We can make this a dry run: a rehearsal, with this one standing in for my sister.*

In the way of dreams, the Jedi Knight understands that the trap into which he has fallen was set for Jaina. There's something wrong with that, though; something he can't quite remember. If they had really wanted to catch Jaina, there must have been a better option, but what it might be he cannot summon.

As always, the Prophet objects to the traitor's plan: even the existence of the traitor is a closely held secret. Too many people, Yuuzhan Vong and slave, would participate in this rehearsal; the secret would inevitably be lost.

Secrecy has outlived its usefulness, the traitor counters serenely. *My conversion to the True Way serves no purpose if it remains secret. I will proclaim the Gospel of the True Gods to the whole galaxy on the day we take my sister—but we must prepare. We must practice, if the ceremony is to be flawless. I must practice.*

Practice what? the Prophet asks. *A sacrifice is not a complex ritual.*

The alien speaks: *The Great Sacrifice, when it comes, will be a willing sacrifice: the Other Twin will walk to her death eagerly, with head high and joy in her heart, knowing that she brings the Truth to this galaxy.*

As will this one, the traitor claims. *This is why you have made me what I am. I must bring him to the Truth. To the Light. He will hear Truth ring from my mouth, and see the Light of the God I Am shine from my eye.*

The Prophet appears skeptical, but he says: *Preparations will take some time.*

Take whatever time you require, the traitor says. *When all is prepared, I will speak to this Jedi.*

And always, the Jedi Knight reaches into the Force here, to pound the traitor's brain with the hammer of his refusal, and receives in return another invisible Force wink. The traitor never makes any other indication he's aware of the Jedi Knight's presence; and here he turns to the Prophet.

On that day, Ganner Rhysode will walk proudly at my heel, as I lead him into the Well of the World Brain, where we will together offer up his death to the glory of the True Gods.

It is always at this point that a familiar clench of dread squeezes him back down into darkness for a time, until he surfaces once more and begins the dream again. So it goes, over and over and over, etched in psychic acid upon his brain.

Over and over and over and over until—

With a great shuddering gasp, Ganner Rhysode awoke.

Waking up hurt.

Somebody had stuck his whole arm to the elbow down Ganner's throat, fingers jammed into his bronchi; now the fingers and hand and wrist and arm slowly withdrew, dry and hard and rough as a scab, grating up the inside of Ganner's throat as he choked and retched and tried to cough. At the same time, tubes and wires and needles pulled out of his veins and nerves and through his stretching skin—

Ganner Rhysode, awaken! Awake and arise! It is commanded!

He knew he had been dreaming, and he knew he was waking up, but he couldn't fight free of the dream. It stretched around him, gluey, clinging, membranes of goo dividing into thin strings and sagging ropes that bound him with impossible things: wild fantasies of having been captured by a dozen Yuuzhan Vong warriors who all looked like Jacen Solo, mad images of sacrifice and aliens and Jaina and that Nom Anor character—

His eyelids cranked open like rusted-shut hatches.

The arm that withdrew from his windpipe was less an arm than it was a branch, its bark coated with blood-tinged slime. The tubes that pulled free of his veins through his skin looked like ovipositors of immense bloated wasps that had grown like galls on the trunks of stunted trees to either side of him. He lay in a hammock that seemed to have been made of vines—but the vines writhed muscularly beneath him, flexing and squeezing like a net woven of snakes.

More vines dangled from the ceiling, long ropy vines, knotted and coiled—but they weren't vines, they were more like tentacles, because vines couldn't uncoil and coil again, untie and retie themselves in impossibly complex knots—and they weren't tentacles, because tentacles don't end in huge round glowing red eyes that even through all the coiling and tying seem to always focus on you with unblinking concentration . . .

Drugs, he thought groggily. *They drugged me. I'm hallucinating.*

"Awaken, Ganner Rhysode! Awaken to the Truth!"

This had to be a hallucination—*had* to be, because when he rolled his head to the side to blearily stare at whoever was giving him these pompous, vaguely stupid-sounding orders, the guy looked just like Jacen Solo.

Ganner blinked, and lifted a hand to wipe sleep gunk from his eyes—which was how he discovered he was no longer paralyzed, nor was he restrained. But he might as well have been: the alkaloids still circulating through his bloodstream made his hand feel only a couple of grams lighter than the Sun Crusher.

When he looked again, with slightly clearer vision, it was still Jacen.

But he was no longer the boy Ganner remembered.

Jacen was taller now, and broader across the shoulders. His brown curls had been sun-bleached to streaks of golden blond, and a dark beard sprang wiry from his jaw. His face had thinned, sharpened, refined: he had lost that impish softness, that playful roguishness that once had made him resemble his father, and replaced it with a cold-forged durasteel expression that reminded Ganner of Leia denouncing a corrupt Senator from the Chief of State's Podium of the Great Rotunda.

He wore a long, flowing robe of black so dark that its folds vanished into formless night. Along his sleeves spidered an intricate design that glowed with a light of its own, chased in scarlet and viridian like a network of external arteries that pulsed light instead of blood. Draped over his shoulders he wore a surplice of shimmering white on which strange, unidentifiable sigils wrote themselves in twists of shining gold.

He opened his mouth to ask Jacen what kind of stupid masked ball he was planning to crash in this ridiculous costume, but before his drug-numbed lips could shape the words, he remembered:

Jacen Solo is a traitor.

"Do not fear, Ganner Rhysode," he said, in a weird dark voice like a bad imitation of a hypnotist. "Instead rejoice! The day of your Blessed Release has arrived!"

"Does . . ." Ganner had to hack a wad of haven't-talked-in-days out of his throat. "Does this mean . . . you're going to let me go?"

"The Gifts of the True Gods are three." His words fell like boulders down a well. "Life They give us, that we may serve Their Glory: this is the least of Their Gifts. Pain They give us, that we may learn Life's value lies only in Their Service: this is a greater Gift. But the Greatest Gift of the Gods is Death: it is Their Release from the Burden of Pain and the Curse of Life. It is their reward, their grace, their mercy, granted liberally even to the unjust and the infidel."

Captured. Drugged. Helpless. About to be murdered. *Boy, it's a good thing I was so cautious and unobtrusive,* Ganner thought muzzily. *Otherwise I might have gotten myself into trouble.*

"Um, yeah, y'know," he said with a weak laugh, "those wacky gods . . . I guess they *mean* well, but they just don't know when to stop. They're *way* too generous. I'm getting along fine with just the *first* Gift. The other two, hey, y'know, I can wait—"

"Silence!" Jacen commanded, stretching forth his arms, hands high, palms forward as though to address a multitude from a mountaintop. "Waste not your breath in prattle! Hear now the lore of the True Way!"

Ganner stared, speechless, but instead of continuing, Jacen's eyes drifted closed. He swayed in place as though he were about to faint.

"Jacen?"

One hand curled to a fist, then extended a forefinger: *Wait.*

"Jacen, what did they do to you? Whatever it is, we can fix it. You have to come back with me, Jacen. You don't know what's been happening. Jaina . . . everyone needs you. I don't know what they've done to you, but it doesn't matter. Whatever you've done, it's not your fault. We can *help* you—"

Jacen's eyes opened, then his left lid drooped in a long, slow wink. Ganner's mouth snapped shut.

Jacen's eyes closed again.

Then slowly, one at a time, so did each eye on the end of each of the tentacle-vines that hung from the ceiling: as the red glow within each orb faded into darkness, a pair of vertical eyelids squeezed across them, and the tentacle-vines gradually relaxed, hanging limp, motionless.

Jacen dropped his arms and opened his eyes. His face seemed to collapse into an exhaustion too profound for any human to bear. "How do you feel? Any strength coming back? You think you can walk?" He sounded like a teenager again—but a teenager old beyond his years.

Old—too old—that's part of what was so strange about him. Something in his eyes: some old, cold knowledge, a broken admission of bitter truths, that made him not resemble a Solo at all.

"What are you—what's going on? Jacen—"

"We can talk now, but not for long. I persuaded all the creatures monitoring us to take a nap."

"Creatures? Monitoring? I don't—"

"They were watching us. That was the point of that silly nerf-and-Wookiee show just now. The Yuuzhan Vong have decided I'm the avatar of one of their Twin Gods."

Ganner stared. His life had become a succession of inexplicable strangenesses.

"I had a dream—a dream about a sacrifice—you were going to kill me, then find Jaina and kill her, too . . . That *was* just a dream, wasn't it?" He swallowed. "Wasn't it?"

Jacen reached into one sleeve and pulled out a pouch similar to the one in which he'd carried that poison pad back on the camp ship; this pouch contained a similar wad of damp fabric, which Jacen began to apply directly to the blood-welling punctures where the tube-vines had withdrawn through Ganner's skin.

"They can't see us or hear us right now. Pretty soon somebody's going to come around to find out why. We have to be ready to go when they get here."

"Go? Go where? Where *are* we, Jacen? What—hey, what are you doing to me? What is that stuff?" Everywhere the moisture of the pad touched, Ganner stopped bleeding. Strength flowed back into his drugged muscles.

"We're on Yuuzhan'tar." Jacen kept wiping him down with the pad. "The Yuuzhan Vong homeworld."

Ganner had heard the name from refugees on the camp ships. "You mean *Coruscant*."

"No. I don't."

"Just changing a name doesn't make it—"

"The Yuuzhan Vong remake everything they touch." Jacen's hand fell to his side, and a dark distance stretched his gaze far beyond the walls of this small chamber. "It's not about names. My name is still Jacen Solo."

Ganner frowned.

An instant later, Jacen seemed to remember where he was. He dropped the pad on the floor and shook out a long, flowing robe of white. "Here, sit up. Put this on."

Ganner discovered, to his astonishment, that he could now move without discomfort. He sat up and swung his legs over the edge of the hammock. The Yuuzhan Vong had left him his boots and leggings, but he was obscurely grateful to Jacen for providing the robe; being bare-chested here made him feel oddly uncomfortable. Vulnerable. He stood and shrugged into the robe, marveling at how *good* he felt. Being dressed. Being able to stand. He never could have guessed what profound joy might spring from such simple pleasures.

A shimmer of motion caught his eye, and he looked down. The robe he wore bore glowing designs like Jacen's, colors pulsing along arterial networks down the sleeves and front, except the designs on Ganner's robe were in black and green upon the white.

He frowned. "What's this?"

"It's your sacrificial robe. For the processional to the Well of the World Brain."

Ganner stared. His dream flooded back to him.

On that day, Ganner Rhysode will walk proudly at my heel, as I lead him into the Well of the World Brain, where we will together offer up his death to the glory of the True Gods.

"Oh, no you don't," he said. He started pulling the robe off over his head.

"Oh, yes I do."

"This is some kind of trick." Wasn't one of the Yuuzhan Vong Twin Gods supposed to be some kind of trickster or something? How much truth was Jacen telling? "This is *all* some kind of trick. You're lying to me."

"Well, actually, yeah. I am."

Ganner stopped, staring at Jacen out through the neck hole of the robe, which was now halfway over his head. Jacen's lips twitched in that unmistakable Solo half smile. "Everything I tell you is a lie."

"What?"

"See, the thing is, everything *everyone* tells you is a lie. The truth is always bigger than the words we use to describe it."

"I knew it! This *is* some kind of trick!"

"Yeah. But not on you."

Ganner shook his head wordlessly. He couldn't connect this Jacen to the cheerful dark-haired kid he used to know. He suffered an instant of wild hope: maybe Jacen *wasn't* Jacen—maybe this traitor who had promised to murder him was some kind of impostor, some kind of clone, something force-grown in a Yuuzhan Vong shaper's vat—

"Uh, Jacen? You *are* you, aren't you? . . ." Ganner grimaced. *That sounded stupid, even for me.*

"No," said the man who looked like a sad, grown-up Jacen Solo. "I'm not. But I was."

"I don't understand."

He sighed. "Thinking of me as Jacen Solo," he said distantly, "will only get in your way. I was the boy you knew, Ganner, but I'm not the boy who knew you."

"But you're alive." Ganner shrugged into the robe, and smoothed it down. "That's the only thing that counts. I found you. After all this time. That's the important thing. You're *alive*."

"No."

"Yes it is," he insisted. "You have no idea *how* important— you have no idea what it'll mean to the New Republic that you're alive! What it'll mean to *Jaina*—"

"But I'm not."

Ganner blinked.

Jacen only looked sad.

"I don't understand," Ganner said.

"I can't help that."

"But, but, but, Jacen, come on, don't be ridiculous—"

That dark distance captured his eyes altogether. "I've been dead for months, Ganner. I died not long after Myrkr. I just haven't gotten around to lying down, yet."

A chill trickled the length of Ganner's spine. "You're . . . *dead*?"

"That's right," Jacen said. "And so are you."

Some of Jacen's quick-sketched explanation made sense. The planted rumors leading to the "trap" on the camp ship had never really been intended to catch *anybody*; Jacen had only been stalling for time. As weeks passed with no results, Jacen hoped Nom Anor would lose patience and pull him out of there. If he'd really wanted to catch Jaina, all he would have had to do was reopen the Force-bond that had linked them since birth. Nothing in the galaxy would have stopped her from finding him.

"Nothing in the galaxy stops Jaina from doing pretty much whatever she decides to do. So I have to hold that part of myself shut down. If she finds out I'm alive, she'll come for me—and that'll just get her killed, too. Like

Anakin. And me." That strange sadness leaked back onto his face. "And you."

Ganner let that pass. It was clear that Jacen wasn't firing on all thrusters—and after what he must have been through, Ganner couldn't blame him. "What if she *had* shown up on the camp ship after all?"

Jacen's eyes closed and opened again, a motion too slow and deliberate to be called a blink. "Then I'd be having this conversation with her. And you'd have the chance to live to a ripe old age."

Jacen had felt Ganner coming days before he arrived, and had done everything he could—under the circumstances—to discourage him. The freezing dread, the growing conviction that he was going to his death, finally even the outright compulsion to turn and run, had all been Jacen's doing, reaching through the Force to push Ganner away.

"But nothing worked." Jacen sighed and shook his head. "If you weren't so bloody brave, you might have lived through this."

"Uh . . . yeah. Right. I guess," Ganner said hesitantly. "But—uh, Jacen? You do understand that I'm not *really* dead, don't you?

"You're the one who needs to understand, Ganner. You *are* really dead. When you came back to the chamber in the camp ship: that's what killed you." Jacen sagged exhaustedly against the wall, and rubbed his reddened eyes. "The warriors who were with me were going to slaughter you on the spot. The only way you could have escaped is if I'd helped you—and if I had, if I'd shown them I was still a Jedi at heart—the pilot would have triggered the dovin basal and wiped out the whole ship."

"And themselves along with everybody else?"

"Suicide missions are an *honor* for the Yuuzhan Vong.

That stuff about the Blessed Release? That's not just dogma. They really believe it."

And the sad, dark distance in his stare made Ganner wonder if maybe Jacen believed it a little himself.

"We've both been dead for a long time, Ganner. And today—" Jacen drew new strength from somewhere. He pushed himself off the wall and stood like a man who knew fatigue only by reputation. "Today is the day we stop breathing."

Ganner scrubbed at his face as though he could massage understanding in through his skin. "Then why not just let them kill me?"

"Because I need you. Because I can use you. Because we both have a chance to make our deaths *count* for something."

Jacen explained that the "sacrifice" was a sham. It was nothing more than an excuse to get into what he called the Well of the World Brain. Ganner understood this "world brain" to be some kind of organic planetary master computer, shaped by the Yuuzhan Vong to manage the ecology of their re-created homeworld. Jacen had been racking his brains for weeks, trying to figure out a way to get inside the Well, which was some kind of reinforced bunker, a sort of impenetrable skull designed to protect the World Brain from any possible harm. The Yuuzhan Vong—especially Nom Anor, who was Jacen's control—hadn't let him anywhere near the place. They didn't entirely trust that Jacen's "conversion" was real.

Ganner understood. He didn't entirely trust that it *wasn't*.

"I've been waiting a long time for a chance to steal ten minutes alone in the Well of the World Brain. You, Ganner—your 'sacrifice'—you're my key in the door to the Well. All I need is to get in there."

"What's so important about this world brain? What are you going to do once you're in there?"

Jacen stood very, very still; his face settled into an unbendable durasteel determination that was pure Skywalker.

"I am," he said with quiet, absolute conviction, "going to teach the Yuuzhan Vong a lesson about the way the universe actually works."

A wave of chill shivered through Ganner then, as though some cold shadow had flowed into the Force. "I don't understand."

"You don't have to. Repeat after me: 'I have seen the Light of the True Way, and go to the Gods with joy in my heart, full of gratitude for Their Third Gift.'"

"You must be *crazy*."

Jacen nodded thoughtfully, as though he'd spent some time considering that possibility and had come to the conclusion that it could not be denied.

"What makes you think I'd go along with this?"

Jacen's durasteel stare fastened on Ganner. "I'm not asking, Ganner. I'm *offering*. I don't need your cooperation. Ten minutes after I walk through the door of the Well, we'll both be dead whether you play along or not."

"So why should I?"

Jacen shrugged. "Why shouldn't you?"

"How do I know I can trust you? How do I know I shouldn't jump you right now?" Ganner shifted his weight onto the balls of his feet, reaching a balanced stance from where he could spring in any direction. "I know you're stronger now, Jacen—stronger than I've ever been. I felt it on the camp ship. I know you can kill me if you want. But I can make you kill me *here*."

Jacen spread his hands. His face was blankly expectant. "Choose, and act."

"Choose? What do you mean, choose?"

"Choose to die here for nothing, or choose to die

in the Well of the World Brain: where your death can change the galaxy."

Ganner licked his lips. "But how am I supposed to decide? How do I know whether I can trust you?"

"You don't." Jacen's face softened again, and a hint of the Solo half smile traced itself ruefully onto his lips. "Trust, Ganner, is always an act of faith."

"Easy for *you* to say—!"

"I guess it is. You want to see how much *I* trust *you?*" He reached again within his robe. When his hand came out, he opened it toward Ganner, offering. "Here."

On his open palm balanced the handgrip of a lightsaber. Ganner blinked. He rubbed his eyes.

When he looked again, it was still a lightsaber. "Take it," Jacen said. "Use it, if you must. Even if you choose to use it on me."

"You're giving me your *lightsaber?*"

Jacen shook his head. "It's not mine." He lifted his hand. "Go ahead. Take it."

"So what is this? A fake? Another trick? Is it going to blow up in my hand?"

"It's not a fake," Jacen said with a sadness so profound it could only be expressed with quiet, dry exactitude. "It's not a trick."

For the third time, he extended the lightsaber toward Ganner. "It's Anakin's."

"*Anakin's*—!" A sharp, hot thrill shot through Ganner's whole body, as though he'd been narrowly missed by a stroke of lightning. "How did you get Anakin's lightsaber?"

"A friend kept it safe for me." Jacen squinted as though mildly surprised to hear those words come out of his mouth—then he nodded, reluctantly agreeing with himself. "A friend."

Ganner could only stare, drop-jawed. Dazzled. Awed. "And you want to give it to *me*?"

"You might need one. Since I destroyed yours."

Ganner's hand shook as he took the lightsaber. It was warm in his hand, warm with Jacen's body heat, smooth and gleaming. He could feel its structure in the Force, could feel the way it fit together, the individuality of design that made it Anakin's. He could feel Anakin in the handle.

And he could feel a gap: where his own lightsaber had held a Corusca gem, this one had only a void, an empty space in the Force—but to his eye and hand, the handgrip held a shining amethyst that seemed to flicker with its own interior light.

He triggered the activator and the blade snarled out to full extension, brilliant, eye-burning, buzzing with a hum he could feel in his teeth.

It lit the whole room with a vivid, unnatural purple glow.

"What about you? Where's yours?"

Jacen shook his head. "I haven't seen my lightsaber since Myrkr. For what I have to do, weapons are irrelevant."

"But—but—"

A dull thudding penetrated one wall, a wall dominated by a huge knurled pucker like a pursed mouth carved from wood. Voices came thinly from outside, snarling in the guttural retching hacks of the Yuuzhan Vong tongue.

"They're here," Jacen said. He nodded toward the lightsaber in Ganner's hand. "Better put that away. If they find it on you, they'll kill us both." A gently ironic smile quirked his lips. "I mean, they'll kill us both too *soon*."

Ganner was floundering, choking on unreality. His dream had made a great deal more sense than did his waking. He waved Anakin's lightsaber as though he'd forgotten what it was. "You have to help me *understand*—!"

"Just remember: 'I have seen the Light of the True Way,' " Jacen repeated firmly, meaningfully, " 'and I go to the Gods with joy in my heart, full of gratitude for Their Third Gift.' "

As Ganner stood gaping helplessly, the puckered mouth on the wall suddenly yawned into a hatchway that opened on an enormous vaulted hall beyond. He jerked, nearly dropping Anakin's lightsaber in his haste to deactivate it and stuff it into one of his white robe's voluminous sleeves.

The hall was full of scarified Yuuzhan Vong warriors standing rigidly at attention, weapons extended in present arms.

Just beyond the opening stood a pair of nervous, sweating Yuuzhan Vong of a caste Ganner did not recognize. Both held leashes attached to reptilian creatures the size of banthas; the reptilian creatures crouched on their haunches while their taloned forelimbs forced the hatch sphincter to full dilation. Several steps farther in, a dozen or more impressively costumed Yuuzhan Vong, caparisoned in identically fantastic arrays of clothing that shone and shimmered and writhed with restless life, formed a half circle that framed two individuals.

One of these wore the immense spiny headdress Ganner had heard was favored by shaper masters; the other wore a long black robe, and grinned a lipless, needle-toothed smile Ganner recognized from his dream.

Nom Anor.

Jacen faced them without the slightest appearance of concern. "What signifies this interruption?" he intoned, once more in the rolling-thunder mode of his Avatar-of-God voice. "How do you dare disturb Me as I share the Light?"

Nom Anor stepped forward, and leaned close to Jacen to murmur, astonishingly, "Very good, Jacen Solo. You wear the mantle impressively." Then he stepped back, and said more loudly, so that those nearby could hear, "The monitor creatures suddenly lost consciousness. We were concerned. Is all well?"

"Your concern is an *insult*," Jacen snapped with magnificent arrogance.

Nom Anor's eyebrows quirked as though he struggled to suppress a smile, but the master shaper and the ring of fancy-dress Yuuzhan Vong—priestly caste, Ganner guessed—seemed to take him considerably more seriously. Several of them flinched openly.

"Nothing can occur that is not My Will. If these creatures slept, it is because *I made it so*!"

Ganner blinked. *Funny,* he thought, *how he can take pure truth and make it come out a lie.*

Jacen turned to Ganner grandly. "Tell these weak, faithless creatures what has transpired within this chamber."

Ganner blinked some more. "I, uh, I uh, I mean—"

"Speak! For I so command!" On the side of his face turned away from the vaulted hall, one of Jacen's eyelids momentarily drooped again.

Ganner experienced an instant of perfect clarity.

He didn't have to know.

He just had to decide.

Death waited for him no matter what. It wasn't a question of *whether* he'd die.

It was only a question of how.

"I have seen the Light of the True Way!" His voice came out surprisingly steady, considering the flutter in his chest and the way his guts had turned to water. Hands within his sleeves, he squeezed Anakin's lightsaber as though it were a talisman that could lend him strength. "And I, uh, I go to the Gods with joy in my heart, and, uh, and *gratitude* for Their Third Gift!"

Do you indeed? Nom Anor mouthed silently, a wicked

gleam in his eye as though he were not in the least deceived, but one of the priests called out in a voice like an air taxi's blarehorn: *"Tchurokk sen khattazz al'Yun! Tchurokk'tiz!"*

The assembled warriors answered with an avalanche roar. *"TCHUROKK!"*

Enthusiastic little beggars, aren't they? Ganner thought unsteadily. They sounded like they were leading a cheer. He muttered softly to Jacen, "What are they saying?"

"They offer me a shadow of my due respect," Jacen replied with regal assurance. "The words mean 'Behold the avatar of the God.'"

"Tchurokk sen Jeedai Ganner! Tchurokk'tiz!"

"TCHUROKK!"

"And they, uh, like *me* too, huh?"

"They do not like you," Nom Anor interjected, as cheerfully malicious as a well-fed Hutt. "No one *likes* you; they merely honor your willing sacrifice to the True Gods."

"Yeah. My, uh, willing sacrifice. The True Gods. That's right. So—what are we waiting for?"

"Nothing at all," Nom Anor said. "Let's get this show started, shall we?"

THIRTEEN

GLORY SICKNESS

Ganner walked one pace behind Jacen's left shoulder, trying to look solemn and dignified rather than scared out of his mind. He was so nauseated his eyes were watering.

He fought to pay attention to something else. *Anything* else. If he kept thinking about how sick he was getting, he'd drop to his knees right here and vomit his guts out.

A broad ring of those Yuuzhan Vong who'd led the cheers back in the vaulted hall—whom Ganner had correctly guessed to be of the priestly caste—surrounded them at a respectful distance of about ten meters. Ahead, ringed at a similarly respectful distance by an honor guard of warriors, walked Nom Anor and the shaper who'd been in the hall: a big ugly beggar with a cluster of tentacles growing out of one side of his mouth.

The vanguard of the processional was a wedge of bizarrely mutilated warriors who carried various creatures of all sizes and indescribable shapes, creatures that the warriors stabbed and squeezed and twisted in time with their march, producing a kind of rhythmic music from their antiphonal screams of agony. And then behind the priests who ringed Ganner and Jacen marched an immense parade of warriors, rank upon rank marching in lockstep, carrying unit banners that were some kind of sapling whose tops sprouted multicolored snakes' nests of writhing cilia, each different, distinctive, weaving patterns of color and motion that made Ganner's queasiness decidedly worse.

But there was more to it than this. The whole business was making Ganner sicker and sicker.

He *hated* it.

Jacen spoke in quiet tones throughout the processional, relating bits of insight he'd gained into Yuuzhan Vong culture and biotechnology, keeping his voice low, half whispered, lips barely moving so that none of their escort would know he was talking. Ganner could only understand half of what he heard, and he was sure he wouldn't remember half of what he understood. He couldn't concentrate on what Jacen might be telling him; most of his attention had to stay focused on walking while his legs wobbled and kept trying to collapse. And did it matter what he remembered and what he didn't? He wouldn't live to tell anyone.

It wasn't fear that was making him sick. He was afraid to die, sure, but he'd faced that fear before—without this knee-buckling nausea.

He clutched the handgrip of Anakin's lightsaber up his sleeve; only that smooth solidity let him keep a composed expression on his face instead of puking down the front of his robe.

Maybe part of what was making Ganner sick was the world itself.

He'd thought he'd be ready for his first view of Coruscant; he'd heard dozens of tales about it from the refugees on the camp ships during his investigation. He'd heard about the insanely prolific jungle that patched the ruined planetary city. He'd been told about the dazzling orbital rings that some of the refugees called the Bridge.

He knew that the Yuuzhan Vong had altered Coruscant's orbit to bring it closer to its star.

But knowing these things was entirely different from walking out of cool shadow into a blue-white noon that jammed needles into his eyeballs and pounded sweat from his hairline, sweat that trickled into his mouth, his ears, trailed like a river down his spine and made his leggings stick to his knees. The air was as humid as a Priapulin's breath, and smelled like the whole planet had been a monkey-lizard den that somebody had buried in rotting honeyflowers.

The processional spiraled through a titanic hedge maze that was still growing, knitting itself into place around them, huge curving walls of interwoven branches that sported needle-pointed thorns ranging from half a centimeter to as long as Ganner's arm. Thousands of Yuuzhan Vong of unknown caste clambered up and down and across these walls, festooning them with brilliantly colored epiphytes and flowering vines, hanging living cages and nests occupied by a bewildering variety of creatures so alien Ganner couldn't even really see them clearly: his eyes kept trying to interpret them as insects or reptiles, rodents or felines or some other type of animal with which he was already familiar, when these were really nothing like anything he'd ever seen before.

He caught some of Jacen's explanation, that this hedge maze would serve a dual purpose: not only was it a ceremonial avenue, but it would also double as an antipersonnel defense surrounding the all-important Well of the World Brain if Yuuzhan'tar were ever invaded. When mature, the hedge thorns would meet overhead, forming a tunnel twenty meters high and thirty wide, hard as durasteel, fireproof, and resilient enough to minimize the effects of explosives—and the thorns would contain a neurotoxin so potent that a single prick could destroy the central nervous system of any unfortunate creature who touched one. Groundborne invaders would be forced to trace the same route along which the processional now marched, facing dozens of ambush points along the way.

Occasionally, through gaps in the half-completed maze, Ganner could catch glimpses of their destination.

Enveloping the Well of the World Brain was a mountain of yorik coral half a kilometer high, spreading in a shallow dome nearly two kilometers across. Even buried, the shape that underlay the coral mountain was, to anyone who'd ever been to Coruscant, unmistakable.

Ganner knew exactly what it used to be. That might have been part of what was making him feel sick, too.

The Well of the World Brain used to be the Galactic Senate.

The Senate had come through the planetary bombardment with only cosmetic damage; its original architect, a thousand years before, had claimed that any weapon powerful enough to destroy the Galactic Senate would crack the planet itself. While this was a boastful exaggeration, there was no doubt that the Galactic Senate was one of the most durable buildings ever designed. Even the total destruction of the original Senate Hall ten years before had left the structure itself barely damaged; the Grand Convocation Chamber of the New Republic had been built directly upon the bones of the old. The Senate's honeycombed construction gave it incredible structural strength similar, in engineering terms, to yorik coral itself. Only direct hits could do any damage at all, and the interior had been designed in crumple zones, localizing damage by minimizing shock transmission.

Jacen explained: once the yorik coral enzymatically digested the Senate's duracrete and transparisteel and finished using the digested minerals to build its own skeleton, the

Yuuzhan Vong would have taken that long-forgotten architect's boast and made it into prophecy.

Any weapon that could harm the World Brain would have to be so powerful that it would destroy the planet, too.

Not that they were content with this: they had also seeded the dome with a defensive array of dovin basals. Even if the New Republic somehow delivered a planet-buster, the Well might survive the planet's destruction as a self-contained vessel, preserving the Brain, with its irreplaceable genetics and invaluable skills.

But the coral conversion was not yet complete. There were still some weak points in the structure—for example, the area damaged by the proton bomb that had detonated in Borsk Fey'lya's office.

"Somebody bombed Fey'lya's office?" Ganner muttered to the back of Jacen's head. "Before or after the invasion?"

Jacen's soft answering chuckle was dry as summer on Tatooine. He nodded toward the jungle-clutched ruin of the Imperial Palace, enough structure still visible to show the half-kilometer bite the bomb had taken from one corner. "They say Fey'lya set off the bomb himself. They say he took out something like twenty-five thousand crack troops and a bunch of high-ranking Vong officers—including the drop commander."

"They who? Who says?"

"The Yuuzhan Vong themselves. They admire that kind of thing. They look on Fey'lya as a kind of minor hero."

"Huh. They didn't know him like we did."

Jacen's shoulders twitched in what might have been a shrug. "And maybe we didn't know him as well as we should have."

Ganner shook his head. This conversation wasn't making him feel any better; just the opposite. "How do you even know this isn't all a test?" he asked. "How do you know there won't be a company of warriors waiting inside the Well to kill you at the first sign you're not going to go through with this?"

"I don't. But I've been told that the Yuuzhan Vong would regard such a 'test' as sacrilege. Warriors would never be allowed to lie in ambush in the Well."

"Told? Told by whom?"

"My—a friend. Her name's Vergere."

Ganner scowled, remembering the alien in his dream. "Is this *the* Vergere? The same one who was the pet of that Yuuzhan Vong assassin?"

"The same one who healed Mara with her tears. The same one whose tears have healed *you*."

"The one who turned you over to the Yuuzhan Vong." Ganner didn't like the sound of this at all. "You're *sure* she's on our side?"

"Our side?" Jacen said distantly. "You mean the New Republic side? I doubt it." Suddenly Ganner was overtaken by a stingingly potent wish that he might see Jacen's face; there was something about the angle of his head . . . "I'm not sure whose side she's on," Jacen continued. "I'm not sure she's on anybody's. I'm not sure she believes in 'sides' at all."

"But you told her what you're planning? How can you *trust* her?"

"Because I have decided to believe she won't betray me."

Ganner heard the echo inside his head: *Trust is always an act of faith.* That swelling ball of nausea in his stomach was getting heavier with every step. The world swam around him like a slow whirlpool of gelatin.

The thorn maze abruptly ended, opening onto an immense wedge-shaped causeway of curving pale ribs that seemed to be the smoothly interlaced horizontal trunks of living trees; leaf-bearing branches tangled toward the sun to either side. The foot of the causeway spanned at least a hundred meters between the branch-walls. It tapered like an arrowhead as it rose, forming a ramp whose point touched the Great Door of the Galactic Senate: a double leaf of durasteel layered like the hull armor of a Star Destroyer, intaglioed with the Galactic Great Seal surrounded by the seals of the Thousand Worlds.

Here the yorik coral had been shaped to preserve access; there grew around the perimeter of the door an immature hatch sphincter of incredible size—though still only half grown—that left the central third of the Great Door exposed.

As the vanguard began to mount the causeway, their music of screams slowed, deepened, broadened in a decorous segue from the briskly martial to the solemnly devotional. The change in the music seemed to suck the last of the strength from Ganner's legs; his knees buckled, and he pitched forward onto the causeway's foot, curled into a fetal ball around the spiny fist of nausea clenched in his guts. Saliva flooded his mouth, and his sides heaved. He squeezed shut his eyes to restrain a retch.

"Ganner? Ganner, what's wrong?" Jacen's voice came from close by, just above, low and worried. "C'mon, Ganner, you have to get up!"

Ganner couldn't get up. He couldn't speak. He couldn't even open his eyes. The smooth, hard trunks that made up the ribs of the causeway were cool beneath him, much cooler than the sun that scorched his other side, and all he wanted was to die. Right here. Right now. If only he could die . . .

The grunting hack of the Yuuzhan Vong tongue sounded in the middle distance, two voices, one imperiously disdainful, the other unctuous, conciliating.

A moment later, he heard Nom Anor's rasp in Basic, closer by: "The Shaper Lord inquires why the Jedi cowers like a brenzlit. I *lied* to him, Jacen Solo. I told him this is how humans show reverence for the True Gods. Make him get up. Make this weak, pathetic excuse for a Jedi get on with this sacrifice—before the Shaper Lord *knows* I lied."

"He's only a man," Ganner heard Jacen reply. "You can't keep a human sedated for weeks and then expect him to march like this. He's weak because he's *ill*."

Ganner burned with shame: even Jacen was lying for him now. The weakness that pinned him helplessly to the causeway wasn't physical. And having Jacen make excuses for him only made it worse.

Everyone has to lie for me, he thought. *Everyone has to pretend I'm not as pathetic and useless and weak as I really am. But I can't pretend anymore. I can't.*

Self-loathing rose up the back of Ganner's throat like vomit, burning, driving stinging tears through his eyes. Within his robe's sleeve, his thumb found the activation plate on Anakin's lightsaber; without really understanding what he was doing, he pressed the lightsaber's crystal against his own ribs. One quick squeeze, and the purple shaft of pure energy would shear through flesh and bone and weak watery guts to spear oblivion into his coward's heart—

"C'mon, Ganner, we're almost there," Jacen whispered. "Don't screw it up now."

". . . sorry . . . can't do this . . ." was all Ganner could say, a low miserable moan. He hugged himself, clutching at his ribs, arms crossed over his rebelliously spasming stomach. ". . . can't do this, Jacen . . . sorry . . . let you down . . ."

His finger tightened on the lightsaber's activation plate—

And invisible hands caught him under the shoulders and lifted him to his feet. Though he hung limp, the processional once more began to move forward, mounting the causeway toward the Great Door. His legs swung without his will to drive them, moving as though he walked under his own power. His body tingled with the touch of the Force.

Jacen was carrying him.

"There, you see?" Jacen said to Nom Anor. "He's fine. Return to your place, and reassure the Shaper Lord."

Ganner hung in Jacen's invisible Force grip, drowning in humiliation as Nom Anor moved quickly away. If only he could die—if only the trunk-causeway beneath his feet would gape like a mouth and swallow him right now . . .

His whole life, he'd chased a single dream. He had only wanted to be a hero. That's all. Not even that—not even a hero—not really. All he'd ever wanted was to walk through a room full of strangers and overhear somebody say "There goes Ganner Rhysode. He's a man who gets things done."

Yeah, I get things done. I get things done to me. Some hero. More like a damsel in distress.

And that was it: that's what was making him sick.

Himself.

He was sick of being Ganner Rhysode. Sick of trying to be a hero. Sick of trying *not* to be a hero. Sick of being a crappy Jedi, a mediocre pilot, and a bloody lousy leader of men. Sick of being a joke.

Just sick.

The vanguard parted as it approached the Great Door, dividing down the middle to line either side of the causeway, as their music of screams swelled toward a triumphal climax. The warriors who accompanied Nom Anor and the Shaper Lord formed another line within. The priests who had surrounded Jacen and Ganner knelt, lowering their foreheads to the causeway.

Jacen paced forward steadily, smoothly, giving no sign of strain, no hint that might betray effort, no clue to the assembled thousands of Yuuzhan Vong that he was carrying Ganner like a child in the invisible arms of the Force.

He came to a stop before the Great Door and moved Ganner to his side. From here, the living city of Yuuzhan'tar spread below them, a vast tangled jungle of every conceivable color and texture of life, shaped by a skeleton built of duracrete and transparisteel.

"Ganner, can you stand?" he asked softly. "You don't have to walk. Just stand. I need to do something else right now."

Ganner clenched every ounce of his will to swallow the rising tide of his shame and self-disgust. He drew on the Force to hold himself upright, and for the strength to steady his voice. "Yeah. Yeah, go ahead. I'm okay, Jacen," he lied, then made himself say, "Thanks."

Jacen flashed him a hint of that quick Solo smile. "You'd do the same for me."

As if I'd ever have to, Ganner thought, but held his tongue.

Solemnity settled back over Jacen's features like a mask. He turned to face the assembled thousands, and lifted his arms. *"I am Jacen Solo! I am human! I was a Jedi!"* His voice boomed out like artillery fire, and the echoes came back in Yuuzhan Vong: *Nikk pryozz* Jacen Solo! *Nikk pryozz* human! *Nikk pr'zzyo Jeedai!*

"I am now a servant of the Truth!"

How he said that made Ganner suddenly scowl; for someone who was only playing a part, Jacen sounded unsettlingly *sincere*—

Ganner felt a surge in the Force like a vast rushing

wind; it passed him without touching him. The Great Door swung inward, to reveal the shadowed reach of the Atrium beyond, and the cavernous mouths of the Grand Concourse to either side.

Jacen turned his palms upward as though reaching for the braided arch of impossible color that was the Bridge overhead.

"*WITNESS!*" he thundered. The echo cried: *Tchurokk!*
"*WITNESS THE WILL OF THE GODS!*"

Before the echo finished roaring *Tchurokk Yun'tchilat*, Jacen had already turned and walked briskly through the Great Door; a swirl of the Force drew Ganner after him. Nom Anor and the Shaper Lord made to follow, along with the priests and the vanguard band, but as soon as Ganner was clear of the doorway, Jacen turned and made a small gesture that Ganner felt as another swift, incredibly powerful rush in the Force.

The Great Door boomed shut.

Echoes faded. Slowly.

The Atrium had become a vast cavern of living yorik coral.

The immense statues that had once represented the varied species of the New Republic had become unidentifiable, misshapen pillars like boils of old lava. Shadows huge and black masked every fold of coral, and the mouths of the Grand Concourse to either side yawned bottomless depths of night; the sole light—a pulsing, sulfurous glow mingling reds and yellows—leaked into the Atrium from an archway opposite the Great Door.

"What's making that light? And, and, and, wait—" Ganner said numbly. "I don't remember any *door* there—that was, uh, the Information Services office, wasn't it? . . ."

"Maybe you've noticed: things have changed." Jacen

was already trotting toward the archway. "Follow me. We don't have much time."

Ganner stumbled after him.

The arch led to nearly half a kilometer of yorik coral tunnel. The roof and sides formed a rough semicircle, a little less than five meters wide at the base and the same in height. Pulsing red-orange light filled the far end, flaring sometimes to an eye-burning yellow. "How are you doing?" Jacen asked as he jogged along; Ganner was lagging, breathing hard. "Keeping up okay? You need any more help?"

"I'm . . . I am—" *not going to screw this up,* Ganner swore to himself. "—okay. I'm okay. I'm right behind you."

The tunnel's roof opened to a vast cavernous red-lit space overhead, and the walls, too, fell away; the tunnel's floor became a cantilevered bridgeway out to a circular platform ten meters across, which hung unsupported in great swirls of sulfurous mist that burned Ganner's throat and scoured tears from his eyes.

"What *is* this place?"

"Look around," Jacen said grimly. If the scorching heat or brimstone-reeking fog bothered him at all, he didn't show it. He seemed to be listening for something. "Give me a minute. I have to concentrate."

Ganner barely heard him. He gaped, turning in a slow, dumbfounded circle.

This used to be the Senate's Grand Convocation Chamber.

A hundred meters below, where once had stood the pillar of the Chief of State's Podium, there now boiled a great pool of glowing slime; huge bubbles roiled to the surface, bursting into flares of scarlet and starflower yellow—it was from this pool that the light came.

Rising around the pool, a gargantuan bowl of yorik

coral climbed the staggered rank upon rank of Senatorial platforms, slowly scaling the walls toward the dim, shadowed vault of the ceiling.

And down in that pool of glowing slime, a vast fleshy bulge *moved*, breaching the surface in a slick black curve before submerging once more.

Ganner jolted back from the edge. "*Gyahh*—*!* Jacen, there's something *down* there!"

"Yeah." Jacen stepped to the front edge of the platform. "Don't worry. It's a friend of mine."

"A *friend*?" Ganner looked down again—and again the creature breached: black, bloated, a ghastly stomach turned inside out, swollen with malice. A yellow eye the size of an X-wing glared up at them, blinking, wiped by a triple layer of transparent eyelids that slid across its surface at different angles to scrape it free of slime.

Then a second eye appeared, blinked, and fixed on them: a parallax, for ranging. A spray of tentacles shot upward from the slime.

Ganner threw himself backward as tentacles hissed through the fog around them, impossibly flexible ropes of muscle slicing the air so fast he couldn't even tell how many there were. Tentacles slammed against the platform, knocking Ganner half off his feet, chipping away head-sized hunks of coral.

Jacen never moved.

"This—uh, *friend of yours,*" Ganner said shakily. "It doesn't seem too happy to see you . . ."

"Yeah, well, I can't say I'm surprised. The last time we saw each other, I was trying to kill it."

"To kill—uh, your friend?" Gazing downward in a daze of horrified revulsion, Ganner tried a laugh; it came out too high, too tight, too close to a hysterical giggle. "How do you treat your enemies?"

Jacen cocked his head, his brown eyes suddenly thoughtful, then he shrugged. "I don't have any enemies."

"What?"

Jacen pointed at an angle, down across the Well. "See that platform—the one sticking out under that fold of coral? That's the platform for the Kashyyyk delegation. They like manual doors. I know you're not as strong as a Wookiee, but with the Force you should be able to get them open."

"Down *there*?" Ganner clutched his guts again. "You want me to go *in* there?"

"Listen: straight back on your right you'll find the Kashyyyk Senator's private office. There's a turbolift shaft behind a concealed door by his desk. Just slide down the inside of the shaft; it'll take you right into the tunnels."

Tunnels? A secret turboshaft? When was Jacen going to start making sense? "What would the Wookiees be doing with a secret turboshaft?"

"I think all the delegates' offices had them: They go into concealed tunnels that are full of shielded conference rooms for secret meetings and stuff. They even connect with Fey'lya's offices in the Imperial Palace."

"How do *you* know all this?"

"Ganner," Jacen said dryly, "those offices used to be my mother's."

"Uh, yeah."

"If you can reach the tunnels, you should at least be able to find a place to hide for a while. You might live a few days. You might even escape."

Ganner went cold. "What are you talking about?"

"I'm talking about making a run for it, Ganner. Give yourself a chance."

"Oh, no no no," Ganner stepped back, shaking his head. "Oh, no you *don't*—!"

"We've only got a minute or two before Nom Anor

decides he can't keep pretending nothing's gone wrong. About two minutes after that, they'll blow open the Great Door. They'll kill me about thirty seconds later."

"What can you do in here that's worth your *life?*"

"I don't have time to explain. I'm not even sure I *can* explain."

"You expect me to make a run for it and let you die? For something you can't even *explain*? You're coming with me, or I'm not going!"

"Still playing the hero, Ganner?"

Ganner winced—that had hit too close to the bone—but he stood his ground. "No. I'm just the sidekick here. *You're* the hero, Jacen. We *need* heroes like you. That's why I came looking for you. The New Republic needs you." He lowered his voice. "*Jaina* needs you. If there's even the faintest ghost of a chance, you have to *live*, Jacen. You have to at least *try!*"

Jacen shook his head. He had that Skywalker dura-steel on his face again. "No, I don't. The only thing I have to do is be who I am."

"What are you *talking* about?"

"Anakin had his path. Jaina has hers." He spread his hands, as though to indicate the futility of arguing with fate. "I have mine."

"I don't care about any stupid *path*!" Ganner said desperately. "They'll blow the door any second—we have to *go!*"

"No. *You* have to go. I have to . . . Ganner, listen. I need you to understand. The only power I have—the only power *any* of us have—is to be who we are. That's what I'm going to do here. Be who I am."

"You're not making any *sense*! How old are you? Seventeen? Eighteen? You don't even really *know* who you are!"

"I don't have to know. All I have to do is *decide*," Jacen answered serenely. "Choose, and act."

"I am *not* leaving you here!"

"That's up to you."

"How long is it going to take, Jacen? How long?" Ganner stepped toward him. "What if they kill you *first*?"

Jacen shrugged. "Then I lose. When you start to become who you are, the first thing you learn is that there is nothing to fear."

A ripping roar of thunder behind him blew away Ganner's reply, and the bridgeway jounced sharply, smacking his feet, making him stagger. Whirling, he saw a roil of smoke belch out from the tunnel's mouth, a reeking gust like burning swamp gas.

"That's the door," Jacen said distantly. "We're out of time. I guess we both lose."

Ganner didn't move.

Illumination burst within his brain.

In that instant, everything finally made sense. He understood what Jacen had been talking about. There was nothing to fear.

He understood the power of being who he was.

He didn't even really have to *know* who he was. He could *decide*.

He could choose, and act.

Suddenly, his life made sense. His life had been a story of pretending to be a hero. *Well,* he thought. *Okay, then.*

His nausea had vanished. It wasn't even a memory. No more weakness. No more uncertainty. Doubt and fear had disappeared along with the nausea.

He hefted Anakin's lightsaber.

"We both lose unless"—he spoke slowly—"unless somebody *doesn't let them in.*"

"You have to play the hero," Jacen said sadly. "Even if it kills you."

Ganner squeezed the blade to life, and stared at its sizzling purple shaft. Here was the weapon of a hero. A real hero. Not a playactor. Not a pretend-hero, like Ganner had always been.

But this weapon was now in Ganner's hand.

I don't have to be a real hero, he thought. A dazzling, old-Ganner, forget-the-consequences-and-have-some-fun smile dawned on his face. He shook himself and years fell from his shoulders; his eyes lit up, sparking like arc gaps in the red-lit gloom. He felt shiny as a war droid and twice as tough.

I don't have to be *a hero,* he thought in silent wonder. *All I have to do is pretend.*

"Like I said, I'm just the sidekick here," he said carelessly. "*My* job is to make sure the real hero lives long enough to do *his*. That whole 'needing to be a hero' thing has always been my greatest weakness."

Jacen stared at him, into him, through him, as though he knew him to his very core, and he nodded. "But you should know that it can also be your greatest strength. Give yourself permission to use that strength, Ganner. You'll need it."

"Yeah." Ganner looked into the lightsaber's blade as though his future could be read in its amethyst shaft. He grinned at what he saw. "You know, I never liked you, Jacen. I thought you were soft. Wishy-washy. An over-intellectual bleeding heart."

"I never liked you either." Ganner looked up to find Jacen answering his grin with a gentle, knowing smile. "I thought you were nothing but a grandstander. A play-acting glory hunter, more concerned with *looking* good than with *doing* good."

Ganner laughed out loud. "You were right."

"So were you." Jacen held out his hand. "So: here's our chance to show the Yuuzhan Vong what a grandstander and a bleeding heart can do."

Ganner took Jacen's hand and gripped it fiercely. "It'll be a show they'll never forget."

Jacen stepped back and lifted his arms, and the pulse of scarlet and green glow from the arterial sigils on his robe synchronized with the shifting light of the bubbling slime below. Tentacles coiled upward behind him, beyond the lip of the platform, arching high overhead, trailing slime that shone and pulsed, framing him with a living corona: Jacen's silhouette became a shadow cross within a bramble of light.

"*Jacen—!*" Ganner gasped, reaching toward him. "*Behind you!*"

"I know." Jacen turned his face upward. The tentacles curved down to meet him; he lowered his hands to accept them as their shimmering coils settled across his shoulders. "Don't be afraid. This is all part of it."

The tentacles now lifted Jacen in their grip, bearing him up and off the platform, cradling him gently—almost lovingly—as they lowered him toward the bubbling slime, but down there those immense yellow eyes still glittered alien malice.

"Buy me ten minutes," Jacen said. "That should be enough."

The clatter of booted feet grew from the tunnel. Ganner paused for one last moment, watching Jacen be pulled beneath the surface of the slime. He felt a burst of power in the Force, a shove from below, an impulse: *Go.*

He bunched the front of his robe in his free hand and tore it off his body. The dark-glowing arterial sigils spasmed, leaking black light. He tossed the robe into a heap on the platform.

He went.

*   *   *

Nom Anor squinted through the smoke that boiled from the shattered gape of what had been the Great Door. Squad after squad of warriors slipped close around the twisted durasteel wreckage that pinged and groaned as it cooled. They spread out within the smoke- and shadow-filled Atrium, weapons at the ready, eyes straining for any glimpse of a target.

A squad of warriors had sprinted down the coral tunnel toward the Well, to reconnoiter.

That had been five minutes ago.

None had returned.

Nom Anor hung back in the doorway. He had not survived so much of this war by underestimating Jedi.

Red-gold slimelight pulsed through the smoke from the Well archway. A figure solidified in that archway: a silhouette approaching lazily through the smoke, haloed by the slimelight.

A human silhouette.

Bonelessly powerful: a sand panther, out for a stroll. Relaxed but alert. Poised.

Predatory.

A superstitious chill climbed Nom Anor's spine.

Warriors fanned out, officers glancing back to their commander, who looked to Nom Anor. "This is *your* event, Executor. What would you have us do?"

"You! You there!" Nom Anor called nervously in Basic. "What are you doing there?"

The answer was a deep, mockingly cheerful growl. "Isn't it obvious? I'm standing in your way."

Ganner Rhysode. Nom Anor began to relax; this was Ganner Rhysode, the weakling who could not even mount the causeway. Ganner Rhysode who got no respect from the other Jedi. Ganner the poser, the playactor. The joke.

Nom Anor snorted. He should just order the fool cut down—but Ganner didn't sound weak now. Or foolish.

And what had happened to the missing recon squad?

And did Nom Anor really want to be responsible for starting a brawl in the Well of the World Brain?

He bit his lip so hard he tasted blood. "Stand aside! There are *thousands* of warriors out here! You cannot hope to stop us."

"I don't have to stop you. All I have to do is slow you down."

A sharp buzzing crackle made Nom Anor jump. From the shadow's hand sprang a meter-long bar of vividly sizzling amethyst.

"You want me to move?" The shadow beckoned with the blade of light. "Come on and move me."

The smoke thinned, and cleared, and the human within the archway didn't look at all like the Ganner Nom Anor remembered. This Ganner wore only faded brown leggings and battered leather boots. This Ganner was tall, broad-shouldered, and the light from his weapon gleamed on the sculpted muscle of his bare chest. The blade in his hand was steady as the roots of a mountain, but it was not this that made Nom Anor hesitate, made him run his thin yellow tongue nervously between his filed-sharp teeth.

It was the light in Ganner's eyes.

He looked *happy.*

"There are *thousands* of warriors out here," Nom Anor repeated, waving a futile fist. "You are only one man!"

"I am only one Jedi."

"You're *insane!*"

The man's answering laugh was deep and long and bright, full of joy and freedom. "No. I am Ganner."

He spun his shining blade in a dazzlingly complex

flourish that illuminated the arch around him, making it shine like a rainbow frame for the pure, animal grace of his body.

"This threshold," he announced through a happy grin, "is *mine*. I claim it for my own. Bring on your thousands, one at a time or all in a rush. I don't give a damn."

His flourish ended with the blade slanted before his chest, and his teeth flashed in the gloom.

"None shall pass."

FOURTEEN

PATH OF DESTINY

They come at him one at a time, an endless stream, each warrior in turn charging toward honorable single combat.

Then—

They come *two* at a time.

By the time they begin to come in groups, they have to scramble over bodies of their dead comrades to reach him. A *pile* of bodies.

A pile that becomes a wall, a rampart.

Ganner Rhysode builds a fortress of the dead.

From a safe vantage point—behind a twisted curve of durasteel that had once been part of the Great Door—Nom Anor watched with appalled fascination. All he could see through the smoke and the mass of warriors who pressed forward to engage the mad Jedi were flashes of brilliant purple, sometimes joined by the Jedi himself as he leapt and whirled and spun, always in motion, always attacking, stabbing and slashing, littering the Atrium with corpses and severed limbs.

"This is *insane*!" Nom Anor turned to the warrior commander at his side. "Can't you simply blow him up? Gas him? *Something?*"

"Nay." The commander's facial scars flushed pale blue. "He faces us with honor. Would you have warriors of the Yuuzhan Vong show *less* honor than an infidel *Jeedai*?"

"*Space* your honor! Don't you *understand*? There's a Jedi in the Well of the World Brain—and that Jedi is *Jacen Solo*!" He used the name as though it could conjure devils . . . and perhaps it could.

Only a devil could have slain the voxyn queen. Only a devil could have slaughtered the dhuryams and shapers and warriors in the Nursery, yet still wormed its evil way into Nom Anor's trust, to the point where he—*he,* Nom Anor *himself*—had ushered this terrifyingly lethal Jedi into the one place on Yuuzhan'tar where he might slay the whole *planet*! "Jacen Solo is *alone* with the World Brain—"

"The World Brain is well able to defend itself." To Nom Anor's other side stood Ch'Gang Hool the Shaper Lord. "Matters of honor aside, we cannot use overpotent explosives, nor poison gases. The World Brain would be in greater danger from a clumsy attempt at rescue than it could ever be from a single *Jeedai*."

"This is no ordinary Jedi," Nom Anor said feelingly. "You have *no idea* what he is capable of! We have to get in there! We have to stop him!"

The commander snapped a series of orders, and a squad of heavy infantry lumbered toward the archway, their head-to-toe overlapping plates of vonduun crab armor gleaming in the slimelight. He glanced back at Nom Anor. "We will be in soon enough. Remain calm, Executor."

"Space your calm, too!"

"You do seem a bit . . . mm, *overwrought*," Ch'Gang Hool murmured. His mouth-tentacles twitched. "One might wonder if you felt, in some way . . . mmm, *responsible* for this?"

Nom Anor opened his mouth, took a breath, started

to say something, changed his mind, started to say something else—then closed it again. The Shaper Lord's mouth-tentacles braided themselves into a shape subtly obscene. Nom Anor looked away. He was about one second away from ripping those ridiculous tentacles right off that smug smirking bureaucrat's face, and *eating* them—

A few strides down the causeway, among the milling crowd of priests and warriors, he saw Vergere. She met his eye, and with a twitch of her head motioned for him to follow. Oh, he'd follow all right, he thought as he excused himself and paced after her. He had some choice words for *that* little creature—

She moved well downslope into the blue-white sunlight, and stopped with one hand holding a leafy vertical branch of the road trees. Nom Anor was already snarling by the time he reached her. "Do you know what your 'student' has done? That sniveling traitor has betrayed *us*—and it's all *your fault!*"

"Perhaps it is." Her fluting voice was cheerful as ever. "But let us be clear on the issue of fault, eh, Executor? What is important is not whose fault this truly is; all that matters is whom Tsavong Lah will choose to blame for it, yes?"

Nom Anor pulled fleshless lips back over needle-sharp teeth. He could imagine all too well what Tsavong Lah would do, once word of this disaster reached his fanatic ears. "And why do you come to me now?"

"Because you should take me with you."

He went absolutely still. "Take you with me?" he asked with studied blankness.

"You'll need me. I saved the life of Luke Skywalker's wife. With me at your side, the New Republic might not simply shoot you on sight."

Nom Anor admitted silently that she might have a

point, but his face revealed nothing. "You think I have—some sort of escape plan?"

"Executor, please," Vergere chided knowingly. "You *always* have an escape plan. This time, you have something even better: a secret coralcraft, grown below the Well."

"I—I—I have nothing of the sort!" How could she possibly know? A concealed accessway on the far side of the Well—that would open only to him—led to the coralcraft he'd bribed a shaper to seed months ago, during the earliest stage of the Galactic Senate's conversion into the Well of the World Brain. "You cannot possibly think—"

"Executor, again: please. Are you the only one who can bribe a shaper? And all the tending and care of your secret coralcraft, while it matured—"

"Hsst! Enough!" He glanced back over his shoulder up the causeway. Though the commander had turned away to observe the battle, Ch'Gang Hool still watched Nom Anor expectantly. To leave now would be too suspicious—he might never make it.

Vergere seemed somehow to read his mind. "Executor, if we do not flee *now*, there will be no flight at all. There will be no *ship*." She stood on tiptoe to lean close to him, and whispered, "Jacen Solo will *steal* it."

The surface of the slime pool closes over Jacen Solo like lips, warm as blood.

He does not feel it.

Knotted ropes of tentacles stretch wide his arms, bind close his legs, circle garrote-tight his throat. Their coarsely scaled hide rasps blood through his skin, blood that trails him in a fractal tree-spiral gelled motionless in the slime. Tentacles twist him and turn him and bend him, pulling him deeper through the slime that fluoresces yellow-gold and scarlet around him, blazing colors that shift with his motion and surge from contact with the heat of his body.

He does not see them.

At the deepest depths of the slime pool, the tentacles hold him face-up, his back to a ring of jagged rubble; that ring of rubble once had been the base of the Chief of State's Podium from which his mother had so often declaimed. The tentacles gather him in, gather him up, toward a body vast and billowing, black curves of flesh bulging between translucent green sheets and ropes of viscera. The tentacles spring from a fleshy ring around a mouth gaping and hungry, and from either side of that emptily chewing maw stare immense eyes that glow yellow with suspicious malice.

Jacen does not notice.

His attention is filled with the hollow in his chest.

His empty center rings with anger and mistrust and hungry triumph: the emotions of the World Brain, which has caught the former friend who tried to murder it.

The former friend it had trusted, and by whom it had been betrayed.

Mobile teeth like swords protrude from humps of muscle like multiple tongues, and begin to circle and clash within the tentacle-ringed mouth.

Jacen can answer only with regret and sadness.

Yes. I betrayed you. I taught you to trust, and I taught you what it means to trust a traitor.

He cannot teach it forgiveness. He has not learned that lesson yet himself: there is too much he will never forgive.

The tentacles contract, drawing him into the gaping maw, and the sword-teeth close upon his flesh.

He does not recoil in fear.

He does not resist.

He does not struggle.

Instead, he opens himself. In his most secret center, that gap in his being that once fed him pain, he offers an embrace.

Into the hollow in his center, he pours compassion. Absolute empathy. Perfect understanding.

He accepts the pain he caused the dhuryam with his betrayal; he shares with the dhuryam the pain that betrayal had caused him.

He shares with the dhuryam all his experience with the spectrum of life: the featureless whiteout of agony, the red tide of rage, the black hole of despair, the gamma-sleet of loss . . . and the lush verdure of growing things, the grays of stone and duracrete, the glisten of gemstones and transparisteel, the blue-white sizzle of the noonday sun and its exact echo in a lightsaber's blade.

He shares how much he loves it all: for all these things are all one thing: pain and joy, loss and reunion, life and death. To love any is to love all, for none can exist without every other.

The Universe.

The Force.

All is one.

The Yuuzhan Vong and the species of the New Republic.

Jacen and the World Brain.

When I betrayed you, I betrayed myself. When I killed your siblings, I killed pieces of myself. You may kill me, but I will live on in you.

We are One.

And Jacen cannot tell if those words come from him to the World Brain, or from the World Brain to him, for Jacen and the World Brain are only different faces of the same thing. Call it the Universe, or the Force, or Existence: those are only words.

They are half truths. Less.

They are lies.

The truth is always greater than the words we use to describe it.

The skirl of lightblade along amphistaff, a thrusting bind that sizzles disintegrating energy through the web of skin between a Yuuzhan Vong thumb and forefinger where hand meets amphistaff—

A world-whirl of airborne somersault over the heads of two warriors lunging side by side, and their boneless collapse as a single lightsaber slash opens the napes of two necks and unstrings their limbs—

The astonished blink of a warrior's eyes as an amethyst shaft of energy spears into his open mouth, angling upward to burn open a three-centimeter-wide tunnel from his hard palate through the roof of his skull—

Of such brief flickers is built the death of Ganner Rhysode.

—burned-milk reek of Yuuzhan Vong blood sizzling into smoke on his blade—

—lines of burning ice that are the slices left in his flesh by amphistaffs—

—cold flame of amphistaff venom consuming his nerves—

These are mere flicks of melody in Ganner's symphony of the Force. The Force does more than give him strength, more than lift him, spin him: the Force surges though his veins to tune his heart to the rhythm of the Universe.

He has become the Force, and the Force has become him.

He is not directly aware of the sequence of his death; time vanished along with fear, and doubt, and pain in that eternal second when he surrendered his self-command. Standing in the archway, waiting for the

Yuuzhan Vong, Ganner realized that this, right now, right here, was what his whole life had been for.

The day of his birth set his feet upon this path; every triumph and tragedy, every foolish stunt and humiliation, each random useless twist of cruel fate built a pressure within him, piled up in tidal surge behind the dikes of his control. Those dikes had been built by his parents, trying to smooth the rough edges of his arrogance; they had been built by the mocking laughter of his playmates, when they jeered his every attempt to impress them; they had been built even by Luke Skywalker's Jedi training— "A Jedi doesn't *show off*, Ganner. Fighting is not a *game*. For the Jedi, combat is *failure*. It is a tragedy. When blood must be shed, a Jedi does so quickly, surgically, with solemn reverence. With grief."

Ganner tried for so long, tried so *hard* to be what everyone told him he was supposed to be, tried to control his flair for the dramatic, for the elegant, the graceful, the artistic, tried to be a good son, a good friend, a humble man, a good Jedi . . .

But in the archway, he finds the end of trying.

There is reason no longer to resist the truth of himself. Playacting the hero's part is not only permissible—

It is *necessary*.

To hold the archway it is not enough to merely wound and kill, is not enough to be calm, and surgical, and grieving.

To hold the archway, he must not only slaughter, but slaughter effortlessly, carelessly, laughingly. Joyfully.

To hold the archway, he must dance and whirl and leap and spin, calling out for more opponents. More *victims*.

He must make them hesitate to face him.

He must make them *fear*.

He had spoken the words: he had found a magical incantation to crack the dikes within him and unleash the flood.

None shall pass.

He wields the blade of a fallen hero, but now he is the hero, and it is others who fall.

He is *rising*.

The Force thunders through him, and he thunders through the Force. Letting slip the bonds of control, leaving aside conscious thought, answering only the surge of his passion and his joy, he finds power undreamed of.

He has *become* the battle.

He is not directly aware of the corpses that litter the tunnel, that his feet nimbly avoid of their own accord.

He is not directly aware of the warped sheets of durasteel that he has drawn from the wreckage of the Great Door, sheets that spin and tumble around him to become anvils for the hammer of thud bugs and shields to shelter his flanks.

He is not directly aware of the coral-embedded statues from the Atrium that he has caught in his Force-powered dance, immense figures of the species of the New Republic that seem to come to life to fight in his cause, statues that lumber and rock and fall, crushing dozens and hundreds, remaking Atrium into abattoir.

No more is he aware of the texture of the coral that lines the walls, or the quality of the light, or the number of his opponents. Has he faced a dozen? A hundred? How many have been pulled back to safety after taking disabling wounds? How many lie dead in the brimstone smoke?

He doesn't remember, for there is no memory. There is no past. There is no future.

He is not even aware of himself. Nor of the Yuuzhan Vong. He has become the warriors he fights, slaying himself with each who falls. There is no longer any such thing as a Ganner Rhysode; there are no more Yuuzhan Vong, no more Jedi.

There are only the dancers, and the dance.

The dance is all there is: from whirl of quarks to wheel of galaxies, all is motion.

All is dance.

All *is*.

Nom Anor motioned for Vergere to wait while he took one last quick look around. Before him rose the coral mountain of the Well. The half-finished thorn maze towered behind, empty of shapers—they'd all probably been drawn to the Well's front by the noise of the battle. Distant explosions popped in stuttering arrhythm, punctuated by fainter shouts.

Satisfied that they were unobserved, Nom Anor pulled aside a soft, mosslike sheet of false coral to reveal a hatch sphincter's nosetongue. He stuck his hand inside it, still glancing around nervously while the nosetongue tasted and analyzed the enzymatic secretions of his skin. A second later it recognized him, and a larger curtain of false coral nearby suddenly dimpled as a small concealed hatch sphincter opened behind it.

He motioned for Vergere to follow, and went in.

Yorik coral gave way to age-grimed duracrete; the corridor became a labyrinth. As they threaded their way along, Nom Anor congratulated himself on the cleverness of his escape plan. No one had been within the Well except master shapers and their assistants since its initial conversion had begun; no one was willing to risk the homicidal wrath of Ch'Gang Hool—except for one shaper whose greed had overcome his cowardice. Of all the Yuuzhan Vong, only that shaper and Nom Anor himself had been aware that immense chambers—once the offices of the Old Republic's Chancellor—lay below the World Brain's pool.

These chambers were blasted and broken. Damaged in the destruction of the Senate above, they had never been repaired. Nom Anor picked his way over mounds of rubble and through a jungle of twisted durasteel and dangling cable, leading Vergere through the wreckage. Down here some of the New Republic glow globes still functioned; they had not been destroyed as heresies because only Nom Anor and his pet shaper had known of their existence.

He pulled himself over a bent girder, and there it was: long and sleek, sculpted for atmospheric speed, twinned dovin basals—one for motion, one for defense—surfaces angled to deflect sensors, flat matte black, nonreflective to defeat visual targeting.

The shaper who had grown it had guaranteed this coralcraft would be as fast as any in the Yuuzhan Vong fleet; Nom Anor had used the concealed hatch sphincter above to secretly visit the craft on several occasions while it grew, so that its pilotbrain could be imprinted with Nom Anor's mental signature. While visiting, Nom Anor had often amused himself by contemplating how he had found a new use for the chambers that had once belonged to the legendary Palpatine . . .

The defensive dovin basal would collapse a tunnel through the duracrete and yorik coral alike, opening it like a gate to the sky. The pilotbrain was trained with the necessary recognition codes to pass the fleet cordon around the planet, and had coordinates for the jump into New Republic space already memorized. Once inside, nothing could touch him.

Once inside, he would be safe.

"Beautiful, isn't it?" he murmured as he put his hand to the coralcraft's nosetongue. Its hatch gaped wide, instantly obedient. "This is the result, Vergere, of contingency planning. I never assume success. This is why I always survive. I always have a contingency plan, to cover any possible disaster—"

"Do you *always*?" Something in her voice froze him in place. "Any *possible* disaster?"

Before he could even draw breath to ask what she meant, his unspoken question was answered by a sickeningly familiar sound—

snap-hiss hummmm

Slowly, glacially, afraid of what he'd see but unable to stop himself, Nom Anor turned toward a new light in the ruined office: light that sizzled green and struck white highlights off the black curves of his coralcraft.

To find himself staring into the terminal curve of a lightsaber's blade, one centimeter from his nostrils.

"A lightsaber is an interesting weapon," Vergere said conversationally. "A blade unique in the history of warfare. A paradox, not unlike the Jedi who wield it: those peaceful warriors, who kill in the service of life. Have you ever noticed? The blade is *round*. It has no edge. But it is a lightsaber—which means it is nothing *but* edge. There is no part of this blade that does *not* cut. Curious, yes? Symbolic, one might say."

"What?" His mouth opened, closed, opened again. He wanted to ask what she was doing. He wanted to ask where she had gotten a lightsaber. He wanted to ask any number of things, but all that would come from his mouth was "What?"

Again, Vergere seemed to read his mind. "It's Jacen's," she chimed cheerfully. "I think he might want it back, don't you?"

"You *can't*—"

"Yes, I can." She nodded toward the gloom beyond

the coralcraft. "I should be able to cut my way into the Well easily enough."

"If you kill me—" Nom Anor began desperately.

"Kill you? Don't be silly." Cables from the dangling jungle of wreckage suddenly writhed to life, whipping through the air to bind Nom Anor's limbs. They wrapped him tightly enough to squeeze a gasp from his lungs, then tied themselves in hideously complex knots. Vergere watched all this happen—*made* it happen, Nom Anor realized—with a humorous expression on her face and a bright orange flare of her crest. "If I want you dead, all I have to do is leave you behind. Tsavong Lah will take care of the rest."

"But you *can't* leave me behind," Nom Anor said. He was beginning to recover his self-possession. "You can't fly my craft. It's imprinted on *me*! Only I can—"

"That may be true," she allowed. "But I doubt it. Your coralcraft is, after all, a living creature—and Jacen, you may have noticed, has a certain gift for making friends."

"You—he—you're *mad*! This can't be happening!"

"Executor," she said severely, cutting him short with a twitch of the lightblade, "didn't I say Jacen Solo will steal your ship?"

Nom Anor could only gape.

"When will you learn," she asked, shaking her head in mock sadness, "that everything I tell you is the truth?"

Abruptly, the dance falters, stumbles, begins to limp.

There is no one left to fight.

Ganner sways, dizzy, dying, poisoned with amphistaff venom from scores of wounds. His blood paints the floor beneath his boots and the walls of the tunnel around him.

Only the Force holds him upright.

A grinding rumble approaches, and soon he can see what makes this sound, what produces these tremors he feels shaking the floor: something huge and dark, trundling on curving knotted legs like buttresses, splayed claws flattening Yuuzhan Vong corpses heedlessly as it approaches. Its bulk is mailed with vast plates of horn, and a vast head swings slowly from side to side like an AT-AT's control cabin in hunter-killer mode. Its massive jaws drip flame.

Warriors advance along its flanks.

I guess it was inevitable, Ganner thinks with a twinge of melancholy. *Sooner or later, the bad guys always bring up their armor.*

This is about to be over; he cannot face such a beast supported by infantry—and yet the Force offers him one last trick.

Though the Force is blind to the warriors and the tank beast and the coral around them all, in it Ganner can feel the duracrete walls of the Senate, which form the Well's skeletal structure; he can feel that the tunnel had been cut through any number of load-bearing members—he can feel that the duracrete around him is crazed with stress fractures, half broken already, and sagging under the unimaginable tons of the coral that surrounds it.

Ganner smiles.

The tank beast roars a gout of concentrated acid; with the Force, Ganner angles a shard of the Great Door to form a durasteel shield that sluices the acid to one side, so that it splashes to one wall. Coral smokes, dying, liquefying instantly. The shard of the Great Door begins to melt.

Blast bugs zing toward him from the warriors, and the melting shard dances before him, deflecting them into the acid-burned wall. Their explosions splash liquid coral and duracrete splinters.

Above their heads, the building groans. Warriors flinch, glancing upward in sudden fear. The tank beast howls.

Ganner laughs. The Force is with him, and he has become once more the dancer.

He has become the dance.

With the Force, he reaches into the duracrete around them all, and he begins to *shove*.

Jacen was surprised by life.

The teeth of the World Brain had not closed upon him. Its tentacles had not ripped the flesh from his bones. He had not drowned in the slime pool, asphyxiating on phosphorescent goo. No Yuuzhan Vong warriors swarmed around him to drag him from the slime and carve the life from him with amphistaffs.

Instead, a bubble of air had formed around him, and tentacles had cradled him like a sleeping child, and lips had closed over sword-edged teeth to touch him with a kiss.

Because he was the World Brain, and the World Brain was him, and each was everything else, and Jacen had learned that one can meet the Universe and all its irrational pain—which means meeting oneself—with fear, or with hatred, or with despair.

Or one can choose to meet it with love.

Jacen had chosen.

But still, he was astonished to discover that the Universe could love him back.

At the far end of an infinite distance—which was the same as *right here*—he felt an oceanic roll of the Force gathering an interstellar fortissimo of symphonic joy; at the same time, within the hollow at his center, he felt rage and pain and fierce hot combat, and he understood another reason why he was still alive.

Ganner—

He reached out with his feelings and gathered power from across the Universe.

Tentacles fell away from his arms and legs, and the air bubble around him collapsed. He brushed the World Brain lightly with his fingertips: a good-bye to a friend. Then Jacen Solo shot from the slime pool as though fired from a torpedo launcher.

He burst into the brimstone smoke, his robe blazing with slime that trailed from him in shining ropes and dripped like falling stars; he sailed over the slime pool to alight at the bowl rim, where the coral met the bare durasteel of a Senate platform. He lifted his head, fixing his gaze upon the cantilevered bridgeway that stuck out into the Well like a tongue, a tongue from a mouth that belched smoke and scarlet flame and the amethyst lightning of a lightsaber biting flesh.

And he could hear a human voice up there. He could not make out words, but the tone was unmistakable.

Ganner was *laughing*.

Deep in the Force, Jacen seized that bridgeway with the hands of his mind. One long, smooth tug would lift him to it, and he could reach Ganner's side, and join in his fight, stand at his shoulder against the Yuuzhan Vong—

"Jacen, *wait*."

The words were spoken not loudly, but so perfectly resonant that they chimed in his ear as though the speaker were at his side. And she might as well have been: in the Force he felt an invisible hand take his shoulder.

He nodded to himself. "I should have known, somehow. I should have known you'd be here."

Vergere stood only a few meters above and to his right, on the coral-draped Senate platform that had once belonged to the delegation from Kashyyyk. "Come, Jacen. Your sojourn in the lands of the dead is at an end. It is time once more to walk the bright fields of day."

Instead of answering, he turned back toward the bridge-way above—but her Force grip tightened on his shoulder.

"You cannot save him, Jacen. All you can do is die with him. He has chosen this destiny. The only aid you can offer is to honor his choice. You stand at the very gates of death; life lies before you. If you turn back now—even for a single glance over your shoulder—you are lost."

"What do you want me to do? I won't leave him! I *won't*!" He turned on her. A wave of trembling started at the back of his neck and shivered out through his arms and down his legs. "I can't let people keep giving their lives for me!"

"He does not give his life for you. He gives *your* life *to* you. Will you refuse the gift of a dying man?"

"I can't—Vergere, I can't just—"

"In the story of your life, is this your best ending?"

He reached into the Force and gave a wrenching shove that twisted him free of her grip. "I won't leave him."

She shrugged. "Then you'll be wanting this."

She tossed something down to him. It spun lazily through the air, flashing silver in the slimelight; he caught it instinctively.

It was a lightsaber.

It was *his* lightsaber.

It felt strange in his hand. Weird. Alien.

He had not seen it since the death of the voxyn queen.

The last time he'd held it, he'd been somebody else. A boy. A sad, conflicted boy, searching desperately for anything he could be sure of, willing to die on a sure nothing rather than live for an uncertain something.

She said, "Choose, and act."

He looked at the flare of battle above. He ached to go, burned to go, to find in himself the pure release, the cosmic symphony that he could feel echoing through Ganner . . . but—

He looked back at Vergere. "Every time you say that to me, it's a trick."

"As it is now," she admitted. "But it's not the *same* trick. The first time, you were but a boy. You did not truly understand what you were throwing away. The second time you were lost in the dark, and you needed flint and steel to spark a torch. Now, though—now, what are you, Jacen Solo?"

In an instant, it all flashed through him, from Sernpidal and Belkadan through Duro and Myrkyr to the Embrace of Pain, the Nursery, the Jedi Temple, and the cavern beast—

He was no warrior, he was certain of that. Not like Jaina was, or Anakin had been. He was no hero like Uncle Luke or his father, no great statesman like his mother or strategist like Admiral Ackbar or scientist like Danni Quee . . .

He remembered that he didn't have to *know* what he was. All he had to do was decide.

"I—I guess . . ." he said slowly, frowning down at the weapon in his hand. "I guess—I'm a student."

"Perhaps you are." Vergere nodded. "Then you are also a teacher, for the two are one. But to be such, you must learn, and you must teach. You must *live*."

She was right. He knew she was right. He could feel it as surely as he'd ever felt anything. But Ganner—

As he looked up, a new sun was born in the Well of the World Brain, somewhere deep in the tunnel above, a rising yellow glare that grew bright, and white, that flared until Jacen had to shield his eyes with his hand and turn away.

The Well shook, and he could feel sudden terror from

the World Brain as the cantilevered bridgeway and platform collapsed, plunging a hundred meters to crash into the slime pool, and the world seemed to rock and tremble, and a blast of smoke and dust burst from the tunnel—

"What—" Jacen gasped, coughing in the dust that smelled of burning blood and duracrete, "—what—? Is that *Ganner*? What's happening up there?"

"It may be Ganner. It may be a weapon of the Yuuzhan Vong. It makes no difference. Your choice is the same: stay, or go."

The glare from above died in a long groundquake rumble and new billows of dust, and when Jacen reached out once more through the Force, Ganner was no longer there.

In the hollow of his chest, the warriors who had fought him were similarly absent.

Jacen stared up at the mouth of the tunnel. He could see it now, choked with rubble. Then the platforms around it began to sag, to crumble, and slide down the bowl toward the slime pool. Even the gloom-shrouded ceiling high above seemed to droop, and he felt a warm hand on his shoulder, and heard a warm whisper in his ear: *Go*.

It sounded like Ganner.

He frowned at Vergere. She returned his gaze blankly.

He would never know what had happened up there.

He would never know if that voice he'd just heard had been Ganner's, or another of Vergere's tricks.

He would never really know—*could* never really know—much of anything. Truth is elusive, and questions are more useful than answers.

But he knew this: life is more a matter of choosing than of knowing. He could never know the eventual destination of his path, but he could always choose in which direction to take each step.

He chose.

"You're the one who's supposed to be my guide through the lands of the dead, right?" he said. "So go ahead and guide. Show me the way out of here."

She smiled down upon him fondly.

"Of course," she said. "I was only waiting for you to ask."

EPILOGUE

LESSONS

Jacen reclined on a couch beast in the coralcraft's cargo stomach, staring through the clear curve of a corneal port at the vast noncolor of hyperspace. Vergere sat curled up in feline repose on the other side of the room. She might have been napping, but Jacen doubted it.

He *still* hadn't seen her sleep.

Every time he looked at her, he remembered coming to the coralcraft hidden below the Well, remembered finding Nom Anor tied up like a field-dressed nerf. He remembered how the Yuuzhan Vong executor had begged to be taken along. "Leaving me here—that's the same as *murder*!"

Jacen had turned his back and walked onto the coralcraft, stone-faced. "Don't think of it as murder," he'd said. "Think of it as your Blessed Release."

Once Nom Anor had understood that no plea would help, his pleading had turned to curses. He'd insisted that only his protection had allowed either of them to live this long. "Take her with you, yes, you vile little traitor," he spat at Jacen. "One traitor deserves another."

Vergere had answered cheerfully, "And what did you expect? How was I to teach treason, had I not learned it already myself?"

And yet, Jacen reflected, there was truth in the epithet

traitor. She and he had both lied, had both deceived, had both pretended loyalty to serve their own ends.

Funny how when Vergere was around, even straight-forward concepts like *treason* became slippery.

Every once in a while he took another sip from his sac-worm of dragweed broth or thoughtfully scooped the flesh from another clip beetle. He wondered idly how his stomach would react to regular old synthsteak and pro-tato. He couldn't remember what regular food tasted like.

He wondered what Jaina might be eating right now, and for an instant he was tempted to open himself to their twin bond—

But he didn't. He couldn't. Not yet.

He wasn't ready.

What could he possibly tell her? What information could pass through the bond that would even hint at who he had become? And more than that: he was afraid to find out what *she* might have become.

He didn't know what he was going to tell people once he got back to New Republic space. He couldn't imagine facing his mother. Or his father. Or Uncle Luke.

He couldn't imagine trying to explain how Ganner Rhysode had died.

He had brooded about Ganner quite a bit during the first few days of their voyage. He couldn't reconcile the pompous, arrogant, slightly silly Ganner he'd known most of his life with the transcendent power and pro-found joy he'd felt through the Force. How had Ganner gone from the one to the other? It didn't make sense. He couldn't even really understand why Ganner had chosen to sacrifice himself.

"He didn't even *like* me," Jacen had told Vergere. "I didn't like him."

Vergere had regarded him from one corner of her bottomless eyes. "You need not like someone to love him. Love is nothing more than the recognition that two are one. That all is one."

Jacen had thought of the dhuryam that had become the World Brain, and he'd nodded.

"Ganner knew that, at the end, more fully than even you do," Vergere said. "That knowledge is the seed of greatness."

Jacen shook his head, smiling ruefully. "I still have a hard time putting 'greatness' and 'Ganner Rhysode' in the same sentence."

"He was born to be a legend."

"Maybe he was." Jacen sighed. "Ganner's Last Stand. Too bad nobody saw it."

"Nobody? You mean, nobody from the New Republic. Let me tell you of a vision I have had," she said. "An image of the far future. It came to me through the Force some time ago, but only now have I come to understand it. In that vision, I saw a new figure in the mythology of the Yuuzhan Vong. Not a god, not a demon, but an invincible giant called 'the Ganner.'"

"You're kidding, right?"

"Not at all. They will come to believe that the Ganner, the Jedi Giant, is the Guardian who stands before the Gate to the Lands of the Dead. It is the Ganner—and his forever-blazing blade of light—who stands eternal guard to prevent the shades of the dead from passing back through the Gate, to trouble the living. The curious part of the vision"—she chuckled a little—"as if it could be any more curious than it is already—is the words engraved on the stone of the Gate, in an arc above the great head of the Ganner: they're in Basic."

"In *Basic*? Why would they be in Basic?"

"Who can say? Such visions are enigmatic, and rarely come equipped with footnotes."

"What does it say?"

Vergere spread her hands, palms up, a shrug of helpless incomprehension. "In deep-carved block letters, it reads: NONE SHALL PASS."

Days passed, each much the same as the last.

Jacen had plenty of time to think.

He thought about being a student. About being a teacher.

Being a Jedi.

Being a traitor.

Being a shadowmoth.

Once he brought it up to Vergere. "Can you tell me, now, what you've been after all this time? What it was you wanted me to be?"

"Of course," she said easily. "I wanted you to be exactly what you are."

"That's not a very helpful answer."

"It's the only answer there is."

"But what *am* I—? No, don't say it, I already know: 'That's always been the question, hasn't it?' If you only knew how *aggravating* that gets after a while—"

"Forgive my curiosity," she interrupted with an air of changing the subject, "but I have been wondering: just what, exactly, did you do in the Well of the World Brain?"

Jacen settled into himself then, and moved around on the couch beast into a more comfortable position. "What were you expecting me to do?"

Her crest flared green. "We know each other too well, you and I. Very well, I confess it: I did not know what to expect. I guessed you would either kill the World Brain, or yourself. The third possibility—that you would go ahead and sacrifice Ganner—I didn't think likely."

"But not impossible."

"No," she said. "Not impossible."

"I chose a different option," Jacen said. "I seduced it."

Vergere's crest flickered to orange. "Indeed?"

"I'm using the dhuryam to teach the Yuuzhan Vong a lesson. A *real* lesson. Kind of like the ones you taught me." Jacen smiled, but it was a hard smile, a cold one, that glinted like pack ice in his eyes. "The World Brain's on our side, now."

"It's going to fight the Yuuzhan Vong? Work for the New Republic?" Vergere asked skeptically. "A genengineered double agent?"

"No. Not the New Republic's side. *Our* side. Yours and mine."

"Oh." Now she settled into her feline repose, and her black eyes gleamed. "We have a side of our own, do we?"

"I think we do," Jacen said. "The dhuryam isn't going to fight them. The Yuuzhan Vong are *fanatics*. For them, everything is Right or Wrong, Honorable or Evil, Truth or Blasphemy. When you fight fanatics, all you do is make them even *more* fanatic than they were when they started. Instead, my friend the World Brain is going to *teach* them something."

He sat upright. "They are about to discover that the Vongforming of Yuuzhan'tar is not going exactly to plan. In fact, *everything* is going to go just a *little bit wrong* for them from now on. No matter how hard they try, nothing will happen quite the way they want it to."

Vergere's crest flickered quizzically. "And this teaches them what?"

"It's that fanatic thing," Jacen said. "That's most of what's wrong with the Yuuzhan Vong. Instead of working with what *is*, they keep trying to force everything to be what they think it *should* be. That's not going to work on Yuuzhan'tar. They'll either have to murder the dhuryam and start over from scratch—which they have neither the time nor the resources for—or they're going to have to learn to *compromise*. Get it?"

"I do," Vergere said appreciatively. "This is the most valuable lesson one can teach a fanatic: that fanaticism is self-defeating."

"Yeah." Jacen looked back out the corneal port into the infinite nothing of hyperspace. "I can think of a few Jedi who could stand to learn that one, too."

Suddenly Vergere was on her feet, and her arms encircled Jacen's shoulders in a surprisingly warm hug. When she drew back, her eyes glistened—not with their customary mockery, but with tears.

"Jacen, I am so *proud* of you," she whispered. "This is the greatest moment of a teacher's life: when she is surpassed by her student."

Jacen found himself blinking back tears of his own. "So is that what you are, finally? My teacher?"

"And your student, for the two are one."

He lowered his head. His chest ached with a hard, cold solidity that wouldn't let him meet her eyes. "Hard lessons."

"It is a hard universe," she said from beside him. "No lesson is truly learned until it has been purchased with pain."

"Maybe you're right." Jacen sighed. "But there has to be an easier way."

She joined him at the port, and stared with him out into the space outside the universe.

"Perhaps there is," she said at long last. "Perhaps that is what *you* will have to teach *me*."

Outside the universe, there is nothing.
This nothing is called hyperspace.

A tiny bubble of existence hangs in the nothing. This bubble is called a ship.

The bubble has neither motion nor stillness, nor even orientation, since the nothing has no distance or direction. It hangs there forever, or for less than an instant, because in the nothing there is also no time. Time, distance, and direction have meaning only inside the bubble, and the bubble maintains the existence of these things only by an absolute separation of what is within from what is without.

The bubble is its own universe.

Within this universe, there are traitors. One is a teacher, and a student; another is a student, and a teacher.

One is a gardener.

This universe falls toward another, wider universe: a universe that is a garden—

Which is still full of weeds.

And don't miss STAR WARS: THE NEW JEDI ORDER: DESTINY'S WAY, by Walter Jon Williams, in which a new government is born, a lost hero returns, and hope comes back to the people of the Star Wars galaxy . . .

For a taste of DESTINY'S WAY, please read on . . .

As she sat in the chair that was hers by right of death, she raised her eyes to the cold faraway stars. Checklists buzzed distantly in her mind and her hands moved over the controls, but her thoughts flew elsewhere, amid the chill infinitude. Searching . . .

Nothing.

Her gaze fell and there she saw, on the controls at the adjacent pilot's seat, her husband's hands. She drew comfort from the sight, from the sureness and power she knew was there, in those strong hands.

Her heart leaped. Something, somewhere in all those stars, had touched her.

She thought: *Jacen!*

Her husband's hands touched controls and the stars streamed away, turned to bleeding smears of light as if seen through beaten rain, and the distant touch vanished.

"Jacen," she said, and then, at her husband's startled look, at the surprise and pain in his brown eyes, "Jacen."

"And you're sure?" Han Solo said. "You're sure it was Jacen?"

"Yes. Reaching out to me. I felt him. It could have been no one else."

"And he's alive."

"Yes."

Leia Organa Solo could read him so well. She knew that Han believed their son dead, but that he tried, for her sake, to pretend otherwise. She knew that, fierce with grief and with guilt for having withdrawn from his family, he would support her in anything now, even if he believed she was delusional. And she knew the strength it took for him to suppress his own pain and doubt.

She could read all that in him, in the flicker of his eye, the twitch of his cheek. She could read him, read the bravery and the uncertainty, and she loved him for both.

"It was Jacen," she said. She put as much confidence in her tone as she could, all her assurance. "He was reaching out to me through the Force. I felt him. He wanted to tell me he was alive and with friends." She reached over and took his hand. "There's no doubt, now. Not at all."

Han's fingers tightened on hers, and she sensed the struggle in him, desire for hope warring with his own bitter experience.

His brown eyes softened. "Yes," he said. "Of course. I believe you."

There was a hint of reserve there, of caution, but that was reflex, the result of a long and uncertain life that had taught him to believe nothing until he'd seen it with his own eyes.

Leia reached for him, embraced him awkwardly from the copilot's seat. His arms went around her. She felt the bristle of his cheek against hers, inhaled the scent of his body, his hair.

A bubble of happiness grew in her, burst into speech. "Yes, Han," she said. "Our son is alive. And so are we. Be joyful. Be at peace. Everything changes from now on."

The idyll lasted until Han and Leia walked hand-in-hand into the *Millennium Falcon's* galley. Through their touch, Leia felt the slight tension of Han's muscles as he came in sight of their guest—an Imperial commander in immaculate dress greys.

Han, Leia knew, had hoped that this mission would provide a chance for the two of them to be alone. Through the many months since the war with the Yuuzhan Vong had begun, they had either been apart or dealing with a bewildering succession of crises. Even though their current mission was no less urgent than the others, they would have treasured this time alone in hyperspace.

They had even left Leia's Noghri bodyguards behind. Neither of them had wanted any passengers at all, let alone an Imperial officer. Thus far Han had managed to be civil about it, but only just.

The commander rose politely to her feet. "An exceptionally smooth transition into hyperspace, General Solo," she said. "For a ship with such—such *heterogeneous* components— such a transition speaks well of the ship's captain and his skills."

"Thanks," Han said.

"The Myomar shields are superb, are they not?" she said. "One of our finer designs."

The problem with Commander Vana Dorja, Leia thought, was that she was simply too observant. She was a woman of about thirty, the daughter of the captain of a Star Destroyer, with bobbed dark hair tucked neatly into her uniform cap, and the bland, pleasant face of a professional diplomat. She had been on Coruscant during its fall, allegedly negotiating some kind of commercial treaty, purchasing Ulban droid brains for use in Imperial hydroponics farms. The negotiations were complicated by the fact that the droid brains in question could equally well be used for military purposes.

The negotiations regarding the brains' end-use certificates had gone nowhere in particular, but perhaps they had been intended to go nowhere. What Commander Dorja's extended stay on Coruscant had done was to make her a close observer in the Yuuzhan Vong assault that had resulted in the planet's fall.

Vana Dorja had gotten off Coruscant somehow—Leia had no doubt that her escape had been planned long in advance— and she had then turned up at Mon Calamari, the new provisional capital, blandly asking for help in returning to Imperial space just at the moment at which Leia had been assigned a diplomatic mission to that selfsame Empire.

Of course it wasn't a coincidence. Dorja was clearly a spy operating under commercial cover. But what could Leia do? The New Republic might need the help of the Empire, and the Empire might be offended if its commercial representative were needlessly delayed in her return.

What Leia *could* do was establish some ground rules concerning where on the *Falcon* that Commander Dorja could go, and where was strictly off-limits. Dorja had agreed immediately to the restrictions, and agreed as well to be scanned for any technological or other secrets she might be smuggling out.

Nothing had turned up on the scan. Of course. If Vana Dorja was carrying any vital secrets to her masters in the Empire, she was carrying them locked in her all-too-inquisitive brain.

"Please sit down," Leia said.

"Your Highness is kind," Dorja said, and lowered her stocky body into a chair. Leia sat across the table from her, and observed the half-empty glass of juri juice set before the commander.

"Threepio is providing sufficient refreshment?" Leia asked.

"Yes. He is very efficient, though a trifle talkative."

Talkative? Leia thought. What had Threepio been telling the woman?

Blast it anyway. Dorja was all too skilled at creating these unsettling moments.

"Shall we dine?" Leia asked.

Dorja nodded, bland as always. "As Your Highness wishes." But then she proved useful in the kitchen, assisting Han and Leia as they transferred to plates the metal that had been cooking in the *Falcon's* automatic ovens. As Han sat down with his plates, C-3PO contemplated the table.

"Sir," he said. "A princess and former head-of-state takes precedence, of course, over both a general and an Imperial commander. But a commander—forgive me—does not take precedence over a New Republic general, even one on the inactive list. General Solo, if you would be so kind as to sit above Commander Dorja?"

Han gave C-3PO a baleful look. "I like it fine where I am," he said. Which was, of course, as far away from the Imperial commander as the small table permitted.

C-3PO looked as distressed as it was possible for a droid with an immobile face to look. "But sir—the rules of precedence—"

"I like it where I am," Han said, more firmly.

"But—sir—"

Leia slid into her accustomed role as Han's interpreter to the world. "We'll dine informally, Threepio," she told the droid.

C-3PO's tone allowed his disappointment to show. "Very well, Your Highness," he said.

Poor Threepio, Leia thought. Here he was designed for working out rules of protocol for state banquets involving dozens of species and hundreds of governments, interpreting and smoothing disputes, and instead she persisted in getting him into situations where he kept getting shot at. And now the galaxy was being invaded by beings who had marked for extermination every droid in existence—and they were *winning*. Whatever Threepio had for nerves must be shot.

Lots of formal dinner parties when this is over, Leia decided. Nice, soothing dinner parties, without assassins, quarrels, or sword fights.

"I thank you again for your offer of transit to the Empire," Dorja said later, after the soup course. "It was fortunate that you have business there."

"Very fortunate," Leia agreed.

"Your mission to the Empire must be critical," Dorja probed, "to take you from the government at such a crucial time."

"I'm doing what I do best."

"But you were head of state—surely you must be considering a return to power."

Leia shook her head. "I served my term."

"To voluntarily relinquish power—I confess I don't understand it." Dorja shook her head. "In the Empire, we are taught not to decline responsibility once it is given to us."

Leia sensed Han's head lifting as he prepared to speak. She knew him well enough to anticipate the sense of any remarks. *No,* he would say, *Imperial leaders generally stay in their seats of power until they're blasted out by a laser cannon.* Before Han could speak, she phrased a more diplomatic answer.

"Wisdom is knowing when you've given all you can," she said, and turned her attention to her dinner, a fragrant breast of hibbas with a sauce of bofa fruit. Dorja picked up her fork, held it over her plate. "But surely—with the government in chaos, and driven into exile—a strong hand is needed."

"We have constitutional means for choosing a new leader," Leia reassured. And thought, *Not that they're working so far, with Pwoe proclaiming himself Head of State with the Senate deadlocked on Mon Calamari.*

"I wish you a smooth transition," said Commander Dorja." "Let's hope the hesitation and chaos with which the New Republic has met its current crisis was the fault of Borsk Fey'lya's government, and not symptomatic of the New Republic as a whole."

"I'll drink to that," Han proclaimed, and drained his glass.

"I can't help but wonder how the old Empire would have handled the crisis," Dorja continued. "I hope you will forgive my partisan attitude, but it seems to me that the Emperor would have mobilized his entire armament at the first threat, and dealt with the Yuuzhan Vong in an efficient and expeditious manner, through the use of overwhelming force. Certainly better than Borsk Fey'lya's policy—if I understood it correctly *as* a policy—of negotiating with the invaders at the same time as he was fighting them, sending signals of weakness to a ruthless enemy who only used negotiation as a cover for further conquests."

It was growing very hard, Leia thought, to maintain the diplomatic smile on her face. "The Emperor," she said, "was always alert to any threat to his power."

Leia sensed Han about to speak, and this time was too late to stop his words.

"That's not what the Empire would have done, commander," Han said. "What the Empire would have done was build a super-colossal Yuuzhan Vong–killing battle machine. They would have called it the Nova Colossus or the Galaxy Destructor or the Nostril of Palpatine or something equally grandiose. They would have spent billions of credits, employed thousands of contractors and sub-contractors, and equipped it with the latest in death-dealing technology. And you know what would have happened? *IT wouldn't have worked.* They'd forget to bolt down a metal plate over an access hatch leading to the main reactors, or some other mistake, and a hotshot enemy pilot would drop a bomb down there and *blow the whole thing up.* Now *that's* what the Empire would have done."

Leia, striving to contain her laughter, detected what might have been amusement in Vana Dorja's brown eyes.

"Perhaps you're right," Dorja conceded.

"You're right I'm right, commander," Han said, and poured himself another glass of water.

His brief triumph was interrupted by a sudden shriek from the *Falcon's* hyperdrive units. The ship shuddered. Proximity alarms wailed.

Leia, her heart beating in synchrony to the blaring alarms, stared into Han's startled eyes. Han turned to Commander Dorja.

"Sorry to interrupt dinner just as it was getting interesting," he said, "but I'm afraid we've got to blow some bad guys into small pieces."

The first thing Han Solo did when he scrambled into the pilot's seat was to shut off the blaring alarms that were rattling his brain around inside his skull. Then he looked out the cockpit windows. The stars, he saw, had returned to their normal configuration—the *Millennium Falcon* had been yanked out of hyperspace. And Han had a good idea why, an idea which a glance at the sensor displays served only to confirm. He turned to Leia and she scrambled into the copilot's chair.

"Either a black hole has materialized in this sector, or we've hit a Yuuzhan Vong mine." A dovin basal to be precise, an organic gravitation-anomaly generator that the Yuuzhan Vong used both for propelling their vessels and warping space around them. The Yuuzhan Vong had been seeding dovin basal mines along New Republic trade routes in order to drag unsuspecting transports out of hyperspace and into an ambush. But their mining efforts hadn't extended this far along the Hydian Way, at least not till now.

And there, Han saw in the displays, were the ambushers. Two flights of six coralskippers each, one positioned on either side of the dovin basal in order to intercept any unsuspecting transport.

He reached for the controls, then hesitated, wondering if Leia should pilot while he ran for the turbolaser turret. No, he thought, he knew the *Millennium Falcon*, her capabilities, and her crotchets better than anyone, and good piloting was going to get them out of this trouble more than good shooting.

"I'd better fly this one," he said. "You take one of the quad lasers." Regretting, as he spoke, that he wouldn't get to blow things up, something always good for taking his mind off his troubles.

Leia bent to give him a quick kiss on the cheek. "Good luck, Slick," she whispered, then squeezed his shoulder and slid silently out of the cockpit.

"Good luck yourself," Han said. "And find out if our guest is qualified to take the other turret."

His eyes were already scanning the displays as he automatically donned the comlink headset that would allow him to communicate with Leia on the turbolasers. Coralskippers weren't hyperspace capable, so some larger craft had to have dropped them here. Was that ship still around, or had it moved on to lay another mine somewhere else?

It had gone, apparently. There was no sign of it on the displays.

The Yuuzhan Vong craft were just now beginning to react to his arrival—so much for the hope that the *Millennium Falcon's* stealth capabilities would have kept it from being detected.

But *what*, he considered, had the enemy seen? A Corellian Engineering YU-1300 transport, similar to hundreds of other small freighters they must have encountered. The Yuuzhan Vong wouldn't have seen the *Falcon's* armament, its advanced shields, or the modifications to its sublight drives that could give even the swift coralskippers a run for their money.

So the *Millennium Falcon* should continue, as far as the Yuuzhan Vong were concerned, to look like an innocent freighter.

While he watched the Yuuzhan Vong maneuver, Han broadcast to the enemy a series of queries and demands for information of the sort that might come from a nervous civilian pilot. He conducted a series of basic maneuvers designed to keep the coralskippers at a distance, maneuvers as sluggish and hesitant as if he were a fat, nervous freighter loaded with cargo. The nearest flight of coralskippers set on a basic intercept course, not even bothering to deploy into military formation. The farthest flight, on the other side of the dovin basal mine, began a slow loop toward the *Falcon*, to support the others.

Now *that* was interesting. In a short while they would have the dovin basal singularity between themselves and the *Falcon*, with the mine's gravity-warping capabilities making it very difficult for them to see the *Falcon* or to detect any changes in its course.

"General Solo?" a voice on the comlink intruded on his thoughts. "This is Commander Dorja. I'm readying the weapons in the dorsal turret."

"Try not to blow off the sensor dish," Han told her.

He looked at the displays, saw the far-side squadron nearing eclipse behind the space-time-distorting gravity mine. His hands closed on the controls and he altered course directly for the dovin basal just as he gave full power to the sublight drives.

The gravity mine was now between the *Millennium Falcon* and the far-side flight of coralskippers. The space-time warp surrounding the dovin basal would make it nearly impossible to detect the *Falcon's* change of course.

"We have about three minutes to contact with the enemy," he said into the comlink headset. "Fire dead ahead, on my mark."

"Dead ahead?" came Dorja's bland voice. "How unorthodox . . . have you considered *maneuver*?"

"Don't second-guess the pilot!" Leia's voice snapped like a whip. "Keep this channel clear unless you have something of value to say!"

"Apologies," Dorja murmured.

Han bit back his own annoyance. He glanced at the empty copilot's chair—Chewbacca's place, now Leia's—and found himself wishing that he was in the second turbolaser cockpit, with Chewbacca in the pilot's seat. But Chewie was gone, the first of the deaths that had struck him to the heart. Chewbacca dead, his younger son Anakin killed, his older son Jacen missing, presumed dead by everyone except Leia. . . . Death had been haunting his footsteps, on the verge of claiming everyone around him.

That was why he hadn't accepted Waroo's offer to assume Chewbacca's life debt. He simply hadn't wanted to be responsible for the death of another friend.

But now Leia believed that Jacen was alive. This wasn't a vague hope based on a mother's desire to see here son again, as Han had earlier suspected, but a sending through the Force, a message aimed at Leia herself.

Han had no direct experience of the Force himself, but he knew he could trust Leia not to misread it. His son was alive.

So maybe Death wasn't following him so closely after all. Or maybe Han had just outrun him.

Stay alert, he told himself. *Stay strong. You may* not *have to die today.*

Cold determination filled him.

Make the Yuuzhan Vong pay instead, he thought.

He made a last scan of the displays. The near-side flight had turned to pursue, dividing into two V formations of three coralskippers each. They hadn't reacted very quickly to his abrupt change of course, so Han figured he wasn't dealing with a genius commander here, which was good.

It was impossible to see the far-side flight on the other side of the gravity-distorting mine, but he had a good read on their trajectory, and there hadn't been any reason for them to change it.

The dovin basal swept closer. The *Falcon's* spars moaned as they felt the tug of its gravity.

"Ten seconds," Han told Leia and Dorja, and reached for the triggers to the concussion-missile tubes.

Antipation drew a metallic streak down his tongue. He felt a prickle of sweat on his scalp.

"Five." He triggered the first pair of concussion missiles, knowing that, unlike the laser cannon, they did not strike at the speed of light.

"Two." Han triggered another pair of missiles. The *Millennium Falcon's* engines howled as they fought the pull of the dovin basal's gravity.

"Fire." The dovin basal swept past, and suddenly the display lit with the six approaching coralskippers. The combined power of the eight turbolasers fired straight at them.

The six coralskippers had also split into two Vs of three craft each, the formations on slightly diverging courses, but both formations were running into the *Falcon* and her armament at a combined velocity of over ninety percent of the speed of light. None of them had shifted their dovin basals to warp space defensively ahead of them, and the pilots had only an instant to perceive the doom staring them in the face, and no time to react. The first vic ran right into the first pair of missiles and the turbolaser fire, and all three erupted in fire as their coral hulls shattered into fragments.

The second formation, diverging, was not so suitably placed. One coralskipper was hit by a missile and pinwheeled off into the darkness, trailing flame. Another ran into a burst of turbolaser fire and exploded. The third raced on, looping around the gravity mine where Han's detectors could no longer see it.

Exultation sang through Han's heart. *Four kills, one probable.* Not a bad start at evening the odds.

The *Millennium Falcon* shuddered to the gravitic pull of the dovin basal. Han frowned as he checked the sublight engine readouts. He had hoped to whip around the space mine and exit with enough velocity to escape the dovin basal's gravity and get into hyperspace before the other flight of coralskippers could overtake him. But the dovin basal was more powerful than he'd expected, or possibly the Yuuzhan Vong commander was actually *ordering* it to increase its gravitational attraction—since there was a lot the Republic didn't know about how the Yuuzhan Vong equipment worked, that was at least possible.

In any case, *Falcon* hadn't picked up enough speed to be sure of a getaway. Which meant he had to think of something else brilliant to do.

The other flight of six coralskippers was following him into the gravity well of the dovin basal, intent on following him. The one intact survivor of the second flight was in the act of whipping around the dovin basal, and wouldn't enter into his calculations for the present.

Well, he thought, if it worked *once* . . .

"Hang on, ladies," he called on the comlink. "We're going around again!"

Savage pleasure filled him as he swung the *Millennium Falcon* around for another dive toward the dovin basal. *Attack my galaxy, will you?* he thought.

They had doubtless seen the beginnings of his maneuver, so he altered his trajectory slightly to put the space mine directly between himself and the oncoming fighters. Then he altered his trajectory a second time, just to be safe. If the enemy commander had any sense, he'd be doing the same.

Both sides were now blind. The problem was that the Yuuzhan Vong were alert to his tactics. They wouldn't just run blindly toward him: they would have their dovin basal propulsor units shifted to repel any attack, and they'd come in shooting.

"Be alert, people," Han said. "We're not going to be so lucky this time, and I can't tell precisely where your targets are going to be. So be ready for them to be anywhere, right?"

"Right," Leia said.

"Understood," said Dorja.

"Commander Dorja," Leia said. "You'll see that your four lasers are aimed so as to fire on slightly diverging paths."

"Yes."

"Don't readjust. There's a reason for it."

"I presumed so. I won't change the settings."

A pang of sorrow touched Han's heart. It was his son Anakin who had discovered that if he fired three shots into a Yuuzhan Vong vessel at slightly diverging courses, at least one shot would curve around the gravity-warping dovin basal shields and hit the target. The quad lasers had been set to accomplish that automatically, without Anakin's eye and fast reflexes.

Anakin, who died at Myrkyr.

"Twenty seconds," Han said, to cover both his own rising tension and the grief that flooded him.

He triggered another pair of missiles at ten seconds, just in case he was lucky again and the enemy flight appeared right in front of him. And then, because he had no choice but to trust his luck, he fired another pair five seconds later.

You are not keeping me from seeing Jacen again, he told the enemy.